# THE MAYBERRY MURDERS

# THE AMANDA RITTENHOUSE MYSTERIES

# THE MAYBERRY MURDERS

## KATE MERRILL

SAPPHIRE BOOKS

SALINAS, CALIFORNIA

*The Mayberry Murders*
Copyright © 2024 by Kate Merrill. All rights reserved.

ISBN Book - 978-1-959929-16-1

This is a work of fiction - names, characters, places, and incidents are the product of the author's imagination or are used fictitiously. Any resemblance to actual persons living or dead, business, events or locales is entirely coincidental.

Editor - Tara Young
Book Design - LJ Reynolds
Cover Design - Fineline Cover Design

**Sapphire Books Publishing, LLC**
P.O. Box 8142
Salinas, CA 93912
www.sapphirebooks.com

Printed in the United States of America
First Edition – April 2024

This book is licensed for your personal enjoyment only. This book may not be re-sold or given away to other people. If you would like to share this book with another person, please purchase an additional copy for each recipient. If you're reading this book and did not purchase it, or it was not purchased for your use only, then please return to your favorite book retailer and purchase your own copy. Thank you for respecting the hard work of this author.

All rights reserved under U.S. and International copyright conventions. Except for use in reviews, no part of this text may be reproduced, transmitted, downloaded, decomplied, reverse engineered, or stored in a storage and retrieval system, data base, including printing, recording either visual or audio, electronic and any future technology invented without written permission of Sapphire Books Publishing.

The author/publisher expressly prohibits any entity from using the production/publication for purposes of training A.I., artificial intelligence, to generate text that may replicate the author's styly or genre similar to this work. The author retains all rights to use this work for purposes of generative AI training and development of any language learning system.

To the extent that the image on the cover of this book depicts a person or persons, such a person is merely a model and is not intended to portray any character feature in this book.

This and other Sapphire Books titles can be found at
www.sapphirebooks.com

# *Dedication*

Grandma Vivian
feisty spirit of strong will and courage
beloved wife, mother, grandmother
providing spice to the past ten Rittenhouse novels
R.I.P.

# *Acknowledgment*

Special thanks to Christine Svendsen and the team at Sapphire Books, Tara Young for her invaluable editing help, and to the unique town of Mount Airy, North Carolina, for sharing "Mayberry."

## Chapter One

### Monday, April 15

Spring had come to North Carolina, with a pure blue sky spilling nurturing sunshine on tulips, redbud trees, and tender young grass. But a scum of pollen floated on Lake Norman. It coated the white skin of Moby Dyke, Amanda's aging cargo van, with green goo and coaxed out her allergies as she drove north.

It was tax day. Amanda Rittenhouse and her partner, Sara Orlando, had already filed. Sara, a successful psychiatrist who made a good salary, owed less than expected. But Amanda, a struggling sculptor, owed nothing. Indeed last year, she had earned less than a living wage from the sale of only one major piece, and she was almost out of money.

Amanda had to get back to work, so she was driving to her studio in Mooresville. Moby Dyke was loaded with newly scavenged metal parts for her welding projects, but she was short on inspiration. She was thirty-two, healthy, still madly in love with Sara after five years, so what was her problem?

As she steered off Interstate 77 at Exit 36, frowning through sunglasses that hyped up the green landscape to a gaudy chartreuse, she came up with a theory—everything was too perfect. Everyone was supposed to be Easter egg happy on a day like today.

If only it would rain, she'd feel better.

Then her cellphone chirped cheerily from the bowels of her purse and instantly goosed the call to the speaker in the dashboard. The caller ID said Diana Rittenhouse, so she pressed the "accept" icon on the steering wheel.

"What do you want, Mom?" she answered testily.

"Gracious, *someone* got up on the wrong side of the bed."

Amanda swerved to avoid rear-ending a pickup truck that cut her off on the ramp. "Sorry, I'm on the road. I just turned off onto River Highway."

"Well, that's convenient, dear. Turns out you're exactly where I need you to be."

Her mother went on to explain that Grandma Vivian needed someone to drive her to a scheduled endocrinologist appointment. Mom, a Realtor, claimed she was tied up with out-of-town buyers, or she'd take Grandma herself.

"Why can't Linc take her?" Amanda whined. Lincoln Davis, Grandma's almost-new eighty-four-year-old second husband was a retired lawyer with nothing better to do.

"Oh, Mandy, did you forget? Linc's out of town at that bar reunion. He won't be home till Wednesday."

Bar reunion? Amanda thought snidely. Sounds like a bunch of old geezers tavern hopping. In fact, it was a sedate group of ex-judges playing golf and swapping courtroom war stories. "But I was planning to work in the studio this afternoon."

Mom snorted. "No offense, dear, but you haven't worked all winter. Can't you put it off for one more day? You're only a mile from Grandma's house."

Amanda couldn't come up with a single good

objection. Not having a real job like everyone else, she was always considered available to run inconvenient errands. She sighed heavily. "Okay, I'm on my way. I'll give her your love."

She hung up and made a quick left onto Williamson, then right onto Brawley. As she neared Silver Bay, the upscale retirement community where Grandma Vivian and Linc lived, her spirits lifted. After all, she loved spending time with Grandma. The lady was outrageous, outspoken, and funny as hell—traits she had passed on to Amanda's mom. But unlike Mom, Grandma never picked on Amanda. She had no expectations, was not judgmental, and frankly did not care how Amanda conducted her life or her love life.

Suddenly smiling, she parked in Grandma's driveway. The semi-detached duplex was tastefully constructed of brick and cedar shingles. Each cluster home maintained privacy from its neighbors provided by a common wall between driveways and by facing in different directions. Grandma's unit angled toward a view of the fifth hole of a public golf course and the dense forest abutting it.

Today the neighborhood was sleepily quiet but for birdsongs and the buzz of a lawnmower down the block. Amanda added the sound of herself whistling a happy tune as she approached the cherry red front door and admired the pansies potted on either side. Sticking her finger into the soil, she noted that Grandma had watered the plants recently, likely that morning, as was her habit. Hopefully, she had also remembered to lock her door, which was not her habit.

Smiling again, Amanda was pleased to find the door locked. Locating the appropriate key Grandma had given her for emergencies, like watering plants when she was out of town, she let herself in and stood in the airy foyer.

"I'm here!" she called loudly, since Grandma was hard of hearing. "Are you ready?"

No response. She heard the television blaring from the upstairs bedroom, so she figured Grandma was still dressing. "Hurry up, will you?" she hollered. "Your appointment's at eleven, and we're running late!"

Nothing. Well, she could check out the kitchen for cookies or other sweets, but success was unlikely since Grandma was a brittle diabetic. Or she could go up and help the woman with her shoes, always an issue, and then they would have a fighting chance of getting to Dr. Patel's on time.

She took off her sandals, one of Grandma's strict rules, and padded across the cream carpet to the stairs around the corner. She smelled fresh-cut flowers, which was usual, but also a foul odor, which was not usual. Rounding the bend, Amanda froze in shock. She could not catch her breath, and her heart seemed to stop.

Grandma lay on the floor at the bottom of the stairs. Rather, her head lay on the floor, her neck twisted at an impossible angle. Her right arm stretched out, fingers splayed, as though she had made a grab for the banister. She had fallen face down, her legs still sprawled on the stairs, her skirt hiked up around her hips.

Amanda's scream echoed off the walls and vaulted ceiling as she dropped to her knees. She fearfully touched the cheek of Grandma's bright red face. *All the blood must have rushed to her head.* Then she saw actual blood, not yet clotted, staining the snowy white crown of Grandma's hair.

Now sobbing, Amanda felt Grandma's neck and her outstretched wrist for a pulse. Nothing. She collapsed to the floor, and through a blur of tears, stared into pale blue eyes frozen in terror.

Grandma Viv was dead.

## Chapter Two

Unthinkable tragedy...

Paralyzed, Amanda lost track of time as horror spread through every cell in her body. Finally, she crawled out of suspended animation, sat upright, found her cellphone, and dialed 911. Barely aware of speaking, she gave the operator details and managed to come up with Grandma's home address.

They promised to come, so she dialed her mother, which had been her first instinct. Without regard to how the news would impact Mom, she blurted it out. "Grandma fell down the stairs!"

Stunned silence, then, "Is she okay, Mandy?"

"No, Mom, she's dead!"

During the next few moments of disbelief and panic, Amanda couldn't recall the words Mom had used, but she knew Mom was on her way.

Next, as she continued to stare into Vivian's disturbing eyes, she was overwhelmed by a need to call Sara. Her lover's response would be emotional but measured. Sara would provide comfort and sanity. Her finger hovered above the phone, with help one touch away, yet she resisted.

Was she a helpless child? She certainly felt like one in this crisis. But Sara, a psychiatrist who worked with the most desperate people the city of Charlotte had to offer, would be conducting her last session of the morning, likely dealing with someone else's crisis. Amanda shoved the phone back in her purse. Surely, she could wait until Sara was on lunch break.

She longed to flee to the safety of the kitchen, but she could not leave Grandma all alone. Instead, she held one of her cold hands for what seemed an eternity until multiple sirens shrieked into the quiet neighborhood. Soon she heard pounding and hollering at the front door.

"Come in, it's open!" she cried.

Suddenly, they towered above her—a man and woman with heavy belts and guns. EMS personnel in green with medical bags, two of those. And firemen. Yet all Amanda could focus on were the seven pairs of shoes standing on Grandma's carpet, breaking her rules.

A gentle hand touched her shoulder and urged her to her feet. The female officer said, "Are you hurt, ma'am?"

Amanda shook her head as the paramedics in rubber gloves knelt and checked Grandma's pulse. They stated the obvious: Her grandmother was dead.

"Let's move away and let these folks do their work," the woman said. "Is there somewhere we can talk?"

Amanda led her to the kitchen, where against all odds, a plate of freshly baked sugar cookies sat on the table under a cellophane wrap. *Grandma can't eat those*, she stupidly thought before realizing they'd likely been baked for Mom, who had originally been scheduled to take Grandma to the doctor.

The woman, who said her name was Judy, asked Amanda what had happened.

Moving like a zombie, Amanda took a seat,

then so did Judy—the cookies between them. As she haltingly explained how she'd come to find Grandma on the floor, the officer nodded and took notes in a little brown book.

"Why are so many people here?" Amanda wondered. "A firetruck, the police?"

"Standard procedure," Judy muttered, then continued to ask questions Amanda could not possibly answer. In the meantime, the male officer, built like a spark plug, had entered the kitchen and stood lounging against the doorjamb. Out by the stairs, the voices escalated in volume.

"Who else was at the house this morning?" he demanded.

"No one."

"Are you sure, ma'am?"

She explained again that Linc was out of town, that Grandma and her husband were the only ones who lived here.

"So what were you and your grandma doing upstairs?"

"I was never upstairs. Haven't you been listening?" She heard more commotion at the front door and then her mother's voice. Jumping up, she pushed past the male officer and stepped around the crew at the stairs, but Mom was already at the body.

"Oh, my God!" Mom screamed, then covered her mouth. It was all the EMS guys could do to keep her from flinging herself on the fallen woman. "You don't understand, that's my *mother!*"

Amanda intervened, pulling Mom into a tight embrace. They were both tall, lanky, blue-eyed blondes. Locked together, they were a formidable force against this unexpected, unthinkable tragedy.

"Let my mother say goodbye to Grandma," Amanda commanded with more heat than she had intended.

It worked. The strangers parted and allowed Mom to touch, kiss, and cry. When it was over, Mom stood erect. "So what the hell happened here?"

At first, the medics and police debated how much to share with the Rittenhouse women, but a second look at their solidarity convinced them otherwise. The smaller medic, a young man with his long red hair in a ponytail, cleared his throat and touched the back of Grandma's head with a gloved finger. "The lady did not fall down the stairs. Someone hit her from behind."

"She was murdered," the surly cop added.

## Chapter Three

### Out of place...

"Murdered? That's impossible!" Mom gasped. "But everyone loves Grandma. She doesn't have one enemy in this world," Amanda cried.

The ponytailed redhead looked sadly down at his hands. "Nonetheless, somebody attacked your grandma. See how she fell face-down? No matter how you reconstruct the scene, she could not have hit her head on the banister. By the look of things, she died instantly and not too long ago."

*Instantly* was good news, but everything else was horrendous. "I wish I'd arrived sooner." Amanda moaned. "Maybe I could have prevented it."

"Don't wish for that, Miss Rittenhouse," Judy said. "You could have been hurt, too."

"Whatever," the male officer grumbled and glared suspiciously at Amanda. "I've called in Homicide. The crime scene techs are on the way. I suggest you women go back to the kitchen till they get here, and for God's sake, don't touch anything."

Mom gave the man a dark look. "Look, officer, I promise you that my daughter's and my fingerprints are already everywhere. You might want to take our prints for elimination."

"Thanks for the tip, ma'am. I reckon we can handle that."

"Let's go, ladies." Judy took their elbows and guided them back to the kitchen where they sat and gazed mournfully at the plate of cookies. "Did Vivian Davis own any valuables?"

Amanda sought Mom's eyes and saw a mixture of shock and defiance in their deep blue depths. The defiance was a good thing. Mom never suffered fools lightly, especially cops like the spark plug . She had done a fair amount of amateur sleuthing and was familiar with police procedure. Unfortunately, Amanda had also been involved in some criminal investigations. She had seen dead bodies before but never someone she loved.

"Did Mrs. Davis own jewelry, gold, or keep money in the house?" Judy persisted.

"You think this was a burglary?" Amanda asked.

"Hard to say, but it's possible. We've seen some vandalism and petty theft in this neighborhood, but no one ever got hurt before. Those incidents occurred while the old folks were out and about, thank heavens."

Mom scowled. Amanda knew she would not appreciate Grandma being categorized as "old folk." Everyone knew Grandma was a feisty fighter, just like her daughter, Diana. Just like Amanda wished she could be.

"Grandma had some good jewelry," Amanda answered slowly. "Mostly stuff Linc had given her." She paused as she recalled holding Grandma's cold hand. "Oh, God, her diamond engagement ring was missing! She always wore it when she went out, and she was fully dressed, ready to go—earrings and all."

"Mandy is right," Mom agreed. "Mama always wore Linc's ring, and it was obscenely valuable. You don't think...?"

As her sentence trailed off, Amanda visualized the thief removing the precious ring from Grandma's finger, a violation almost as vile as rape. The late-in-life romance between Linc and Grandma was awe-inspiring, and then it hit her. "Oh, no, we have to call Lincoln."

Mom moaned. "Oh, Lord, you're right. How can I ever tell him?"

"Do you want me to do it?" Judy kindly offered. "Sometimes it's easier coming from a stranger."

"Thank you, but that's unacceptable. I'll do it now." Without requesting permission, Mom stepped out onto the patio off the kitchen and closed the French doors behind her.

Judy said, "I don't envy her that task. Your mother is a brave woman."

*Yes, she is.* Amanda watched through the glass doors as Mom took out her cellphone, bowed her head, and collected her thoughts. Beyond her silhouette, the golf course was picture perfect, with a foursome of carefree players strolling along the edge of the forest, where a light breeze made the trees sway. The contrast was surreal, so wrong. She glanced at her watch. It was almost noon. Soon she could call Sara.

While Mom was on the phone, Amanda heard the firetruck leave and several new voices talking at the stairs.

"That will be the crime scene techs," Judy informed her. "Now tell me about Mrs. Davis's cash and other valuables."

"Grandma and Linc have a safe in their bedroom, but it's nearly impossible to open. It has a combination lock and requires two keys, which they carry with them on separate chains." They also had some valuable books and art, which she doubted most common thieves would recognize. Their electronics, like the huge flat-screen TV, were so big and bulky no one would dare haul them away in broad daylight.

"Well, when your mother finishes her call, we'll do a house tour, up and down, see if anything is out of place."

Just as Mom came in, looking pale and shaken, two men in nice suits came looking for them.

Amanda ignored them. "Mom, is Linc okay?"

Mom slowly shook her head and held up a trembling hand. "He's on his way home" was all she would say.

The detectives were out of central casting, one young and blond, while the officer in charge, John Winston, was dark with gray at the temples. She paid little attention to either man. She wanted this to be over. She needed fresh air.

They handed Mom and Amanda rubber gloves and booties. "Wear these, please, ladies. We don't want to contaminate the scene."

Nothing seemed amiss downstairs. Unlike her female progeny, Vivian was excessively neat. She had a weekly maid service, so all the wooden surfaces gleamed with polish, the carpet bore vacuum tracks, and a cut glass vase with fragrant flowers glittered on the hall table.

When it was time to go upstairs, Amanda braced herself. With Detective Winston leading the way, they averted their eyes and stepped carefully around Grandma, who had not been moved. When she peeked at her grandmother, she saw how thoroughly her spirit was gone. Grandma wasn't there. The body had little to do with the vibrant woman Amanda had loved. That person was elsewhere. Although she was not religious, she hoped that "elsewhere" was someplace good.

When they reached the landing, in an open alcove the couple used as a home office, Mom squeezed her hand in encouragement.

"Please concentrate, ladies. Do you see anything odd up here?"

All Amanda saw was that one drawer of a tall metal file cabinet was slightly pulled out from flush. She reflexively pushed the drawer in, as Grandma would have done, restoring the space to perfect order.

"Not a thing," she and Mom agreed as they toured the guest bedroom and bath, then moved on to the master suite.

At a glance, nothing seemed untidy except a pair of blue heels and matching sweater laid out on the floor and bed, respectively. Obviously, Grandma had tried on the ensemble but then opted for the beige outfit she currently wore. The bed was neatly made. The clock radio, notepad, and cup of pencils were in their usual place on Grandma's bedside table. The dish on Linc's side was still full of spare pennies.

"Wait!" Amanda cried as they were about to give up. "Grandma's magic box is gone. It was right here on her dresser last week."

"Are you sure, Mandy? I thought Mama kept it in the closet."

"Magic box?" The detective's eyebrows shot up.

She described the ornately painted Chinese jewelry box where Grandma kept her treasures. It had fascinated Amanda since she was a little girl. "It's about six inches square and ten inches high. It has burgundy lacquer with tiny oriental people all over it and a big brass clasp."

Mom said, "I think most of the contents were costume jewelry and personal mementos, but there might have been a couple of valuable pieces."

Winston frowned. "So it was a burglary. Can you two come up with a list of the items in the box?"

"Perhaps, Detective, but not today," Mom said firmly. "It's time for Mandy and me to leave and catch our breath."

Winston did not look happy but was not inclined to argue. He took down information about Linc, including his phone number. He promised to keep in touch and then dismissed them.

As they moved back downstairs, a camera flashed, and techs dusted for prints and chattered as they went about their business. Amanda noticed that the blond detective and the original two officers were gone. "Where is everyone?"

Winston told her the officers were canvassing the neighborhood, while his blond partner had gone to the office of the golf course. "We'll get this bastard," he promised. "But we'll need you and your mother to come down to the station tomorrow."

"The list of jewelry, we know," Mom said.

"Yes, and we'll take your fingerprints at that time."

As someone took Mom aside and requested the name of a preferred funeral home where they could send the body once the autopsy was done, Amanda drifted toward the ponytailed redhead.

"You didn't happen to find a murder weapon lying around up there?" he wryly asked.

She gaped at him.

"I mean, it looks like she was hit by something heavy and narrow, like a rebar."

She waved him off, removed the rubber gloves and booties, and stuffed them into an umbrella stand at the front door. Stepping outside, she found herself enclosed in a spider's web of yellow crime tape and stood at a loss between the potted pansies. Staring out at the street, she saw Judy knocking on doors and her partner, the spark plug, jawing with the lawn care guys who had been working in the neighborhood. Lifting her gaze to the fifth hole, she saw a flag waving on the green and thought: *Hit with a rebar? Or maybe a golf club.*

## Chapter Four

Therapy session...

Sara let her cry. She held Amanda close and urged her to let it all out. She asked her to share good memories about her grandmother. As they snuggled in bed and Amanda thought about that request, she realized her history with Grandma Vivian fell into two distinct categories—early childhood and her current adulthood—with big gaps in between. Amanda had run away from home at eighteen and did not reunite with anyone in her family until a decade later. Even when they'd lived in close proximity to one another, then and now, she'd never spent a great deal of time with Grandma.

"That's true for most kids," Sara reassured her. "We have lives of our own."

"Yes, we do." They were lying on their sides, Amanda's bottom tucked into Sara's lap. She captured Sara's arm and guided it up and around so that her hand cupped her breast. "The best part was Grandma's farm. I don't remember much about Grandpa Whitaker, but he let me collect eggs from the henhouse. After he died, once I was in elementary school, Grandma Viv taught me how to milk the cows."

Sara laughed and gave her nipple a little squeeze. "It's hard to imagine Viv yanking cow titties."

"It sure is." By late in life, Grandma had sold the

farm and become much more citified and cultivated, the kind of wife suitable for a Southern gentleman like Lincoln Davis. She had already told Sara the background about how Grandma, a native Southerner, had fallen hard for Yankee farmer Will Whitaker. She had followed her husband to live in the frozen northern fields of Pennsylvania, in Chester County just outside Philadelphia. Amanda's mother, Diana, was their only child.

Years later, after Mom divorced her husband, Robert Rittenhouse, Amanda's father, she had moved to North Carolina to start a new life, and Grandma had come with her. Grandma said it was like "coming home." Amanda had never visited North Carolina until Mom's second marriage to Matthew Troutman. She had attended the wedding and ended up staying. *Good thing I did. Or I'd not have met Sara.*

"What else about Viv?" Sara scooted closer and nibbled Amanda's earlobe, which made it hard to concentrate.

"Well, there was my ballerina pin." Amanda giggled. "Grandma gave it to me as a reward for my first recital."

"You a *ballerina*?"

"Don't laugh. I quit after the first year because the crinoline tutus were prickly. But I loved that pin. It was about an inch long, encrusted with fake diamonds, and her little blue skirt swiveled."

"Do you still have the pin?"

She thought about it. "No, but Grandma definitely had it. I gave it back to her for safe keeping when I moved into my tomboy phase. I'm sure Grandma kept it in her magic box."

"The one that was stolen, right? So that's how

you can start your list."

"Right."

They fell silent. So far, they had not talked much about today's tragedy. But that would change, Amanda knew, because Sara was a great shrink, and when she determined Amanda was ready, she'd coax out the gory details and make sure she confronted them head-on. Just now, it was a gentle therapy session.

"Where is Linc staying?" Sara suddenly asked. "Surely, he didn't go back to their town house."

She wished Sara would stop talking and keep nibbling. "He's staying at the lake cottage with Mom and Trout. My stepdad will cook some comfort food to help take their minds off Viv." At least she hoped this was true, but it would take much more than one of Trout's slow-cook pot roasts to make this better.

"Thanks for the Thai food, Sara."

"No problem."

Thai was their favorite. As soon as she'd called Sara today, Sara had canceled her afternoon sessions and come straight home to their condo. She'd brought Sea of Love, a signature seafood dish they'd eaten the night they first made love. But tonight they hadn't been hungry. They had picked at their food, then went to bed.

Sara gently turned Amanda so they were breast to breast. She held her tight and moved her knee up between Amanda's thighs. Her green eyes were luminous in the dim light. Her raven black hair curved around her porcelain face, framing her full sensuous lips. "So what happens tomorrow, Mandy?"

"I have to be at the Mooresville Police Station at ten in the morning. Mom and Linc will meet me there." She really did not want to think about that now, so she kissed Sara's lips and inserted her tongue.

Sara gasped and pulled away. "Wait, let's talk about this."

"About *this*?" Amanda's hand strayed to the silken patch between Sara's legs.

"No, about tomorrow." Sara stopped her hand. "I'm coming to the police station with you. I took the day off."

Amanda was surprised and ridiculously relieved. "What? How can the clinic do without you, Dr. Orlando?"

"Point is, "Sara said, guiding Amanda's hand back where it belonged, "Dr. Orlando can't do without you."

## Chapter Five

### End of the line...

Tuesday was another bittersweet, perfectly beautiful spring day. Amanda awoke nestled in Sara's arms but was suddenly shell-shocked when she remembered Grandma. They showered, then picked at English muffins while staring unseeing at the sparkling blue lake beyond their condo patio. What could be said about senseless death? They knew nothing about the circumstances surrounding the crime but hoped to learn more today.

Sara drove her red Miata convertible to the police station and parked between Mom's old Crown Victoria and Lincoln Davis's fancy Chrysler.

"Are we late?" Amanda wondered nervously.

"Nope, we're early. Relax, babe."

Resisting a childish urge to cling to Sara's hand, Amanda climbed the short flight of stairs to the entrance of the small modern station. They passed through glass doors under an American flag flapping in the breeze. The polished floors glistened and smelled of disinfectant. She noticed a clear plastic drop box filled with bottles of prescription meds, which had been "responsibly" turned in by the public. Would she or Mom dispose of Grandma's meds that way?

Putting that depressing thought aside, she saw the handsome blond detective from yesterday lounging against the reception desk, waiting for them. She pointed him out to Sara.

"The guy who looks like a young Ryan Gosling?"

"That's the one. It seems like he wants us to go down that hallway."

To emphasize his intent, he approached and reintroduced himself as Detective Shine. He lightly touched Sara's arm and glanced at her generous bosom, which was respectfully covered by a loose peach cotton shirt. When he followed them down the hallway, Amanda could almost feel his gaze on Sara's ass. She rolled her eyes. *Give me a break.* Men and women alike were drawn to Sara's raw sensuality, through no fault of her own. While Amanda's tall, slim, boyish athleticism inspired a less visceral kind of admiration.

Shine directed them into a conference room, where Amanda's family was already seated along one side of a long table, with Detective John Winston presiding at the head. Linc and Trout immediately rose to greet them. Grandma's husband, a vigorous octogenarian, was dapper as always. His luxuriant white hair and stylish mustache made him look like a well-groomed lion in a Brooks Brothers seersucker suit, but his green eyes were rimmed with red. Amanda's stepfather, decidedly more casual, seemed grief-stricken yet solid as he hovered protectively near Mom, who did not stand at all. When she caught Amanda's eye, her expression of numb disbelief matched Amanda's sentiments exactly.

Amanda introduced Sara to Winston, establishing her right to participate in the family debrief, and then Winston brought the meeting to order. He offered water or coffee, which everyone refused, and then told Shine, Sara, and her to sit across from the others.

"Vivian Davis's body is with the coroner," he gently advised. "The autopsy will be done in the next few days. So you can go ahead and make funeral arrangements for the weekend, if you like."

The stark words elicited a strangled gasp from Linc, who then pulled himself together. "Viv wanted to be cremated, though the choice is unusual for folks 'round here."

Amanda and Mom nodded. While it was true that many traditional Southerners needed the body, casket, and gravesite for closure, they had heard Grandma say many times that she did not want to be potted like a plant, she preferred to be scattered like fertilizer.

"Your brother, Robby, is coming," Mom said abruptly.

"Robby's coming?" Naturally, Amanda had expected Mom to inform her older brother about Grandma's death, yet she was surprised he planned to attend the funeral. He was busy practicing law in Philadelphia. The only time he'd visited North Carolina since Mom moved down was for her wedding to Trout. That was the last time Amanda had seen him.

Mom smiled. "Sometimes it seems weddings and funerals are the only events that bring our family together. I'd like to see that change."

It had certainly changed Amanda's life when she reconnected and moved to North Carolina. Now she was comforted in the nest of family and wished the same for her brother. "So did Mrs. Davis have a will?" Winston asked.

Everyone looked at Linc, but Linc shrugged

and spread his hands. "I know y'all expected that I'd drawn up my wife's will. Certainly I offered, but Viv said no. Instead she got that young lawyer, Mecklin Adams from Statesville, to do the honors."

"That's strange," Mom bluntly commented.

Linc giggled nervously. "Yes, she said a woman needs a few secrets from an old dog like me. Said she wanted to keep me in line, keep me guessing."

Shine laughed, but Winston remained serious. "But you know for a fact she left a will?"

"Yes, sir. Mecklin would have a copy, and I believe she left a sealed original in our home office filing cabinets."

"Are you the administrator, Judge Davis?"

"I assume so, but I haven't peeked at the document."

"Okay, but as the husband, you're our default for now. Let me know when you've retrieved the will. Now are there other family members?"

Mom said, "You're looking at all of Mother's surviving relatives right here at this table, except for my son, Robby, and he's on his way."

"What about great-grandchildren?" Winston pressed.

"None of those, either. Unless Robby has secretly gotten married and surprises us." Mom winked at Amanda.

Amanda felt guilt-tripped, though she should not have. The fact that neither she nor Robby had provided progeny was of no importance to Mom, or so she claimed. Yet it was sad because as far as Grandma's genes were concerned, it seemed to be the end of the line.

## Chapter Six

### About the investigation...

Winston promised to bring them up to date about the investigation, but first he requested the lists Mom and Amanda had compiled of the contents of Vivian's jewelry box. Turned out their lists were very similar and included items with only sentimental value, like Amanda's ballerina pin and an old railroad watch that had belonged to Mom's dad, Will Whitaker.

"I didn't know Grandpa worked for the railroad," she commented.

"He didn't. I don't know where Daddy got that watch," Mom said, "and I sure don't know why Mama saved so many stray buttons in that magic box."

Linc blushed. "That would be my fault. Those were extras for my shirts and suits. I made poor Viv keep them in case I needed one sewn on."

"Don't worry about it." Trout squeezed Linc's shoulder. "I'd make Diana save my extras, too, only she wouldn't have a clue how to sew one on."

Everyone laughed, breaking the tension. Because while Mom definitely could not sew, it was also true that Trout didn't have many dress shirts or suits, let alone extra buttons.

Sara cleared her throat and spoke up for the first time. "Mandy said you did a door-to-door. Did any of

Vivian's neighbors see anything unusual?"

Winston described how Officer Judy had indeed knocked on every door, but of the residents who had been home that morning, the only suspicious thing they had seen was Amanda's van. "Judy will follow up again this evening to catch up with any folks she missed," he added.

"What about the lawn service people?" Amanda asked.

"Same deal. That crew is hired by the Silver Bay HOA to maintain the whole subdivision on a regular basis. They recognize all the vehicles belonging to the residents, and they claim that apart from your van, no outside traffic drove in or out."

She thought about how the surly spark plug cop had been yukking it up with the crew. "Are you sure he asked the right questions?"

"Absolutely sure, ma'am." Detective Shine intervened. As he leaned around Sara to talk, he "accidentally" brushed Sara's arm and said, "Don't you have confidence in us, Mandy?"

"Sure I do," she answered sarcastically. "But clearly something has been overlooked."

Sara said, "So it seems whoever attacked Vivian came in the back door. He must have approached on foot, perhaps from the golf course."

"Bingo!" Shine exclaimed. "And that's where my expertise comes into play and why you can have one hundred percent confidence, Sara." He stood, puffed out his chest, and began to pace. "Detective Winston sent me to the golf clubhouse, and the man in the office was very helpful."

He paused to pour himself a cup of coffee. "Lucky for us, it was a quiet Monday morning with few players, so he remembered everyone who signed up."

Shine went on to describe an elderly couple who did nine slow holes, the foursome—two men, two women—whom Amanda had seen while sitting at the kitchen table, and a single man who played through earlier. "The cashier had never seen that guy before. Said he seemed in a hurry and paid cash."

Mom's ears pricked. "Did this stranger bring his own clubs and shoes?"

"Yes, ma'am, but he did rent a golf cart."

"If he didn't use a credit card, did the cashier take his name?"

Shine consulted his notes. "Ralph Morgan, though it could be an alias."

No shit, Sherlock, Amanda thought uncharitably. "Did the cashier see his car or a license plate?"

"No, he did not, but yours truly thought to check the videotape from the parking lot and caught the guy coming and going. I can report that he was tall, maybe 6'2" with a whitish blond crew cut, crisp new blue jeans, and a pale green Lacoste shirt. He was tan and fit, looked kinda like you, Mandy."

She sincerely hoped her grandmother's killer looked nothing like her. "What kind of car?"

"White, late model Ford Fusion. The plates tagged it as a local rental."

Shine rocked on his heels, grinning like a Cheshire cat. Luckily, Winston intervened before she decked the smug SOB, who seemed to be playing to an audience of one—Sara.

"We checked it out. It was rented in Charlotte to one Ralph Morgan, who had what appeared to be a valid license issued by NCDOT, which included a home address. Unfortunately, when we dispatched a unit to that address in Gastonia, it proved to be a deserted warehouse on an overgrown lot."

"So it was bogus," Linc choked out the words.

"I'm afraid so, and again he used cash, so the agent got no other form of ID but the fake license." Winston explained that the rental car customer had been a walk-in, so the agent never saw his original mode of transportation. "So if he had his own car, he must have left it out of sight down the block. Cagey bastard."

Sara asked, "So you definitely like the tall blond stranger as the killer?"

Shine spun a chair around to face Sara and sat in an aggressive, knees-apart posture. "He's our number one suspect." Then he turned to Linc. "The back door was another issue, Judge. Did your wife always leave it unlocked?"

Linc groaned. "God, how many times did I warn her about that?"

Mom confirmed. "Yes, I recall it was unlocked when I stepped out onto the patio to call you, Linc."

Trout sadly shook his head. "I've walked that golf course a time or two, so I know how easy it would be for someone to wait until no one was looking, then duck into that thick forest near the fifth hole and come up to Viv's patio unnoticed."

"None of the other golfers saw him, that's for sure," Shine said. "The time stamp on the video caught Morgan arriving at 9:16 and leaving the lot at 10:37. Allowing for check-in, he only had an hour or so on the course, not enough time to play nine holes."

*But plenty of time to sneak up and kill Grandma.* "I hate to say it, but if Morgan did it, he left only minutes before I arrived." The very idea made Amanda queasy. "What about fingerprints?"

Shine looked down at his spit-polished shoes. "Nothing. He wore gloves the whole time—golf gloves, I suspect, to attract no suspicion."

"What about Grandma's magic box? Was he carrying anything when he left?"

"Yes, he had a sports bag big enough to hold two boxes."

She again thought of the possibility of a golf club as the murder weapon. It now seemed more likely than not.

As the clock on the conference room wall ticked toward noon, Detective Winston finished up, and Amanda was impressed with his thoroughness. They had located the jeweler who sold Linc Grandma's engagement ring. The store even had a digital photo of the expensive diamond in their records. The police had already circulated the picture to all the local and not-so-local jewelers and pawn shops, advising them to be on the lookout for the stolen merchandise. They had posted the grainy parking lot video of the suspect to law enforcement online and put out a BOLO for his apprehension. Now they seemed to be in a holding pattern, waiting for the next clue to pop.

Mom spoke up as they all prepared to leave. "I still wish you'd come home with us, Linc. I don't like the idea of you being alone in that house."

"No, Diana, I have to do this." He turned to Winston. "And I'll get a copy of that will to you, sir."

"Thanks. I promise I'll contact all of you the moment I know more."

The meeting broke up, and the family headed out to the parking lot. They hugged, cried a little more, then got into their respective cars.

At least Sara tried to climb into the driver's seat of her little Miata, but Shine put his hand on the door, blocking her entry. He nodded toward Amanda and said, "Hey, are you guys *together* together? Like a couple?"

Sara's eyebrows shot up like startled raven's wings as she shoved his hand away. "Yes, Detective Slime, we are *together* together."

As they pulled away, they heard him shout, "The name's *Shine*, not *Slime!*"

"Isn't that what I said?" Sara winked as they sped off.

## Chapter Seven

A near stranger...

Amanda eased into the passenger pickup lane at Charlotte Douglas International Airport. The place was busy for a Wednesday night, with a string of headlights in Moby Dyke's rearview mirror and winking red taillights as far ahead as the eye could see. Robby was coming in from Philly on Delta and she was nervous about meeting her big brother—a near stranger.

"I haven't seen him for five years," she mumbled.

Sara lay her hand on Amanda's thigh. "I understand, babe, and you hadn't seen him for ten years before that. Don't worry. It'll be okay."

*Don't worry?* Sara didn't understand the half of it. Once upon a time, she and Robby had been close, clinging together like two small survivors of their parents' messy divorce. But she, the tomboy, had wrongfully sided with her father, Robert Rittenhouse, who taught her to fish, play sports, and even tinker with cars. Robby had rightfully sided with Diana. At the time, she'd been unaware of her father's abusive alcoholic behavior toward Mom, an oversight that caused Amanda to run away from home at age eighteen and stay gone for a decade.

She grabbed a parking space at the curb near Robby's gate, her heart racing in overdrive. "He doesn't exactly know about you, Sara," she confessed. "I mean, he knows we share a condo, but he doesn't know about *us*."

Sara belted out her Liberty Bell laugh. "So you haven't told him we're a couple?"

"Hell, I haven't told him I'm a lesbian."

Sara rolled her eyes. "Jesus, Mandy."

Amanda hated herself. She had always had trouble "coming out," especially to family. She only told Mom two years ago, and somehow, it never came up with Robby. Her cowardice had sometimes caused friction between Sara and her.

"I'm sorry, but was I supposed to just blurt it out in a phone conversation? I speak to Robby maybe three times a year."

"Well, I would have told him on the phone," Sara said. "Besides, I'd be shocked if he doesn't already know."

What did Sara know about her conservative, buttoned-up brother? It was possible that Robby had even voted for President McDonald. She was composing a sharp retort when she saw Robby elbowing through the crowd. He was carrying a briefcase, dragging a pull-along, and looking as scared as she was.

"That's him, right? I recognize him from your pictures." Sara pointed at the very tall, bespectacled young man loping giraffe-like through the crowd. Amanda exited the van, waving her arms like a windmill. "Yo, Robby, over here!"

Before Amanda could process, Sara had introduced herself, helped him load his luggage, and directed him into the backseat. Amanda barely had time to say hello before she had to tap her turn signal and steer into the frantic traffic leaving the airport.

Once she made it through the worst of the vehicular suicide games, Robby leaned across the seat and pecked her on the cheek. "That sign says we're traveling on the Billy Graham Parkway," he drawled. "Gotta love North Carolina. Did you guys hear how Graham's clueless son, Franklin, called out our fine progressive candidate from Indiana for being gay? The asshole said he should repent his sins."

"Which one is the asshole?" Amanda could hardly believe her ears.

"Franklin Graham's the asshole, of course," Robby replied. "Screw those idiots."

Sara laughed. "Amen to that. Robby, you do know Mandy and I are a lesbian couple, right?"

He took a moment to answer. In the interim, Amanda was so shocked she almost missed the on-ramp to the expressway.

Finally, he said, "Well, of course I knew that. I lived with Mandy for eighteen years before she took off, and I wasn't blind. I'm really happy for you both." He punched Amanda's shoulder. "And I approve of your taste in women, sis. Too bad you were such a wuss, or we could have compared notes on our lady loves long before now."

Amanda groaned and pulled into the slow lane, allowing the aggressors to speed on by. Leave it to Sara to "out" her. It was both outrageous and a relief, but she definitely refused to say one more word about it now. She now knew that Robby had definitely not voted for McDonald, and that was a blessing. Considering the tragic occasion that brought them together, now they could relax and not worry about sexual orientation or politics. They could concentrate on the sorrow at hand.

That sobering thought seemed to hit them all as they drove north on I-77. All bantering stopped as they stared into the night.

"I can't believe it," Robby said at last. "Who would want to hurt Grandma? I haven't seen much of her lately, but the lady I remember was sweet and loving and hadn't one enemy in the world."

"Yeah, I know," Amanda agreed. She had actually gotten to know Grandma a lot better these past few years—as an adult, not a child. She'd seen the woman's feisty side, as well as the independence that allowed her to start over with Linc. Still, with the exception of the spats she sometimes had with Mom, Grandma fought with no one.

"Let me tell you what the police know so far…" Sara then proceeded to fill Robby in on the investigation, the suspect, and the lack of any additional progress in the case.

"So it could have been a simple robbery since the diamond ring and the jewelry box were missing," Robby said.

"Unfortunately, it seemed to be premeditated since the guy drove a rental car, used only cash, and had a fake name and address," Amanda said.

"Unless the suspect from the golf course was completely innocent," Sara said. "What if he was just some random businessman using a rental car who needed a golf break?"

"What about the fake ID?" Robby objected.

Sara countered, "What if he's just a jerk who doesn't want his wife to know about his extracurricular activities? It happens."

Amanda smiled. "*It happens?* What are you

keeping from me?"

"You're not my *wife*."

"C'mon, be nice, girls. What you're trying to tell me is that the authorities don't have much but circumstantial evidence."

"You're the lawyer, and you're right." Suddenly, tears pressed behind Amanda's eyes. "I'm sorry, Robby, this is all so horrible. You're staying with Sara and me, right? We have a guest bedroom."

"I'm afraid not. Mom's really torn up about Grandma, and she begged me to stay with them up on the lake—get to know Trout and the rest of your new family."

"It's your family, too."

"Whatever."

Checking the rearview mirror, she saw tears in Robby's eyes. For the hundredth time in three short days, she was dumbstruck by the absurdity of the nightmare that had descended upon them all.

"There's another reason I'm staying up in Mooresville," Robby added. "Since I'm an attorney, they want me to advise them. It seems some guy named Mecklin Adams is coming to their home tomorrow to read Grandma's last will and testament."

This was news to her. "Already? Did Linc find Grandma's will? Why aren't we going to Mr. Adams's office? Why is he coming to Mom's house?"

"I don't know, Mandy, but I know this much—you will have to be there at 3 p.m. tomorrow afternoon. Grandma's new husband will be there, too. Never met the guy."

"May I come?" Sara asked.

Robby winked. "Gosh, I don't know. You're not Mandy's *wife*, are you?"

## Chapter Eight

*A storm was brewing...*

A storm was brewing when they drove onto the gravel driveway at the Troutmans' lake home. The oppressively hot spring day was heavy with humidity, and the tender new leaves on the willow oaks were limp green rags gasping for breath. The sky and water were placid blue, the stillness broken only by the laughter of Amanda's stepsister, Ginny, as she dribbled water on her toddler son, Thomas, and splashed her eleven-year-old daughter, Lissa, down on the beach.

"You better put the top up," Amanda cautioned Sara, who complied by pushing a button on the dash that rolled up the canvas roof on the little red convertible.

"Looks like we're late to the party," Sara said as she clipped down the top, ran fingers through her windblown hair, and touched Amanda's nose. "You got some sunburn."

Amanda smiled and glanced at her bare arms as they climbed stiffly from the car. Looked more like freckles to her, and yes, it seemed like everyone else was already there for the reading of the will. She recognized all but one car, a gray Honda Accord that likely belonged to the lawyer. She did not see any official-looking vehicles that might indicate the presence of either Detective Shine or Winston. For this, she was grateful since she'd half expected them to crash this private party. "We're only fifteen minutes late, but they might have started without us."

"Don't be so sure, babe." Sara winked. "It's likely Vivian remembered you in her will."

Amanda doubted it, didn't really care. All she wanted was her grandma back.

As they entered the air-conditioned kitchen, Ursie, the ancient Doberman, shoved her cold nose into Amanda's hand and wiggled her stubby tail. She hobbled in their wake to where everyone was seated at the long dining room table, and the muted atmosphere instantly struck Amanda as all wrong. Usually this room was filled with animated voices, music, or the cartoon sounds of video games when Lissa was around. She assumed the stranger seated at the head of the table was Mecklin Adams, with Mom, Trout, and Linc to his left—Robby to his right. All the men stood when Sara and she entered, a formality that also seemed off key.

Robby introduced the lawyer, who was a country version of Robby himself. Mecklin appeared to be several years older than her brother, perhaps forty. He was tall, slim, with horn-rimmed glasses and a seriously geeky persona—yet the man projected slightly less polish than her lawyerly brother. After introductions were made, Adams indicated they should all be seated.

Sara hesitated. "Should I be included here?"

"Significant others are welcome," Robby assured her and patted the seat beside him.

"Are you sure?"

"Asked and answered," Mecklin said and then blushed.

Thankfully, someone had told him the score, so

they sat beside Robby, the younger generation facing the older. No one seemed to know quite how to start until Linc cleared his throat and began with a joke.

He grinned at Mecklin. "Now I outrank you, son. I recall you coming before my bench as a baby fresh out of law school, so why did my wife go to you, not me, to draw up her will?"

The family laughed, but the Statesville lawyer was obviously flustered. Yet he got it together and said, "I did some work for Mrs. Davis before she married you, Judge." Other than that, he offered no reasonable explanation and began apologizing.

Linc said, "Apology overruled, Mr. Adams. I am perfectly satisfied with Vivian's decision, but looking at that thick pile of documents before you, I hope you did not charge by the page."

"No, Your Honor." The poor man gulped.

At that point, Trout elbowed Linc. "Give him a break, Lincoln. Let the man do his job."

In the meantime, Amanda stared through the picture window and watched Ginny playing with her kids. Trout's daughter, who was exactly her age, had proven to be a soulmate. Ginny was so much a part of her family now that it seemed she too deserved a place at the table for this sad occasion. But she was not blood to Viv, Mom, or her—as if blood relationship was any measure of the bond of love.

After shuffling the documents into three distinct piles, Mecklin explained that he was starting with the disposition of Grandma's home and contents in Silver Bay. "Mrs. Davis's share in that real property reverts to her beloved husband, Lincoln, along with all the furnishings, art, and personal property they have purchased together since their marriage."

That seemed reasonable, Amanda had expected nothing less. As much as she had loved Grandpa Will Whitaker, who died many years ago in Pennsylvania, she had never resented Grandma for remarrying.

The next pile of papers concerned Grandma's financial assets—cash, stock, and life insurance acquired before her marriage to Linc. Wealthy in his own right, Linc had signed a prenuptial agreement allowing that all Viv's premarital assets would pass on to her only daughter, Diana Whitaker Rittenhouse Troutman—Mom. When Mecklin stood and silently reviewed those figures with Mom, tears filled her eyes.

"But this can't be right. I had no idea Mama had so much money in her checking and all this stock!" Mom seemed floored as she shared the sums with Trout. "And one hundred thousand in life insurance? No way!"

Amanda was thrilled. Trout was nearing retirement, and Mom's real estate career was demanding and financially uncertain. Though they never complained about needing cash, she knew their aging home needed some minor and major repairs, like a new dock. So the money would be welcome.

"I can't accept all this," Mom said to Amanda and Robby. "You kids must take some."

She and Robby loudly objected, while Sara chuckled softly at her side. Mecklin, wanting to get on with his presentation, quickly closed them down and waved the last few pages from the second stack.

"This is a list of personal property, some antiques and stuff originating from the old Whitaker home in Pennsylvania. Many of these pieces are earmarked for Amanda and Robert." He paused to smile at the brother and sister. "But your grandmother said to warn you that these items aren't valuable, yet they may have sentimental worth. She said if you don't want something, pass it on or throw it away."

Amanda would never give up anything Grandma left her. She knew her favorite ballerina pin was gone along with the magic box, but she was hopeful about finding the hobby horse Grandpa had made for her. She realized Grandma had a storage unit where she'd hoarded old possessions and could easily picture the brightly colored wooden horse in their eclectic condo.

"I wonder if Grandma kept any of Grandpa's fishing rods or hunting rifles," Robby mused.

As Mecklin passed the list around the table, Mom promised to take them to the storage unit before Robby left town. "So I guess that's everything," she asked the lawyer.

Linc pointed at the third stack of papers. "Nope, it appears the young man's not done yet, but he better pick up the pace if he wants to beat the storm."

Right on cue, thunder clapped nearby. Down by the lake, Ginny squealed and scooped up baby Thomas. She and Lissa ran toward the house, while Ursie hid under the table. Amanda was accustomed to sudden afternoon storms in the summer, but April was early—global warming, she decided as the sky turned dramatically dark and the wind picked up.

"Okay, then..." Mecklin nervously picked up the stack and captured everyone's attention before speaking. "This last part involves the disposition of Vivian Davis's real estate holdings in Surry County, North Carolina, which represent the largest portion of her estate by far."

Mom quickly interrupted. "Mr. Adams, you are mistaken. Mama didn't own real estate up in Surry

County."

He held up a trembling hand to silence her. "Please let me finish, Mrs. Troutman. This is hard enough for me as it is. You see, this was the work I did for your mother when she first moved back to North Carolina, before she married the judge."

Linc appeared stunned. "My God, maybe Viv really did keepsome secrets from this old dog!"

"Please let me continue, sir," Mecklin said. "The property is just over two hundred acres located near the small town of Mount Airy, in the triangle between interstate highways 77 and 74. It includes the original homestead, barn, and several outbuildings."

"This is not possible," Mom objected.

"I have the deeds and maps right here, ma'am, and your mother asked me to read this next part aloud: *The farm, called Mayberry, shall pass to my grandchildren. The real and personal property may be retained or sold, according to a mutually agreeable compromise between the heirs. In any case, ownership shall be divided into three equal shares for my three grandchildren: Amanda and Robert Rittenhouse and Judd Taylor. May this surprise bring you all great happiness. Love, Grandma.*"

As thunder clapped and rain pelted the roof, it seemed all the oxygen had been sucked from the room, leaving its occupants gasping for breath.

Robby spoke first. "No way, man. Something is wrong."

"What *farm*, what *Mayberry*?" Amanda cried as Sara gripped her hand.

"What *third grandchild*?" Mom was deathly pale. "And who the hell is Judd Taylor? I've never heard of this person."

## Chapter Nine

Attorney-client privilege...

"What's happening?" Ginny and her kids burst through the door, soaking wet. She saw Sara on her feet, attempting to calm Amanda and Robby. Her dad's arm encircled Diana as he patted her shoulder. Linc's face was buried in his hands, while the lawyer from Statesville paced. She took one look at the shell-shocked group and headed for the dry towels in the guest bathroom.

"I'm sorry," Mecklin Adams said at last. "I see you're all upset, but is this such bad news? After all, you've just received substantial inheritances, especially Amanda and Robert."

They all glared at him.

Linc shook his head. "How could Vivian not tell me she had a third grandchild? Diana, could you have a brother or sister you don't know about? Could he or she have given birth?"

"Absolutely not. I had no siblings. I was an only child."

Trout gently asked, "Was your mama married before she married your daddy?"

"No! Aren't you listening? Daddy was Mama's first love. She was only eighteen when she married him. This is all complete nonsense."

Amanda didn't know what to think, except she

couldn't imagine how Grandma could have kept such a huge secret from them all those years. She leaned back against Sara and found her hand. She was amazed that for once her partner had nothing to say because usually Sara's practical, analytical mind would have offered possibilities no one wanted to hear, at least not right now.

Seated beside her, Robby was running on emotional overload. She braced herself for one of his inappropriate jokes, which was his default behavior when his world spun out of control. She did not have to wait long.

"Hey, Mom, did you have any kids we don't know about?" he teased.

"That's not funny, son," Trout scolded.

But Mom took it in stride. She understood Robby's insecurities better than anyone. "Are you asking if I gave birth to any bastards in the closet? No, Robert, your father was more than enough to deal with, thank you very much."

"Sorry, Mom."

Amanda kicked him under the table. Robby yelped and then shut up.

Linc asked, "Mr. Adams, did you find any birth records, or did you take my wife at her word?" Perhaps his long career as a judge, overseeing the best and worst in human nature, allowed him to even consider the possibility of an indiscretion in Vivian's past.

"No, sir, no birth certificates. I didn't look that far. However, the chain of ownership for Mayberry may offer some clues. Vivian's maiden name was Yount. She inherited the farm from a woman named Alice Yount—"

Mom interrupted. "Yes, that would be my great-aunt Alice, but I never knew the woman because she died before I was born."

Mecklin said, "Yes, and when Alice died, Vivian inherited Mayberry. The very next year, Vivian added the name Thomas Taylor to the deed, granting him a twenty percent ownership."

"Who the hell is Thomas Taylor?" Robby demanded.

"No idea," Mom said. "Never heard of the man."

"Some years later, Vivian dropped Thomas Taylor and reinstated the twenty percent grant to one Andrew Taylor. Ring any bells?"

"No bells whatsoever," Mom petulantly responded. "Why would Mother do such a thing? I was four years old at the time. Mama was happily married to Daddy. It makes no sense."

Sara left her post standing behind Amanda and Robby, then took a seat and turned to Mecklin. "Did you find any death certificates? For instance, do you know when the first co-owner, Thomas Taylor, died?"

The lawyer grinned. "Yes, ma'am, I did get that far. Thomas died in 1968 at age 40, the same year Andrew got substituted."

Amanda's head was exploding from information overload. The meaningless names and dates ricocheted as she pieced together the implications. If she made a chart, maybe it would be easier to place these Taylors in time. "So where does Judd Taylor, the supposed grandchild, come in?"

Mecklin gleefully rubbed his hands together. "Judd got onto the deed replacing Andrew in 1974. In 1985, she added Robert, then two years later, she added you, Mandy. By that time, Vivian had reduced her ownership from eighty to forty percent, giving you grandkids twenty percent each. That was the last time she altered her will, until she retained me. I drew up the final version, which explains how her forty percent is to be divided equally among you, Robby, and Judd upon her death. Mrs. Davis also retained me to make sure there were no challenges down the line."

Amanda quickly did the math. Assuming Grandma added her grandchildren when each was born, it meant that Judd was eleven years older than Robby and thirteen years older than she.

Obviously, Robby was doing the math, too. "This dude Judd is forty-five. He's, like, middle-aged."

"So are you, dummy!" she pointed out.

"Stop it, kids," Mom scolded. "Remember, this person is *not* related to you, so forget it."

The family members around the table gazed at one another, seemingly at a loss. At the same time, the sun came out and sparkled on the lake. It washed the fresh young leaves in a golden glow seen only after storms. Amanda didn't know how she felt. If any of this were true, this Judd person would be her cousin. Indeed, in a family as small as theirs, with a gene pool that had probably reached the end of the line, was new blood such a bad thing? Clearly, Mom wanted no part of it.

"So what's next?" Linc inquired.

"I'll leave this paperwork with you, a copy for everyone," Mecklin said. "I'll keep my copy in my safe, and I'll register the will with Iredell County. I'll also make the deed changes for Mayberry in Surry County." He pointedly looked at his wristwatch. "But now I gotta run. I'm sure you'll have lots of questions, so feel free to call me anytime."

As Mecklin Adams rushed a little too eagerly

toward the door, Amanda jumped to her feet. "Hey, wait, *I* have a question. You must have spent hours with Grandma, and she knew the introduction of Judd Taylor would send her family into a tailspin. What did she tell you about this surprise relative of ours?"

He was halfway out the door and not slowing down. "Mrs. Davis did tell me a few things, and it wasn't easy for her. But I'm afraid I can't share those confidences. They're attorney-client privileged."

And then he was gone.

## Chapter Ten

Everyone was guessing...

No one spoke when Mecklin closed the door behind him, started his car, and backed out the gravel drive. Not until Ginny and the kids burst into the room did the dumbfounded family blink.

"So he's gone, let's order a pizza!" Ginny cheerfully called out. Her punk-cut black hair was towel dried and stuck out in spikes; her nose stud glittered.

Amanda, a fan of classic comics, decided she looked like a barefoot Daisy Mae, with her bosom ballooning from a red checked halter top and her hips clad in shredded denim shorts. Ginny's husband, Trev Dula, owned a nightclub and was working late that night, so likely Ginny would be with them all evening.

"Yeah, I'm starving!" Lissa, with her lake-frizzed red curls, resembled Raggedy Ann.

Their comical entry, including baby Thomas swaddled in a faded vintage Stones T-shirt, made Amanda feel much better.

"Now tell me what Vivian said in her will." Ginny struck a pose.

Trout shook his head, kissed Mom on the cheek, and rose stiffly from his chair. He walked up to Ginny and took his grandson into his arms. "I reckon I'll let the others bring you up to date, while I take this young'un for a stroll up the road." He whistled for

Ursie, who was always up for a walk, and they left together, the screen door slamming behind them.

Sara said, "Trout's got the right idea. They'll be throwing some surprising news at you, Ginny, and I'm in need of some fresh air myself." She turned to Lissa. "How about you and I take a ride up to Mama's Pizza Shop in my red convertible?"

Lissa squealed with delight. "Can I go, Mom?"

Ginny seemed taken aback by the sudden abduction of her children, but she gave Lissa permission and watched as Amanda followed Sara to the door.

"What are you doing, Sara?" Amanda demanded once she was out of earshot. Sara had never before demonstrated much of a maternal instinct and tended to shy away from kids.

"Look, Mandy, this is a family matter. I don't need to sit in on every detail. Besides, I've had enough drama for one day." She took Lissa's hand, both grinning broadly, and suddenly, they were gone.

Next, Amanda almost bumped into Linc, who was also on his way out. "You're leaving, too?"

He ran a hand through his luxuriant white hair and fixed her with tired eyes. "You know, today has been a little too much for me." With that same hand, he patted the banded documents tucked under his elbow. "Viv's will has thrown me for a loop. I need to take these papers home and try to make sense of it all. Though we were only married five years, I thought I knew the woman. I was wrong."

Amanda didn't know how to comfort him. She'd been with Sara that same length of time and didn't know everything by a longshot, but so far, nothing remotely like Grandma's skeleton had popped from Sara's closet. "It'll be all right, Linc," she lamely told him.

He shrugged and pulled a chain from his pocket. While she struggled for better words, he removed a small key and pressed it into her hand. "This opens Viv's unit at Lake Norman Storage, just up the road on River Highway. You all need to take what you want before Robby goes back to Philly. When you're done, turn in the key for me, please. Have them send me a bill."

"Don't you want to come with us?"

"No, I want no part of it, thank you very much."

She watched in silence as he climbed into his Chrysler and drove away. She understood how he felt. She also hoped they would all get through this—whatever this was. By the time she returned to the table, it was abundantly clear that Ginny had received her update.

"Holy shit!" Ginny kept repeating as she paced. "Who the hell is Judd Taylor?" She turned to Amanda. "Hey, do you realize you have a first cousin you never knew? And you, Diana, have a brand new nephew."

"We'll see about that." Mom scooped up her copy of the will and headed for the sunroom, where the golden light left the far shore in dark silhouette, then drifted into the dazzling lake. As she moved into the room, she snagged her laptop and then closed the door behind her.

"Mom's in denial," Robby said as he thumbed through the list of personal property.

"Aren't we all?" Amanda said. "Mom just needs time out to absorb all this, and who can blame her? It's gotta hurt that Grandma never confided in her about giving birth to a baby boy."

Ginny interrupted. "What makes you think

it was a *boy*? "Shame on you, Mandy, feminist that you claim to be. From what I've been told, this third grandson is likely third generation. Viv could have abandoned a baby *girl*, who then had a child, and that child gave birth to Judd Taylor. Isn't that possible?"

She and Robby stared at Ginny as they considered her hypothesis. Amanda's mind raced as she recalled the string of heirs Mecklin had described on the deed: Thomas Taylor, Andrew Taylor, and Judd Taylor. "I see your point, Ginny, but if Grandma's baby girl eventually got married and had a child, that child's name would not be Taylor, right?"

Ginny laughed. "Who says the girl got *married*? Seems like folks back then, your grandma included, didn't necessarily bother with the formality of matrimony before getting pregnant."

Amanda's face grew hot with shame, or was it anger? Ginny, who got pregnant with Lissa out of wedlock, was in no position to throw stones.

Robby, also a little flushed, looked up and said, "I think you're wrong. The deed implies that Thomas was Grandma's lover, and their child was Andrew. I'm guessing Judd was Andrew's son from a legal marriage, and that's why he also bears the surname Taylor."

Everyone was guessing, but in the meantime, Ginny had suddenly gone pale. "What's wrong?" Amanda asked her.

"I just remembered. My son is named Thomas, right? Guess who suggested that name."

"Grandma?"

"She did. In fact, Viv almost insisted I use that name, said it was noble, strong, and romantic. God, did she convince me to name *my* son after *her* lover?"

The question had an obvious answer, but

Amanda decided to change the subject. "Hey, Robby, you've been reading the gift list. Did Grandma leave you Grandpa's rods and guns?"

"Yeah, she did, and I suppose she stashed them in that storage bin she rented."

"Speaking of which, I have the key." She opened her hand and showed them. "Maybe we can all go check it out tomorrow."

"Yea, can I come?" Ginny asked. "I'll take the scraps. Anything you don't want, I'll keep or donate to Goodwill."

"Sure you can come, Miss Dumpster Diver," she said.

"More the merrier," Robby mumbled as he moved on to perusing the deed to Mayberry. "I'll have to leave on Sunday, after Grandma's funeral on Saturday."

Mentioning the funeral lowered a veil of sadness on the group. Amanda didn't know much about the plans. Mom and Linc had been quietly making the arrangements, while she could barely stand to think about it—it was her own form of denial. The shock of a mystery grandchild, bizarre as that was, was a welcome distraction from the fact of Grandma's violent death—her murder.

"Whoa, this is interesting," Robby said, interrupting her sorrow. "We grandchildren hold the title to Mayberry as *joint tenants*."

"So what?" Amanda sighed.

"So that means that the thirty-three and a third percent we each own passes on to the other two if one of us dies. In other words, our shares can't pass on to any outside heirs."

"I still don't get it."

"Well, if Grandma had made us *tenants in common* instead, then, say, if I died, my portion would pass on to my children or to whomever I had willed it to."

"Look, can you take off your lawyer hat for one minute and tell me in plain English what Grandma intended?"

"Mandy, you can be so dense." Robby stuck out his tongue at her. "Grandma wanted you, me, and Judd to get Mayberry—nobody else. If one dies, the other two get it. If two die, survivor takes all. Get it?"

"Got it!" Mom shouted from the sunroom and then quickly joined them. "It's Real Estate 101. Listen up, kids, your grandmother absolutely wanted you and this Judd person to have this place, and I don't understand one damn bit of it."

Mom slid her laptop down onto the table between them, then flipped the lid open to a shot from Google Earth. "Look at this. I entered the coordinates of the Mayberry property, and here's what I found."

She jiggled her mouse. All Amanda saw was a blur of green treetops nestled with its triangular point between two major highways.

Mom continued, "These are the two hundred-plus acres described on the deed, bordered on the two long sides by interstates 77 and 74." She zoomed in closer, so that some defined fields and forests appeared. "Looks to me like nobody's farming most of these fields anymore. They've gone to seed, nothing but brush and weeds. What a waste."

Amanda searched her mother's face. Clearly, the curiosity of the real estate agent had won out. Mom was angry, still in denial, but couldn't help but investigate.

"So where's the house?" Ginny was as excited as a kid on Christmas morning.

Mom grunted and moved in closer on the roofs of what appeared to be a dilapidated barn and some chicken coops. Soon a rural road appeared at the wide base of the triangle, with a winding dirt path branching off it into a heavily forested area.

"I can't see a thing," Robby complained.

Mom guided the cursor down the twisted path until, set far back from that path, a crooked wooden porch, sagging door, and a few raw boards of siding came into focus.

"Looks like a dump," Robby commented.

Amanda squinted. "Can't you get closer?"

"Sorry, dear, that's the best view this technology can offer." Mom snorted. "Maybe someday you'll meet this Judd person, and he'll show you more."

"One hour ago, we didn't even know Judd Taylor existed," Amanda pointed out.

"Hey, guys, that's not the big question," Ginny said. "Does Judd Taylor even know *you* exist?"

## Chapter Eleven

### Treasures and trash...

*Did* Judd Taylor even know they existed? It was a good question. It troubled Amanda all through the night and into the next morning as she watched Sara dress for work. In Sara's opinion, Judd did not know they existed, but he soon would.

"Chances are Judd will find out about his surprise cousins from Mecklin Adams, just like you did," she told Amanda.

"Mecklin's coming to Grandma's funeral, so we'll find out then if he's told Judd. God, I guess he'll be as shocked as we were."

They were all still guessing, but Amanda put the unknowable aside the moment she stepped into the big steel building that housed Grandma's storage unit. Once she entered the dimly lit, climate-controlled hallway, with locked units on either side, it didn't take long to locate Grandma's. She just followed the laughter.

Mom, Robby, and Ginny were already there. Their enthusiasm spilled out into the hallway, along with stacks of cardboard boxes filled with the treasures and trash of a lifetime. Robby had taped the gift list to the unit's wall, and they were sorting their loot. His pile was clearly identifiable, with old rifles, rods, and tackle boxes. Mom had started hers and was lovingly fondling an ornately painted china pitcher.

"My grandmother Whitaker painted this chocolate set!" she exclaimed. "See the six little cups? Each one is decorated with a different fruit. She was so talented."

While Mom waxed eloquent about how ladies of that period were extraordinarily skilled at painting china and floral watercolors, Amanda spotted her beloved hobby horse in her own special pile. She also found a tiny crib Grandpa had made, along with the "Ginny" dolls who slept in it. Even more exciting was the plastic set of cowboys, Indians, and horses she used to play with. They almost made up for Robby getting the electric train.

In the meantime, Ginny separated out the books, some of Grandma's most adored possessions, each with her name: *Vivian Leigh Yount* neatly printed inside each cover. Robby got the "first editions," some signed by the authors. Amanda got the Nancy Drew and Trixie Belden mysteries, with Mom's name stamped inside. Ginny, who was assembling her own stack of discards, got the well-worn paperbacks and pulp fiction.

"Wow, look at this!" Mom had unearthed a carton of family photos. The most recent were neatly displayed in numbered albums, the old ones in those yellow cardboard boxes that reams of typing paper were once sold in. Everyone dug in and gaped at the pictures.

Amanda and Mom were most intrigued by the old ones, including Polaroids and little square black and whites of life on the Whitaker farm in Pennsylvania. Grandma and Grandpa were so young—Robby a toddler, Amanda a baby.

Conspicuously missing were any photos of Grandma's "secret" life. Amanda was sure that Mom, like she, was looking for those clues to Mayberry and the time Vivian spent living with Aunt Alice. But there were none. There was, however, a sealed linen envelope, stained by time, with Amanda's name on it.

Mom ceremoniously handed it to her. "You better open it, Mandy."

Inside were a small key and a note from Grandma: *Dear Mandy, This key unlocks the fold-down writing surface of Aunt Alice's antique slant top desk. You will find a second key, one that unlocks the pigeonholes inside the desk, inside my jewelry box at our Mooresville town house. You called it my "magic box," remember? What you find in Aunt Alice's desk is yours to share with the others in our family but only when they are ready. Until then, keep this letter and its contents to yourself. I trust you on this. Love, Grandma.*

Amanda quickly hid the key and the note deep in her pocket. "Hey, has anyone found an antique slant top desk?"

"What did the note say?" Mom demanded.

She ignored Mom. "The desk must be here in the storage unit."

"Nope." Robby barely looked up from the old red Swiss army knife he was playing with.

"I haven't seen a desk," Ginny echoed.

"It's not here," Mom stated with certainty. "Besides, I don't remember Mama ever owning a slant top desk."

Amanda sank to the cold concrete floor and leaned against the security gate to the storage unit. Even if they found the mysterious desk, she only had one key and was completely out of luck. Because Grandma's jewelry box had been stolen the day she died. The killer had the second key.

## Chapter Twelve

A beautiful ceremony...

Grandma's service at Trinity Lutheran in nearby Troutman was beautiful and brief—just the way she would have wanted it. The morning was fresh and clear. The stained-glass windows were brilliantly illuminated, sending dancing colored sunbeams onto the shoulders of the mourners nearest the wall and onto the pastor's lectern.

The church was packed with friends, acquaintances, and the family seated upfront. Amanda was surprised to see so many people, but then Vivian and Linc had grown up in North Carolina. A preponderance of elderly congregants attested to that fact, and the pastor, who seemed to know Grandma well, had actually attended grammar school with her. Amanda recognized Grandma's doctors, a few neighbors, and even her hairdresser.

She gazed at the simple wooden urn holding Grandma's ashes and reflected on her many years on this earth. The pastor was emphasizing the happy highlights of a life fully lived. Until that week, no one had realized quite how full that life had been.

Mom whispered, "Linc's taking your grandmother's ashes to Paris, where they spent their honeymoon. She wanted him to scatter them at some undisclosed location in the city that was special to them."

"Can they even carry ashes on an airplane?"

"Apparently, the funeral home gave him a certificate that's airline-approved. I wonder if he'll sprinkle her into the Seine."

Amanda groaned, wondering how many tons of human ashes had been dumped into that historic river. If that were Grandma's final resting place, she figured she'd be among some famous and infamous company.

Sara jabbed her gently in the ribs and pressed a finger to her lips, urging her and Mom to respect the solemn occasion. Amanda nodded and winked, yet she knew full well Grandma would enjoy the irreverent banter.

After the service, the family and a few select guests drifted into the church's activity room, where a light brunch awaited. She was disturbed to see detectives Winston and Shine lurking behind the buffet like birds of prey in dark suits.

"What do they want?" Amanda asked Sara.

"Maybe they're watching to see if the perp will show up to affirm the outcome of his handiwork."

"Very funny."

Just then, Robby came up from behind and took their arms. "Why don't we go ask them what they're up to? Maybe they have news about the investigation."

Detective John Winston was solemn and respectful as they approached, but Shine zeroed in on Sara's breasts, which were especially lovely in a low-cut, jade silk blouse.

Mecklin Adams also loped up to the table, again looking much like the country version of Robby, only his linen suit was more rumpled than her brother's. The lawyers shook hands and Linc joined their group, completing the law enforcement community.

After expressing his condolences, Winston got right to the point. "I'm afraid we have little of consequence to report. After reinterviewing the neighbors, the golf course personnel, and the rental car company, nothing new has turned up."

Linc frowned. "Are you giving up?"

"No, sir, not at all. We'll stay right on top of it." Shine was responding to Linc, yet his gaze had not left Sara. He chose a miniature egg salad croissant and stuffed it into his mouth.

Mecklin dug into a battered briefcase and handed Winston a document. "This is the copy of Vivian Davis's will you requested. I think you might find some threads to pull here."

"What do you mean?" Winston took the papers.

The Statesville lawyer shifted uncomfortably foot to foot. "Well, it's unusual and completely unexpected. You see, a property in Surry County and a third grandchild have popped up. The family had no knowledge of the place or the person."

"I'll take a look." Winston tucked it under his arm. Managing to look both intrigued and confused, he tried to free a hand to fill a plate, but in the end, he gave up. Signaling Shine that it was time to leave, he dragged his reluctant sidekick away from the food—and Sara. Then soon, after a courtesy word with Mom, they both left.

"Well, that was not helpful," Linc grumbled. Moments later, he too departed to join a table of friends already eating their salads and finger foods.

Feeling ill at ease and not at all hungry, Amanda looked around the room of relative strangers, while Sara helped herself to a heaping platter. "Now what?"

"Why don't we sit with our family?" Robby suggested.

The three, with Mecklin tagging along, pulled up chairs with Mom, Trout, Ginny, her husband, Trev, and Lissa. Lissa wasn't at all shy about sampling all the dainty desserts, including strawberry shortcake that precisely matched her hair and red-stained lips.

"That was a beautiful ceremony," the child said in her best grown-up voice.

"Yes, it was, honey." Trev wrapped a protective arm on the back of her chair.

Mom still looked shell-shocked, and her appetite seemed no better than Amanda's as they both sipped iced tea. Mom turned to Mecklin. "Have you contacted Judd Taylor yet?"

"Yes, ma'am, I have. And I gotta say, the man was just as surprised as you were to hear about his, uh, extended family." He cleared his throat. "In fact, Mr. Taylor was largely speechless as he listened. I had to repeat everything several times."

"You contacted him by phone, but you haven't met him?" Mom demanded.

"No, I haven't met him. I sent a copy of the will via FedEx to a law office in Mount Airy, and I suspect Mr. Taylor has read it by now."

"He actually lives in Mount Airy, right near Mayberry?" Sara asked.

"Yes, Judd Taylor was born and raised there—third generation, just as we expected."

Mecklin explained that Thomas Taylor was indeed Judd's grandfather. Andrew, son of Thomas and Vivian, was his father. "Unfortunately, Andrew died young, in Vietnam, and since then, the Mayberry Farm has fallen on hard times.

"Judd is married with three children, and here's the thing...he wants to meet all of you as soon as possible. He can't wait to show you the old home place and get to know you."

"Oh, good Lord!" Mom rolled her eyes, but Amanda sensed her attitude toward her mystery nephew was softening.

"Well, *I* can't wait to meet him," Amanda said and suddenly meant it with all her heart. "When can we drive up there?"

Robby blinked several times. "I want to go, too. I've already decided to delay my return to Philly by one week and have informed my law office. I intend to rent a car and drive home with all my inherited loot. Can't very well carry a couple of rifles onto an airplane, can I?"

"Oh, good Lord!" Mom repeated.

Everyone else agreed the plan sounded wonderful. They would rent a couple of motel rooms and explore.

"It's an adventure!" Lissa squealed. "Can I come?"

"You're still in school, young lady," Ginny said. "Maybe you can go during summer vacation."

Amanda glanced hopefully at Sara. "Any chance you could take a few days off?"

Sara squeezed her hand. "Not sure, babe, but I'll see what I can do."

Even Mom seemed curious. After some vacillation, she said. "I have out-of-town buyers." It was her go-to excuse.

Just then, Linc walked over with a man who looked familiar. He was young, meticulously groomed, and appeared to be of Indian or Pakistani descent. "This is Dr. Patel, Vivian's endocrinologist."

After Linc introduced him, Amanda remembered. She had taken Grandma to his office several times.

"I am so sorry about Miss Vivian," he said. "I cannot believe she died the same day we had an appointment."

That horrible morning rushed back to Amanda. "That's right. I was supposed to get Grandma to your place by eleven that morning. I thought we were going to be late."

"Miss Vivian also feared she would be late." Dr. Patel sadly shook his head. "That's why she called the office around nine thirty to ask if she could come one hour later, at eleven. Ordinarily, we would not allow such a last-minute change, but your grandmother was special."

Mom added, "I remember. I would have taken my mother myself had she not changed the time. That's why I needed you, Mandy."

"I hope the time change did not inconvenience *you*, Judge Davis," Dr. Patel said.

"Why would it be any concern of mine?" Linc gruffly retorted.

The young doctor registered surprise. "Well, you did specifically call the week before to inquire as to the date and time of Miss Vivian's next appointment. You told the receptionist you would like to sit in on the consultation."

"I did no such thing," Linc barked. "I was never aware of my wife's various medical appointments. She handled those things."

"With all due respect, sir, the receptionist who spoke to you was very specific. She told me Judge Lincoln Davis had called. And she told *you* that Miss Vivian's next appointment was Monday, April 15, at ten a.m."

Linc became dangerously red in the face. "I never called your office, Dr. Patel."

"Then who the hell did?" the distraught physician barked back.

## Chapter Thirteen

Jumping to conclusions...

"Who called Dr. Patel?" Amanda again asked Sara as they sipped wine and munched on leftover goodies from Grandma's funeral. They were sitting on the patio of their condo, watching the sun sink into the lake.

"It doesn't make sense that his receptionist would make a mistake with the name, and obviously, the caller was male. Is it possible that Linc forgot he made that call?" Sara frowned as she rearranged a plate of veggie sticks, separating the carrots from the celery.

"It's not possible, Sara. I'm sure Vivian never bothered Linc with the details of her day-to-day appointments. In that way, she was very independent. But why would some man pretend to be Linc or care about Viv's appointment?"

After the doctor's odd revelation at the reception, Mom had rushed from the activities room and caught up with detectives Winston and Shine to tell them about the suspicious event.

"Well, the police will check it out. Maybe the receptionist can help them pinpoint when the call came in, and they can trace it to a phone number."

"Yeah, right," Amanda responded sarcastically. She read crime novels and watched cop shows, so she knew about untraceable burner phones. Her skepticism about the investigation and the apparent sophistication of the killer dampened her hope that a connection could be found.

"Maybe the call to Dr. Patel's office was unrelated to the murder," Sara murmured after downing a cold chicken salad canape.

"Of course it was. Grandma's killer wanted to find out when she'd be gone from the house, so he could break in and steal the jewelry box." Sara was the only one she'd told about Grandma's note, how she now possessed one key to open the missing desk, while the other key required had been inside Grandma's jewelry box. Why did Sara not get it?

Sara wiped her fingers with a napkin, took Amanda's hand, and searched her eyes. "I'm worried about you, babe. You're jumping to conclusions. First, if this monster knew Viv was diabetic and even the name of her doctor, he would almost have to be a close friend. Second, how would anyone but you know about needing two keys to open some desk? That sealed letter you found at the storage unit was intended for your eyes only. How on earth would anybody else know about it?"

"I don't know!" Amanda cried out in desperation as the sunset left bloody red streaks along the far shore. "But I do know one thing. If it *was* the killer who called Dr. Patel's office, he was told that Grandma's appointment was at ten. Unless he's psychic, he had no way of knowing she'd changed the appointment to eleven. In other words, he thought she would be gone when he broke in..."

"And maybe Vivian would not have died," Sara finished.

## Chapter Fourteen

The road to Mayberry...

The next day, Monday, Robby steered his rental car, a white Ford Focus hatchback, north on Interstate 77, on the road to Mayberry. "I'm sorry Sara couldn't come."

Amanda sighed. "I'm sorry, too." But Sara had already taken a week off work, and her patients were getting anxious, or "going crazier," as she often teased. With some luck, she could counsel her neediest clients, and then juggle her schedule to join Amanda and Robby by midweek. "How long till we get there?"

"Google says we'll be there in an hour and a half."

To say she was nervous about meeting Judd was an understatement. What could she possibly have in common with a straight, middle-aged father living in the boonies? Clearly, her brother was nervous, too, judging by the uptight square of his shoulders, his starched and buttoned-up shirt, and his incessant tapping on the steering wheel. He acted like he was heading into a contentious courtroom battle, rather than reuniting with a long-lost relative.

She saw the comb marks in his expensively cut, light brown hair, and smelled his cologne. His freshly shaved cheeks were flushed with excitement, or perhaps nerves.

"I wish Sara was with us," he repeated. "I really like her. Are you guys, like, serious?"

She squinted at him. Late morning sun streamed through the passenger-side window and heated the back of her neck. "Duh, we've been together five years. What do you think?"

He grinned. "What do I know? You're not married or anything."

"Well, neither are you!" Why was this subject so difficult? Over the past several days, she'd come to realize that Robby was one hundred percent fine with her lesbian relationship. Perhaps she, Amanda, was the problem. How many times each day did she imagine the joy of being married to Sara? Maybe she thought about it pretty much nonstop, yet they had never seriously discussed it.

"*I'm* not married because I enjoy my eligible bachelorhood," Robby quipped. "What's *your* excuse?"

"Who would want to marry you?" she shot back.

He laughed. "Maybe Sara would say I'm relationship-averse or scared of commitment."

"Aw, you're just shy." She punched his arm. The shyness, she figured, was closest to the truth. As a boy, Robby got brilliant grades and won every scholarship, yet lacked self-confidence and social skills. He clearly liked women, but even now, in spite of his handsome looks, prestigious job, and high salary, he still did not seem entirely comfortable in his own skin.

"This is weird, right?" He glanced at her from the corners of eyes one shade darker blue than hers.

"Yeah, it's all weird." It was weird talking about their love lives, weird being on this bizarre mission to Mayberry, and weird being with Robby. She had been a young teenager the last time she rode alone in a car with him. She remembered this because it was the week she got her period, the same week he left for a fancy, pre-college prep school. "How much do you remember about Grandma?" she suddenly asked. "I mean, from those early years when we visited Grandma and Grandpa's farm in Pennsylvania?"

He rolled his neck and attached clip-on sunglasses before answering. "I've been thinking a lot about them lately. I still can't believe Grandma had a child out of wedlock. It had to have been before she met Grandpa Whitaker, and she was only eighteen then. So she must have been a kid when she had the baby."

"Right." Indeed Grandma must have had her first period not long before she got pregnant, a depressing thought. "Is it true Grandma was living with her aunt Alice then?"

"So the story goes," Robby answered. "Mom never talked about it because she never knew her great-aunt Alice. I only know Grandma Viv's parents died in a car wreck when Viv was really young, so she went to live with her daddy's sister, on Mayberry Farm, I suppose."

Robby was two years older than Amanda, so his memories were a little clearer. "So how did Vivian end up in Pennsylvania with Grandpa Will?"

"Again, this might be nothing but a pretty fairy tale, but Mom said Viv came up to Philadelphia with a church group and met Grandpa Will then. He was fifteen years older than she, and her aunt Alice did not permit them to marry until Will traveled down to North Carolina several summers in a row to woo both Viv and her aunt."

"It's a romantic story."

"It is, isn't it?"

"Do you think Grandma loved Grandpa Will? Considering she'd already had that baby, and he was so much older…" She let the sentence trail off, hoping the "fairy tale" they'd been told had some basis in reality.

"I think they were very much in love, don't you? Don't you remember how they were always touching and smiling and kissing? You used to point and giggle at the way they carried on."

"I guess." Robby seemed firm in his memory, but Amanda was unsure. She knew love was a tricky business and not always what it seemed. "Do you think Grandpa Will knew about Grandma's 'love child'? And if he did, why didn't they adopt it?"

He didn't answer. How could he?

## Chapter Fifteen

Back to the 1960s...

As the terrain became hillier, with small mountains in the distance, Robby took Exit 100 to NC89, Mount Airy. Amanda recalled that the two hundred acres comprising Mayberry Farm lay somewhere in the immediate vicinity of this major intersection. Nearing town, she saw forests, fields, and a few typical roadside businesses in an area far from developed.

Robby made a grand gesture. "Reckon we own that land over yonder, sister?"

"Could be."

The idea was preposterous. As NC89 became Pine Street and increasingly more commercial, Amanda became increasingly uneasy. They had not informed Judd Taylor they were coming but intended to "get the lay of the land" first and then set up a meeting. She sensed that Robby also needed to put off the face-to-face with their cousin until they were both geographically and emotionally prepared.

"Sara made reservations for us at a bed and breakfast called Bee & Bee, what's that about?"

Robby chuckled. "It's named for Aunt Bee, Sheriff Andy Taylor's aunt."

She stared at him. Ever since they'd got the news in Grandma's will, Mom and Trout had been jabbering about an old black and white television series called *The Andy Griffith Show*. "I suppose you know all about it, Robby?"

"Well, I've heard of Andy Griffith."

"Sure, but what about the show?"

"C'mon, Mandy, I looked it up. The show ran from 1960-1968, twenty years before we were even born."

"Yeah, I've never seen it, either."

"Well, you might want to keep that guilty secret to yourself around here." He pointed to a prominent sign as they entered a charming small town that time warped back to the 1960s. It said: "Proud Home of Andy Griffith." Soon they saw another directional pointing toward the Andy Griffith Museum. "Wanna check it out?"

"I think we better. It seems like Andy's fictional town was called Mayberry, just like our farm! Do you think they named it after our farm?"

"I guess."

In fact, the town of Mount Airy itself seemed to have been renamed Mayberry. The word was everywhere. She said, "If we're to be landowners here, we should try not to act like ignorant tourists."

They parked in the lot of an impressive brick building with a life-sized bronze statue of Andy and his son, Opie, headed on a fishing trip. Amanda said, "I just remembered that Ron Howard played the role of Opie all those years ago. He went on to become a famous actor and director."

"Sure, everyone knows that."

"Okay, but before we go in, you should lock your car."

"Why?"

She pointed at the two antique rifles wrapped in a blanket in the back, their long barrels sticking out for everyone to see. "This is gun country. Wouldn't someone want to steal those?"

"In Mayberry? If we're really back in 1960 Andy World, everyone's as innocent as apple pie. Surely, there's no crime." Nonetheless, he made an effort to better hide the weapons and then clicked his lock fob as they headed to the building.

They shelled out eight bucks each and entered a large room where an elderly gentleman in a white short-sleeved shirt and red suspenders pointed out treasures from *The Andy Griffith Show*, *Matlock*, movies, and Broadway and comedy albums where the beloved native son had played a starring role.

"Betty Lynn used to come here the third Friday of every month," he proudly exclaimed.

"But she's ninety-two now."

"Oh, great!" But Amanda was clueless.

He must have sensed her confusion. "You know, Betty Lynn played Thelma Lou on the show, Barney Fife's one true love."

"Oh, right." Robby gulped.

They picked through souvenirs at the gift shop, where Amanda almost bought a T-shirt heralding the show she'd never seen, but a disdainful look from Robby stopped her. Not to be intimidated, she asked the elderly gentleman, "Hey, do you know Mayberry Farm? I guess they named Andy's town after it."

Now the guide seemed clueless. "No, ma'am, never heard of it. If such a place exists, the *farm* was likely named after the *show*."

She and Robby glanced at each other, crestfallen.

"Well, then, sir, where should we go for lunch?"

Robby said. "I'm starving."

He offered two choices: Barney's Café with special chicken n' dumplings or Snappy Lunch with a world-famous pork chop sandwich.

Hands down, they chose Snappy on North Main Street, the heart of the tourist district. They parked, locked the car, then waited in line outside a small gray board building with red shutters, where they could see a woman cooking on a grill just inside a small window. They were among the last to be seated before Snappy closed at 1:45 and were hustled through the crowded lunch shop to a narrow second hallway. The harried college-aged waitress seated them at a square steel table with old-fashioned red vinyl chairs with chrome legs, amid walls crammed with posters featuring all the actors from *The Andy Griffith Show*.

While they both chowed down on pork chop sandwiches oozing mustard, chili, slaw, and onions and sipped sweet tea, Amanda spotted a photo of a young Oprah eating at Snappy Lunch. "Now that's one character I *do* recognize," she said, grateful for the dozens of napkins she dug from an old-fashioned silver dispenser.

They stood in line to pay, and on the way out, an old lady informed them that Snappy was the only shop mentioned by name in the show: "It was an early episode called *Andy the Matchmaker,* when Andy tells Barney they should go to Snappy for a bite to eat."

"Wow!" they said in unison.

Back on the bustling sidewalk, they stopped into Floyd's Barber Shop and had their pictures taken in the barber chair where Andy got his hair cut. The barber told them their photos would be among upward of six thousand he'd taken over the last several years, locals and tourists. They stopped into Opie's Candy Store, where Amanda bought a Moon Pie and a box of bubblegum cigarettes. They saw the Earle Theatre, where locals came for "pickin' and grinnin'" on Thursday nights.

"Can you fetch me one of your Tums?" Robby begged. "That pork sandwich ain't sittin' quite right."

She laughed. Ever since he was a little kid, her brother had a knack for putting on a hayseed accent at the slightest provocation. "I'll give you a Tums if you take me to Wally's garage for a tour in the squad car."

They'd been told that Goober and Gomer worked at Wally's on South Main, and a tour in Sheriff Andy Taylor's 1967 Ford Galaxy would be conducted with sirens blaring.

"Can we take a raincheck, sis? I'm plum tuckered out."

They arrived at the Bee & Bee around five, when many folks were heading out for supper. The red brick Victorian home, with an ornately trimmed wraparound front porch, was set on a beautifully manicured lawn shaded by ancient trees. They took their small suitcases, locked the car, and strolled up a flowered path onto the wide porch.

"This town is unreal," she said. "Are we in Disneyland?"

"More like Mayberry Land."

They entered an ornate foyer with floral wallpaper, grand piano, oriental rugs, and an old timey check-in counter with a vintage cash register and mail pigeonholes. The space smelled like lemon oil, dust, and a pie in the oven. A plump woman, her long white hair secured in a bun, was behind the desk. She looked for all the world like a reincarnation of the Aunt Bee character they'd seen on posters throughout the day. She eyed Amanda over rimless reading glasses. "Do you have reservations, sweetie?"

"Yes, ma'am. The name's Rittenhouse," she answered, while noting a humorless, stock-like man hovering behind the lady. She guessed he was her husband, but he seemed none too friendly as he paged through a large handwritten ledger.

He looked up through suspiciously narrowed eyes under bushy white brows. "Says here reservations for two were made by one Dr. Sara Orlando. She's the one who paid for them with a credit card."

Robby said. "Dr. Orlando made the reservations for Robert and Amanda Rittenhouse."

"He's right, Lou. See there?" The wife ducked under her husband's shoulder and pointed at the names. "Welcome to our home, Mr. and Mrs. Rittenhouse."

Amanda choked in disgust. "Ew, no! He's not my *husband*, he's my *brother*."

"If you say so," the man grumbled. "We have you in the same room."

Robby whispered in her ear, "Don't tell me Sara was too cheap to spring for two rooms."

"Why should she?" Amanda hissed back. "You're rich enough to pay for your own separate room if this doesn't suit you."

Robby giggled and faced their hosts. "Hey, seeing how me and sis bunked together as little kids, I reckon I can tolerate her for a few nights…long as she behaves herself."

"Well then, breakfast is six to nine," Lou grudgingly told them. "Don't be late."

Two sets of eyes followed their every step as they giggled their way up the grand staircase.

## Chapter Sixteen

Bee & Bee...

Their suite had two queen beds with burgundy tapestry covers, lace pillowcases, green damask wallpaper, and antique walnut furniture. They pushed off their shoes, dropped onto the beds, and after a brief pillow fight, regarded the big flat-screen TV, which seemed out of place in their circa 1900 luxury.

"I don't know about you, Mandy, but I'm beat. Why don't we order in a pizza?"

"Fine by me." More than fine, in fact. She was suffering sensory overload, her head spinning with visions of candy jars, tourist trinkets, Mayberry-themed T-shirts, and junk food. She didn't want to think about Grandma's murder or meeting Judd or anything beyond the fantasy world in which they'd been living all day. She unpacked her rum and warm tonic, then sent Robby out looking for an ice machine.

Of course the second he left, she called Sara and caught her just getting home from work. "You won't believe this town, honey!" she began. As she tried to describe the bizarre atmosphere of "Mayberry," Sara laughed and exclaimed she couldn't wait to see "the circus."

"When can you come?"

"I'll drive up on Wednesday. Should I book another room at Bee & Bee?"

Amanda considered. "Can I tell you tomorrow? One of the owners made it clear he strongly disapproved of hanky panky. He even suggested my relationship with Robby might not be kosher. I'm not sure how he'd take to the two of us sharing a bed."

"Well, I guess there weren't many open lesbians gallivanting around in Andy Griffith's day. And I do intend to share a bed and gallivant with you, babe."

Their conversation was just getting good when Robby returned with a bucket of ice. He said he found the modern convenience hidden in a dumbwaiter at the end of the hall. "Give my love to Sara," he hollered.

Amanda hung up soon after, promising to call Sara again when she could find some privacy.

Two drinks later and having enjoyed a delicious local pizza, they felt mellow enough to turn on the TV and catch up with the latest scandals in national news. Instead, the set was tuned to a channel airing endless reruns of what else—*The Andy Griffith Show.* "I'm game if you are," she said.

"We said we didn't want to behave like clueless tourists, so why not?"

Three hours, six episodes, and one stiff drink later, they were in their PJs laughing their heads off at the antics of characters who, by then, were almost like family members. They'd watched outrageous, skinny Deputy Barney Fife advising Sheriff Andy not to date a rich woman named Peg, while Andy advised Barney to drop a bargirl named Juanita.

Aunt Bee, always in aprons or floral Sunday go-to-meetin' clothes, had baked countless pies and generally catered to her bumbling menfolk. Gomer and Goober had clowned their way around Wally's

Service Station, while Andy's son, Opie, had stumbled in and out of trouble, including leaving a dead fish in Andy's office drawer just when the mayor had scheduled an inspection visit.

They learned the Mayberry jail cells were left open to accommodate friendly drunks like Jess or to function as playpens for local babysitting. In a nutshell, the only real mysteries in the idyllic little town were which of the ladies baked the best pie or what lucky woman would finally catch the charming widower, Andy Taylor.

"I love it," Robby said when they finally turned off the set.

"What's not to love?" Amanda yawned when they eventually turned off the lights.

※ ※ ※ ※

Breakfast was apple crisp with yogurt, peach or blueberry crepes with fresh whipped cream, roasted butternut squash, redskin potatoes, and homemade sausage.

"I could get used to this." Robby smacked his lips.

"Yeah, I bet even Aunt Bee never imagined a spread like this."

Turned out their hostess from the day before was named Lois, and the grumpy Lou was not her husband, but rather a distant relative whom she employed. In fact, Amanda had learned from the maid who came to make their beds that the bed and breakfast had originally been owned by Lois and "a very dear woman friend," who had since died. Her gaydar at full power, Amanda sensed Lois was a kindred spirit who would have no problem welcoming Sara and her. She made a mental note to call Sara and have her reserve another room, one with a single king bed.

When Lois served them seconds of rich coffee, Robby said, "Say, do you happen to know a local farmer named Judd Taylor?"

The woman's big smile dimpled her cheeks and made her old eyes sparkle. "Of course, I know Judd and much of his family before him. He's a wonderful man, one of my favorite people."

Amanda blinked in surprise. "We've come here to meet Judd, actually," she blurted, but said no more. She and Robby had already agreed not to tell anyone about their blood relationship to Judd—not yet.

"You'll like Judd," Lois continued. "He's an organic farmer—at least he's trying to succeed, which isn't easy in these parts. I buy his veggies for my guests—you're eating them now—but many locals don't see the value in spending a few extra pennies for the quality."

This bit was news. Amanda wondered if Judd made ends meet by selling his produce beyond the Mount Airy town limits.

"Judd's also a deputy sheriff but only part time," Lois added.

"Like Barney Fife?" Robby joked.

Lois blushed. "Oh, Lordy, he's not at all like Barney. I hope you meet his wife, Ella, too. She's a real doll, teaches at the high school. And their kids—Micah, Lori, and Jana—are the sweetest things you'll ever see."

Clearly, Lois was a Taylor family fan and an excellent source of information. "You seem to know a lot about these folks," Amanda ventured.

"Well, I should. Only ten thousand souls live

here, so when you're in business and live to be my age, you get to know a goodly number of the residents."

Robby asked for directions to Mayberry Farm, but Lois had never heard of an actual property by that name.

Lou approached the table. "If you're talkin' about that rundown old place the Taylors have rented for generations, it's out west off Highway 89." He gave them detailed directions but then added, "Nobody lives in that rotten old homestead anymore, but old lady Yount built her a brick rancher back in the sixties and lived there till she passed. Judd and them have been there ever since, cultivating the land behind the house."

"So there's a ranch house on the property, too?" Robby asked.

"Where else would it be?" Lou scoffed and then left, seemingly bored with the subject or perhaps not a Taylor family fan.

"Don't mind Lou, he's an old poop," Lois reassured them. "His brain is stuck way back in the previous century when it comes to folks like the Taylors and their newfangled ideas."

I wonder what she meant by that, Amanda reflected when, a half hour later, she and Robby left the bed and breakfast and drove back toward fantasy land.

## Chapter Seventeen

Loam and straw...

"Shouldn't we call him first, instead of just showing up at his doorstep?" Robby hovered at the stoplight at NC89, indecisive as to whether to turn right or left.

"Judd's probably at work this time of day," Amanda hedged. "Let's at least wait until after five."

"You're procrastinating, Mandy. You're just scared to meet him."

"So are you." She figured they were both right. "You promised I could ride in the Mayberry squad car, and we still need to eat at Barney's Café."

He quickly joined her in avoidance and steered to South Main Street, where they booked a tour in the 1967 Ford Galaxy 500. While Robby paid their driver, Amanda called Sara and asked her to reserve the extra room at the Bee & Bee for the following night.

"Have you met Judd yet?" Sara eagerly asked.

"Not yet. I think it would be better to wait till you're here tomorrow, then we can meet him together."

Sara belted out her famous Liberty Bell laugh and said, "Put on your big girl panties and just do it. You're his cousin, not me."

Their driver proved to be the longtime owner of Wally's Service Station and claimed he could do the tour and scheduled stops in his sleep. As the sun beat down on the vehicle, which had no air conditioning, he pulled up to the first stop and indeed fell asleep while Robby and she shopped. Amanda bought a T-shirt sporting an image of Aunt Bee holding a steaming pie, while Robby got a ball cap with a picture of their squad car on it.

When they finished the ride, they went to Barney's Café and enjoyed PB&J and grilled cheese sandwiches from a section of the menu called "Opie's lunchbox." By then, it was two o'clock, and they were fresh out of excuses.

"Are you going to call him, Mandy, or should I?"

"Sara wants us to wait till she gets here tomorrow," she lied.

Robby seemed relieved. "Well, why don't we follow the directions Lou gave us and do a drive-by at Judd's place? That way, we'll know our way tomorrow. Even if someone sees us, they don't know who we are."

"Sounds like a plan."

They drove west out of town about three miles to a left on Pine Ridge Road, then a right on Yount Farm Trail.

"This is it!" Amanda exclaimed. She imagined Mom's image from Google Earth and calculated they were driving toward the big highway 74, along the base of the triangle defining Mayberry Farm. Off to the right, she saw scrub fields and pine forests punctuated by oaks, maples, and other hardwoods. "Slow down and turn off the air so I can roll down my window. I want to hear it and smell it."

When Robby complied, she heard birds, crickets, and far-away traffic. The earth and fields smelled like loam and straw. "Do we really own part of this?"

"Two-thirds is ours." He grinned enthusiastically, pointing to a gravel road bisecting the next field. It was landmarked by a rural mailbox labeled with the name Taylor. "This is where we turn." He took a right, bumped across a shallow drainage ditch, then moved into a forested area.

"He'll spot us if we get too close," Amanda warned.

"No, I think this leads to the old homestead. Judd doesn't live there."

But suddenly, they rounded into a clearing where a modest brick rancher was clearly occupied. An older model dusty green Ford 150 pickup truck was parked in the driveway, and a big yellowish dog of indeterminate breed was bounding toward them, barking and baring his teeth.

"Oh, no, we're busted." Amanda groaned.

"Look, there are men working out in the garden." Robby sank down in the driver's seat, as if he could hide his tall self from the human and canine eyes. "Should I turn around and drive away?"

"Too late now." She felt her face flush with embarrassment. "One of the guys is headed our way."

Of the three workers, this was a tall, muscular African American, who had been nearest the gate. He wore jeans frayed at the knees and a sleeveless white undershirt. Both items of clothing showcased everything from his powerful biceps and pecs to his quads and glutes. A sheen of sweat oiled his skin to a shiny ebony.

As he strode rapidly toward them, he removed a wide-brimmed straw hat and wiped his forehead with his forearm. With the sun burning behind him,

Amanda absurdly imagined she was watching a scene from *The Color Purple*, and the dog was almost upon them.

"Shut up, Cob!" the man shouted in a deep bass voice. The creature, with a boxy head like a lab and a stringy tail like a collie, instantly ceased barking and charging and began walking and whining. "He doesn't bite!" the man called out.

Yet Amanda and Robby remained in the car. By then, the other two men—one white, one Hispanic—were also drifting curiously toward the fence.

The big man leaned down to Robby's open window. His head was clean-shaven, with salt and pepper stubble on his square jaw. His prominent cheekbones were sunburned the color of ripe plums, and his amazing eyes were dark amber.

He squinted in at them. "How can I help you folks?"

Finally, Amanda spoke up. "Sorry to bother you, sir, but we're looking for Judd Taylor."

He stood upright and laughed. "Well then, seems like you're in luck. I'm Judd Taylor."

## Chapter Eighteen

### Iced Tea...

"You're black!" The words flew unbidden from Amanda's mouth, and she longed to take them back.

Judd seemed unfazed. He looked down at his big hands, turned his palms up and said, "Yep, I'm black. Been that way since I was born."

Amanda rocketed from the car, rushed around the hood, and offered Judd her hand. "I'm so sorry, Mr. Taylor. We just didn't know. I'm Amanda Rittenhouse, and that's my brother, Robby. We're your cousins. We share a grandmother, the late Vivian Davis."

"You're white!" He grinned, shook her hand, but seemed not the least surprised. He laughed, showing off his perfect white teeth. "I figured you would be because I already knew I had a dollop of cream in my coffee. That is, I knew my biological grandmother was a white woman. Just never thought much about it."

Robby also quickly exited the car and shook Judd's hand. "Pleased to meet you, Mr. Taylor. We should have called ahead."

"Not a problem, but call me Judd." The big man then turned and scowled at the two men gaping at them from the field. "Michael, Miguel! Y'all get back to work while I visit with my cousins." The men waved, stifled their curiosity, and went back to planting. "We call those guys the M&M's, like the candy. We've been working together for a long time."

"What are they doing?" Robby mumbled.

"Planting snap and lima beans, beets, and broccoli. Next week, we do collards, corn, and cucumbers. Now do you folks really want me to go through the whole alphabet of veggies while we stand out here in the sun? Or will you come inside for some iced tea?"

"Tea sounds wonderful," Amanda said.

They followed Judd up a sidewalk lined with daffodils, then stepped onto a narrow concrete stoop. He opened a screen door directly into a living room carpeted in harvest gold shag. Cob, now their best friend, pushed past them and streaked into the kitchen.

"Sorry about the dog. We originally intended for him to live outdoors, but now he's part of the family. We live pretty casual and haven't made many repairs to this old place. Don't plan to live here forever."

"It's great," Robby said.

"Yeah, we love dogs," Amanda added.

As he ushered them toward an outdated kitchen with a pink linoleum floor, chipped porcelain farmhouse sink, and red Formica countertops, she noticed a narrow hallway leading to what she guessed were three bedrooms and one bath. The house had popcorn ceilings, with worn avocado green upholstery on the sagging armchairs and couch. But everything was neat and clean and smelled fresh.

"Have you lived here long, Judd?" Amanda asked.

"Too damn long. Our son Micah was born in the old Yount homestead. He's nineteen now and off to college. By the time Lori came three years later, the place was in such disrepair we decided to move here. For Jana, our baby who's twelve now, it's the only home she's ever known."

"You have three kids, that's cool." Robby seemed nervous as Judd got them settled at a big kitchen table, where the whole family obviously ate.

Judd laughed. "You think that's cool? It sounds like you guys don't have any children."

"We're not married, we have no children," Amanda said without apology.

Judd smiled and nodded. "Stay put while I get the tea." He stepped out onto a wooden deck that included a hot tub and barbecue grill, then returned with a gallon-sized glass pitcher filled with several teabags and lemon slices. "This is sun tea. It's been steeping all day, so it's pretty tasty by now." He filled two tall, colorful aluminum glasses with ice, poured the amber liquid, and placed the glasses on the table and the jar in the fridge. "Drink up!" he urged.

"Aren't you having some?" Robby wondered.

"Shower first, then tea." With that, Judd strode quickly down the narrow hallway.

"Good golly." Amanda sighed.

"Holy moly," Robby agreed.

They hadn't used those expressions since they were kids. For Amanda, it was too daunting to broach the subject of a surprise African American family, at least in Judd's kitchen, so she said, "Do you think Judd wants to keep this property?"

"Well, he said he'd lived here too damn long and didn't plan to stay forever."

"Yes, but he makes his living as a farmer, and judging by all the crops ready to go, he plans to be here in the near future."

"I don't know how he feels about selling Mayberry, let alone how he feels about having white relatives who own such a big chunk of it."

She didn't know, either, but figured they'd find out in short order. As she pondered that unknowable, she sipped the deliciously rich tea and stared outside, where the M&M's had moved on to a different part of the garden. She then peered back to the dim living room, where a number of family photos graced the walls and tabletops. She saw no pictures of the parents, but the three kids were displayed at every stage of growing up—from toddlers on swings, to prom dates, to graduation for the son. They were handsome, happy-looking children. All appeared lighter skinned than Judd, perhaps because Grandma's genes were exerting themselves.

"He seemed very welcoming," Robby mused. "He doesn't seem to resent us or anything."

"I agree." Yet she knew the whole situation had to be awkward for the Taylor family, just as it was for them. First their shared grandmother was murdered, then came a sudden transfer of power to two strangers. It shifted the gravity out from under everyone.

Before she could speculate further, Judd reappeared barefoot in clean tan shorts and a blue and white-striped sports shirt. He smelled like Ivory soap.

"Now I'm clean enough to hug my cousins!"

He did just that, hugged them both before pouring himself a glass of tea. He then pulled out a chair at some distance from the table and sat, his long brown legs stretched out before him. He studied them both. "This here is really something, isn't it?"

"You can say that again." Robby chuckled.

Judd's hug seemed to have calmed his jitters.

"Lots to catch up on," Amanda stated the obvious.

"Amen, sister, but not before my wife, Ella, gets home." He glanced at the round clock above the back door, which said 3:30. "She's a high school teacher, so she and the girls will be here any minute."

Right on cue, Cob's toenails skittered on the pink linoleum as he jumped up from a sound sleep and galloped to the screen door in the living room. As he whined in anticipation, Amanda heard tires crunching gravel and saw an older model gray Subaru Outback pull into the slot between Robby's rental and the green pickup.

"Speak of the devil!" Judd got up and loped to the door. They followed him, and all stepped outside just in time to see a stunning blond woman in a navy pantsuit leave the driver's seat. She was petite, well-endowed, and burdened with an oversized bookbag. A tall, long-legged girl climbed out of the passenger seat. She had a stylish, squared-off Afro cut shaved at the sides of her head to showcase enormous gold hoop earrings, and she wore a pouty expression. Finally, a younger girl bounded from the backseat like a frisky colt. Her amazing head of long braids swayed above a sequined orange T-shirt that offset her darker complexion and wide open smile.

Wow, a mixed-race marriage, Amanda thought. Maybe that's what the grouchy old man at the bed and breakfast meant by "newfangled ideas."

"We have company, girls," Judd hollered, opening his arms.

His family approached with varying degrees of suspicion. The youngest rushed into her daddy's arms with a huge "Hey!" to the strangers, the mother was smiling but openly curious, while the teenager was borderline hostile.

"Who are they?" the teenager asked her dad.

"These are your cousins, Amanda and Robby Rittenhouse."

"But they're white!"

*So's your mother,* Amanda wanted to say, but kept her mouth shut.

"Behave yourself, Lori," the mother warned as she warmly shook Amanda's and Robby's hands. "Lori's at *that age*," she explained, rolling her eyes. "I'm Ella Taylor, and our youngest, Daddy's Girl, is Jana."

"Pleased to meet you," Amanda said.

"Likewise," Robby echoed.

"We've been looking forward to meeting you," Ella said. "There's so much to talk about, can you stay for dinner?"

Amanda was taken aback. "Thanks so much, but we can't do that. We came unannounced and uninvited. It was terribly rude."

"Well, you're invited now," Ella insisted.

"Please stay!" Jana begged.

"Oh, no, ma'am." Robby shifted foot to foot and told a white lie. "We need to get to the Bee & Bee by check-in time. But thanks anyway."

Judd said, "Hey, I'm friends with Lois at the Bee & Bee. I'll call and ask her to hold your rooms."

No, please, it's honestly too much," Amanda countered. "We've had a long day. Maybe we can get together tomorrow."

By that time, Lori had grown bored and walked sullenly into the house, and Ella knew when she was beaten. "Okay, then," Ella said. "Come hungry, tomorrow at six."

"But I'll have a friend with me tomorrow," Amanda said, not wanting Sara to be left out.

"Then we'll set the table for three extra," Judd said with finality.

Soon thereafter, they departed the Taylor home.

"Wait till I tell Sara about our surprising new family," Amanda said on the way back to the bed and breakfast.

Robby sighed. "Oh, yeah? And who's gonna tell Mom?"

## Chapter Nineteen

Police conversation...

So how did your mother react to the news about the Taylor family?" Sara emerged from the shower, her long black hair rolled up in a towel, a fluffy terrycloth robe loosely sashed on her damp body.

Sara had driven to Mount Airy directly from work and checked into the Bee & Bee, where Amanda was anxiously waiting. Sara insisted she needed a shower before meeting the Taylors, and they now had only a half hour to dress and join Robby in the lobby.

"Mom reacted just like you'd expect. She's thrilled to have a mixed-race family, it only enhances her liberal credentials." Amanda did not intend the remark to be snarky because indeed her mother was truly inclusive and lived by the credo that diversity of culture was both the strength and spice of life. "Mom did wonder about Grandma, though. She couldn't fathom how a sixteen-year-old Vivian got involved with a black man in the 1950s South."

Sara dropped her robe and began to dress. "Yes, that was before integration, before blacks and whites could legally marry, and if a black man dared flirt with a white woman, it was a hanging offense, at least according to the Ku Klux Klan."

"I can't imagine how it happened," Amanda

said, yet she was finding it difficult to concentrate while watching Sara.

"I hope their sex was consensual," Sara said ominously.

Amanda had never considered the possibility that her grandmother might have been raped. "But it had to be consensual. Otherwise, why would Grandma have arranged for shares of Mayberry to be deeded to the Taylors through the years?"

"Good point, but there is another possibility. Maybe the man who got Viv pregnant was white, and it was their child who entered into a mixed-race relationship?"

The speculation was giving Amanda heartburn, or perhaps it was the sight of Sara pulling on her panties and fastening her bra that was causing the burn much lower in her anatomy. She crossed the room and took Sara into her arms, savoring the press of her soft breasts, the silken damp of her skin, and the hint of lavender in her freshly washed hair. "God, I've missed you, Sara. I wish we had a little more time." She looked wistfully at the king-sized bed.

Sara smothered her words with a kiss, pulled her closer, and dropped her hand to between Amanda's thighs. Just as quickly, she pulled her hand away. "Not now, but soon, babe. Right now it's time to meet your family."

※※※※

They rode in Robby's rented Focus since Sara's Miata was a two-seater, and when they arrived at the Taylor's driveway, the Subaru was just pulling out with Lori at the wheel. Amanda waved at the teenager, who scowled and reluctantly waved back.

"She must have a hot date," Robby muttered.

"Is she even old enough to have a driver's license?" Amanda asked.

"If she's turned sixteen, just barely," Sara said.

As they filed up the daffodil walkway, Amanda hoped Lori was not like the sixteen-year-olds Sara counseled, girls who regularly used drugs and alcohol and got arrested for DUIs. They had barely reached the stoop when Judd barreled out the screen door, seemingly on his way to a five-alarm fire, yet he was dressed like a cop, not a fireman. He wore a dark gray shirt with a gold Surry County sheriff's badge patch on the arm, light gray pants with a dark side stripe, and a holstered gun on his black belt.

"Judd, what's happening?" Amanda asked with alarm.

"So sorry, Mandy, I've been called up. I'll try to get home by dessert."

Then he was gone, spraying gravel behind his truck tires before Sara could be introduced. Amanda had completely forgotten he served as a part-time deputy.

"We really are sorry," Ella echoed as she held the door open. "Please come in. I never dreamed Judd would be called in on a Wednesday night since he's officially only on standby for the weekends. Must be something big."

"No problem." Robby winked at Jana, who was wearing a pretty blue dress for the occasion. She shyly took Robby's hand and led him toward the kitchen after Amanda introduced Sara.

"Mama's made chicken parmesan pasta," Jana proudly announced. "She cooks it all in one pot, and all the veggies come from our own garden. Since Lori and Daddy are gone, it means more for the five of us."

After Ella unobtrusively removed two place settings from the table, she positioned herself at the head, Robby and Jana on one side, and Sara and Amanda together on the other. It occurred to Amanda that Ella seemed to be rushing the event, skipping hors d'oeuvres and pre-dinner chitchat. Either she was flustered by the sudden departures of her husband and daughter, leaving her with three strangers, or perhaps that was how it was done in the Taylor house—the rapid feeding of school kids and a husband hungry from the fields. She did, however, uncork a bottle of red wine and poured it all around, including a taste for Jana.

Refusing offers of help from her guests, she placed a big salad and a steaming hot casserole, which really did smell delicious, on the table, and then rapidly took a seat. "Do y'all say grace?" she asked, and when met with ambivalence, Ella instructed Jana to do the honors.

Jana then blessed everything from the food to the company of new cousins to the dog Cob, who was enjoying his meal on the back deck.

Afterward, between bites, Amanda noticed a light sheen of perspiration on Ella's flawless porcelain forehead and how she angrily brushed back a lock of straw blond hair that kept escaping from her barrette. The woman was truly attractive, obviously wicked smart, but seemed distracted from the polite conversation. She asked all the right questions about her guests' professions, registering respect that Robby was a lawyer, delight that Amanda was an artist, but wariness when Sara explained that she was a psychiatrist.

They learned that Ella was a local girl, with family just down the road, whom she seemed reluctant to talk about. She'd met Judd at Surry County Community College, where he'd studied agriculture, and later received his law enforcement certificate. Ella's pursuit of a teaching degree had been sidetracked by the births of her first two children, but Judd had later paid for her to go back to school to complete her education. Reading between the lines, it seemed the family struggled to make ends meet.

Amanda wanted to talk about what had happened to Grandma, to ask a million questions about the history of her improbable family, but Ella seemed determined to keep the conversation light.

It was Robby who hit the first nerve and got a rise from their hostess. Their plates had been cleaned with gusto, all the wine had been drunk when he said, "We should really discuss the future of Mayberry Farm."

"Absolutely not!" Ella snapped, her color heightening. "Not until Judd gets home."

Amanda and Sara glanced at each other in alarm, but Sara calmly asked, "Do you like living here, Ella?"

"It's our home, isn't it? Where else would we go?"

Robby cleared his throat. "But Judd said he'd lived here too long and didn't plan to stay here forever."

Ella's complexion turned a deeper red. She stood and abruptly began clearing the table. "I assume he meant we don't want to stay in *this house* forever."

"So you eventually want to sell the farm?" Robby pressed.

As Ella roughly shoved dishes into the sink, it sounded like one of them had broken. "Over my dead body!" she exclaimed. "Didn't you hear me the first time? You wait to talk to Judd."

With that, Ella stormed from the room, stunning the company and leaving Jana's dark eyes filled with tears.

## Chapter Twenty

Hot button issue...

"What just happened?" The last thing Amanda wanted was to offend the Taylors on their very first date.

Sara said, "Cleary, Ella's upset by the prospect of you and Robby selling Mayberry out from under them."

"Where will we live?" Jana seemed near panic as she twisted her paper napkin to shreds.

Robby, seated beside the girl, placed a big hand on hers to stop the shredding. "Don't worry, you have a home here for as long as you want it."

Amanda was surprised by the fatherly gesture and by his assertion that Jana would not lose her home. After all, other decision makers were involved, and he shouldn't make empty promises.

At that moment, the screen door banged against the living room wall, and Lori made a grand entrance. She wore low-rise ripped jeans that looked painted onto her long legs and little butt and a red shorty blouse exposing a navel piercing with a gold stud. Her full plum lips were set in a perpetual pout as she approached the table.

"Where's Mom?" she demanded.

"She had a meltdown." Jana shrugged. "She's having a timeout."

Amanda noted Lori's effect on her little sister, transforming her from a vulnerable child to a sass pot. She also noticed that Lori's amber eyes, so much like her father's, were sleepily unfocused as she stared at her and Sara, whom she'd not yet met. So Amanda introduced Sara as her "friend."

"That right?" Lori crossed to the fridge, grabbed a can of Diet Pepsi, and then slouched into the chair previously occupied by her mother. "Is she, like, your *girlfriend*?"

"Hey, that's none of your business," Robby interrupted.

But Amanda held Lori's gaze. "Yes, Sara is my girlfriend. Is that all right with you?"

Lori grinned and stared even harder. "I respect it. I'm a dyke, too."

Jana's dark eyes grew enormous. "Shut up, Lori. Mama will hear you!"

Sara had had enough. "Are you high, Lori?"

The teenager held the cold aluminum soda can against her forehead, and her eyelids drooped. "I'm good. I ate a Big Mac. Now will someone tell me why Mama's torqued?"

"It's about the Mayberry property," Jana said.

Lori grimaced. "Shit, that again?" She dragged her eyelids open and confronted the outsiders. "It ain't for sale. Everybody wants a piece, but it ain't for sale."

"Well, who says we're selling?" Robby made the mistake of engaging with the girl. "Only my sister here, me, and your daddy can make that decision."

"And my husband isn't selling." Ella appeared immediately, as though she'd been eavesdropping around the corner all along. She took one look at Lori, snagged her arm, and pulled her upright. "I can smell it on your breath, young lady. Now go to your room, please. Don't you have homework, Jana?"

Miraculously, both girls instantly obeyed their mother. Amanda had recognized Ella's formidable "school teacher voice" from her own distant past and would have obeyed her, too, in a New York minute.

Once the kids were gone, Ella turned to her guests. "Please forgive my behavior, it was inexcusable. You see, the subject of Mayberry Farm is my hot button issue. Lately, it seems everyone, especially the big developers, are after our land. It has Judd and me crazy, and we didn't know how you felt about it."

"We want what you want," Robby stated with magnanimity.

While Amanda wondered, *Who died and made him boss?* So far, no one had consulted her, and she was a one-third owner.

Visibly relaxing, Ella collapsed onto the musical chair Lori had just vacated. "I'll put on coffee, and we'll have dessert when Judd gets home. In the meantime, I want to tell you a story."

As they sipped strong coffee, Ella spun a yarn about Mayberry and how much the land had meant to generations of Taylors, particularly her and Judd. Promising to detail the family history at a later date, she described her early years of marriage lived in the old Yount homestead. She said the house had "good bones," including heart of pine floors, bead board paneling up to the chair rails downstairs, roomy country kitchen, mud room, screened porch in the rear, and three bedrooms upstairs. The tin roof and much of the original siding needed replacing. The house required all new paint in and out, some plaster work, and complete modernization of the kitchen and bath.

Ella was describing a very expensive renovation, but it was the couple's ultimate dream. The forest encroaching on the old garden needed culling, and there was an old fishing pond hidden in the woods. By the time Ella finished, Amanda could almost smell the morning glories growing on trellises, see the ferns hanging on the wide front porch and hear the mockingbirds showing off their repertoire from the ancient shade trees.

"It sounds idyllic," Sara said.

Ella said, "Judd would continue to farm these fields around the rancher since they're already cleared and ready, but the old Yount place would be our home."

After Ella's recitation, Amanda had pretty much decided that it would be horribly wrong for her and Robby to deprive the Taylors of their dream. On the other hand, she and Sara had also talked about owning a home of their own—possibly, maybe, someday—and if that were ever to become a reality, some big bucks from eager developers could hurry the idea toward reality.

"You said something about dessert?" Robby prompted.

Ella glanced out to the driveway, where headlights approached. "Looks like Judd's coming. I guess I can get the blueberry pie out of the cupboard."

Amanda's mouth was already watering and Sara's green eyes sparkled when Judd walked into the living room, but one look at his tense posture, troubled amber eyes, and clenched jaw changed all that.

"What's wrong?" Ella gasped.

If a black man could be described as pale, Judd fit the bill.

"I'm afraid the pie will have to wait, folks," he said. "There's been a murder."

## Chapter Twenty-one

Murder in Mayberry...

"A murder in Mayberry? That's impossible," Lois said as she served them eggs Benedict on the screened-in back porch. Early morning sun dappled the pink and white tulips and purple freesias in the garden beyond. "We haven't had a murder here in years."

"Now that's just plain wrong, Lois," Lou grumbled as he placed their cups and poured steaming coffee. "We've had ten homicides in the past fifteen years in Surry County. Seeing how it's already late April, we're overdue."

"I didn't know you were into crime statistics, Lou." Lois's apple doll face crinkled in disapproval. "You might want to keep it to yourself, it's bad for business."

"Well, *they* brought it up." He cocked his head at their three guests, then frowned and departed for the kitchen.

Lois rolled her eyes and smoothed her apron with plump hands. "Don't mind Lou. He's an old poop." She lingered expectantly. "Did Judd tell you who died?"

Amanda said, "No, he was upset and didn't want to talk about it." That was an understatement. Indeed, he had almost pushed them out the door. Luckily, Ella had graciously put three slices of blueberry pie onto a paper plate, covered them with foil, and muttered copious apologies as they left.

Lois hovered a little longer, angling for more tangible gossip, but finally moved on to the other tables. As soon as she was gone, Robby took a big gulp of coffee and said, "Judd really was upset, wasn't he? Do you think he knew the victim?"

"Who knows? I guess we'll find out eventually." Amanda sighed. She was suffering from a slight headache. Last night, they had returned to the Bee & Bee, shared the pie in Robby's room to discuss the disturbing turn of events until midnight, but had no better answers in the morning.

Massaging her temples, Amanda decided she was suffering from sleep deprivation. After their visit with Robby, she and Sara had stayed up even later sharing impressions of the Taylor family, particularly the rebellious teenager. Lori had stated she was a lesbian, and they believed her. They worried about her possible substance abuse and hoped her parents supported her being gay. Amanda had joked, "You're a therapist, Sara. Maybe you should hang around to mentor and counsel the kid."

"Oh, yeah? Maybe we should both just move to Mayberry and serve as role models," Sara had fired back.

Next they made love until the wee hours of morning, which was both restorative and debilitating.

Interrupting Amanda's train of thought, Robby said, "But clearly, Judd and Ella don't want to sell their land, and I don't think we should force them to. We don't need the money, Mandy."

"Speak for yourself, bro. What makes you think

*I* don't need it? Lori said some developers had been sniffing around, and that could mean big bucks."

Suddenly, Sara squeezed her knee under the table and gave her a look. It seemed Sara did not want to open that particular can of worms, at least not until they'd had a chance to explore the options. Sara's salary was sufficient to provide for the two of them, but Amanda wanted to carry her own weight. Before they met, Amanda had ended a long-term relationship with a wealthy older woman in Sarasota, Florida. The disparity in their incomes had contributed to the breakup, and she never wanted to depend on Sara in that way. Amanda's income as a sculptor was uncertain at best. Grandma's legacy could even the playing field, and she rather liked that idea.

Robby spooned extra hollandaise sauce onto his muffin and eggs. "Well, I spoke to Mecklin Adams early this morning and asked if he knew about any rental agreement Grandma might have had with the Taylors through the years. They must have paid her some kind of rent, right?"

"You'd think so, wouldn't you?" Sara said as she finished her orange juice. "When Vivian inherited the farm, she not only arranged for the Taylors to stay on her land, she also included them in progressive wills. What did Mecklin say?"

"He didn't know much, frankly," Robby said. "It seemed Grandma played her cards close to the vest when it came to the Taylors. Mecklin suggested I visit the local lawyer to whom he faxed the will."

Amanda recalled Mecklin explaining to them that Judd would get his copy at some law office in Mount Airy. "So he thinks this attorney represents Judd?"

"Could be. There's only one way to find out." Robby took out his phone and Googled. "The guy's name is Howard Hayes, and his office is on South Main Street not far from the Bee & Bee."

"Well, I could have told you that!" Lois had sneaked up on them and held out a plate of Danish pastries, which they all politely refused. "I've known Howey since he was a little boy. They say he's a fine lawyer, but I wouldn't know. His place is within walking distance. Just go out the front door and turn left toward town."

It seemed they were all startled by Lois's sudden appearance, and Amanda wondered how much the woman had overheard.

Robby finally said, "Thanks for the directions, ma'am, but I plan to drive. I intend to check out the Mount Airy Quarry after speaking with Mr. Hayes."

Lois beamed and proceeded to give them a history lesson about the famous white granite quarry called The Rock. She claimed it was the largest open face granite quarry in the world. It had been mined for one hundred twenty years and made Mount Airy famous before Mayberry did.

As Amanda's headache intensified, she tuned out the words and dreamed of taking a long nap with Sara. Unfortunately, Sara was eager to see all the Andy Griffith tourist stuff and wanted a souvenir T-shirt of her own. She also wanted to attend the Open-Mic Jam at the historic Earle Theatre that night. They had all agreed not to bother Judd until they were invited because it seemed their cousin had enough on his plate at the moment.

While Amanda was plotting how to do both the nap and the tourist stuff, grouchy old Lou descended upon their table. The tall, stork-like man was clearly agitated as he elbowed Lois and thrust a newspaper into her face.

He said, "The paper just got delivered, and Lord have mercy, look who went and got himself killed!"

As Lois read the headlines, her small fat hands fluttered, her face reddened, and her lips made little puffing sounds of disbelief. "God bless him! Poor Mr. Landry was only fifty-three, leaving a wife and three kids. I didn't know the wife and kids, mind you, but I've been to his big fancy house and seen that swimming pool. How could a man drown in his own pool?"

The couple's distress attracted the attention of the other guests enjoying breakfast. A single mom got up and hustled her two small children out of the room, while a well-dressed older man with a head smooth and white as a hard-boiled egg rushed up to read over Lois's shoulder.

"This can't be right," he said. "I was at Myron Landry's party yesterday afternoon. He was perfectly fine when I left, but I did leave early."

As the three fought over the paper, Amanda, Sara, and Robby gaped at one another. Could this death be the "murder" Judd told them about? As they listened, they learned the deceased had been a very important man about town, one of the five members of the Surry County Board of Commissioners.

"I voted for Myron last year," Egghead continued. "He was a fine man, an upstanding Republican."

Lois pressed the man for details. "Was it a big party?"

He told them about thirty people had attended the casual picnic. Hot dogs and beer were served. All nine members of the planning board were there but no children.

"Was it a pool party?" Lou asked disapprovingly. "Were folks drunk?"

"No, sir," Egghead insisted. "No one was swimming, and as far as I could tell, no one was misbehaving. In fact, it was boring. That was why I left."

Amanda longed to jerk the paper from their hands and see for herself. They said the man had drowned, and considering the party took place in broad daylight, foul play seemed unlikely. On the other hand, the timing was right. Judd had rushed off yesterday about six, when such an event would be winding down. Wasn't such a high-profile death in a small town too much of a coincidence? Certainly, it would explain why Judd had been so upset.

"Was Mr. Landry murdered?" she blurted out, apparently loud enough for everyone to hear, because a stunned hush fell on the room.

Lois's eyes and mouth formed perfect O's of shock. She finished the article, then said, "Absolutely not, young lady. It says right here that Myron Landry's death was a tragic accident."

## Chapter Twenty-two

Dead woman's account...

After breakfast, Robby went his separate way, while Amanda and Sara hit the tourist joints. He was giving them some quality time alone, and since no one had heard from Judd, the three decided to meet up that evening at seven for the Open-Mic Jam at the Earle Theatre.

Though Amanda would have preferred some quality nap time, her curiosity was piqued by the death of Myron Landry. They purchased a copy of the *Mount Airy News* first thing and confirmed that the paper had indeed described his death as a "tragic accident." It also said an autopsy would be performed by the medical examiner and promised updates regarding the investigation.

"So why do they need to investigate an accident?" Amanda wondered as Sara bought fudge at Opie's Candy Store.

"Standard procedure. Nothing to get excited about." Sara moaned in ecstasy as she licked smears of chocolate off her fingertips.

But as the day progressed, they overheard a steady stream of speculation from the locals. The clerk at the T-shirt shop exclaimed that "Landry was an excellent swimmer. No way would he have drowned." The waitresses at Snappy knew somebody who knew somebody who had attended Landry's party, and that guest swore up and down that the commissioner had been "stone cold sober—no way would he have tripped into the pool." The barber at Floyd's said, "Myron was strong, an ex-football player. No one could have wrestled him off that edge."

Hearing that, Amanda glanced at the photo of the deceased in the paper. The man was an average, pleasant-looking fellow who did appear to be a jock who could fight back. "What do you think?" she asked Sara.

"I think this town is a gossip mill. Everyone has a theory, and no one has a fact. We'll have to wait and see."

All the townsfolk agreed that Landry had been the powerful swing vote of the five Surry County commissioners, who often had the final say on whether a project got approved or not. It seemed the town was as polarized as the rest of the nation, therefore Landry's decisions made friends and enemies in equal proportion.

They returned to the Bee & Bee that afternoon with barely enough time to shower and change before meeting Robby at the theater. When they got there, they found him sitting in a courtyard alleyway adjacent to the Earle. His bench faced a huge mural advertising vintage Coca-Cola, which had been painted on the brick wall of the theater. When he beckoned them over to sit beside him, he was clearly excited about something.

"Wait till you hear what the lawyer Howard Hayes had to say!" he exclaimed. Robby was less buttoned-up than usual, in cut-off jeans and a brand new Mayberry T-shirt, which still reeked of the candles and incense of the store.

They waited as he let the suspense build, a mischievous grin on his face.

"Well?" Amanda finally demanded.

"Grandma was a fox. She had a secret bank account." He leaned forward, elbows propped on his bony knees. "All these years, the Taylors have been paying rent to Mr. Hayes, which he then forwarded to Grandma. Can you imagine? Even Linc didn't know."

Amanda couldn't make sense of it. "But why didn't they pay Grandma directly?"

Sara answered softly, "Because Viv didn't want the Taylors to know who she was or where she lived. She couldn't even confide in her own husband."

"That's right," Robby said. "They always made the check out to the law firm, then Hayes took out a small handling fee and auto-deposited the funds into Grandma's account. It's been going on that way since Grandma's Aunt Alice died in 1960, when Grandma put Thomas Taylor on the deed. So that's almost sixty years."

"Did Hayes understand Grandma's relationship to the Taylors? For instance, did he say Thomas was Grandma's lover?"

Robby scoffed. "If he knows, he's not saying. The old guy has actually met all the players, but he evidently believes attorney/client privilege extends beyond the grave."

"Well, that's not much help," Sara said. "Would he tell you how much rent they paid?"

"Yeah, he shared that information. Thomas paid five hundred per month. When he died in 1968, his son Andrew went on the deed and paid seven hundred fifty. Judd replaced Andrew in 1974, and one family member or another's been paying one thousand ever since."

Amanda was still confused. "No matter what the generation, that seems like pretty cheap rent for a two hundred-acre farm, two homes, a barn, and the various outbuildings."

"It's dirt cheap," Robby agreed. "I guess Grandma wanted it that way."

Sara said, "So is Judd still paying? Assuming rent comes due the first of the month, then the next thousand is due in four days. Does Hayes expect to auto-deposit it into a dead woman's account?"

Amanda and Robby startled at Sara's description of their grandma as "a dead woman," but Robby quickly recovered. "Actually, Hayes and I discussed that problem. First we'll have to contact Linc and tell him about Vivian's secret account—"

"Well, that should be an interesting phone call," Amanda snidely interrupted.

Robby continued, "Yes, and no one knows how much money is in there. She could have saved it or spent it. North Carolina law favors spousal inheritance above all other family members, so Linc will have his say in all of this. But in the meantime, since you and I are the principle owners of Mayberry now, along with Judd, of course, we may be entitled to future rent and any cash in the account."

"It sounds complicated," Sara noted.

"It sounds crazy." Amanda growled, unsure why the subject upset her so. Splitting a thousand bucks per month with Robby was not her idea of a windfall, and she certainly did not want to become embroiled in a pot of legal paperwork. "I don't care about the damn rent!"

"Well, neither do I," Robby countered, "but we need to give Judd some guidance." He looked to Sara, seemingly for support. "We've seen how frugally Judd and Ella live, and likely, the thousand bucks may be all they can afford. I say we keep the arrangement as-is indefinitely."

Sara nodded, apparently sympathetic to Robby's position. In silent turmoil, Amanda watched as a group of children carrying cases for guitars and violins burst from the theater and spilled into their narrow courtyard. They were giggling, pushing and shoving, and chattering about the music lessons they'd just completed inside the building. They passed through and moved into the parking lot beyond.

The evening air had turned chilly, and the performance was about to begin. Amanda realized that Robby and Sara expected a response from her.

"Okay..." she slowly began. "I disagree. I think we should seriously consider selling the property to the highest bidder, or at the very least, raise the rent to a fair market value."

With that, she got to her feet and began walking. Robby and Sara followed, disapproval radiating off them like a train dragging behind an unhappy bride.

## Chapter Twenty-three

### Fun or disaster...

They were surprised by how few people were filing into the theater. As they stepped onto a classic black and white tiled floor, they saw interior glass doors leading to an exhibit titled *Old Time Heritage Music Hall,* a red and chrome ticket booth, and an old-fashioned popcorn machine—none was open for business, and admission was free. Along with a handful of other clueless tourists, they were the only ones not carrying an instrument case. All the regulars seemed to know one another, yet they greeted the outsiders with welcoming smiles and guided them into the nearly empty theater. They began ushering everyone toward the very front.

As they walked self-consciously down the aisle, Amanda noticed the framed black and white photos of old-time music greats hung on both walls. Plaques said they were Tommy Jarrell, Fred Cockerham, Kyle Creed, Earnest East, and others. All were playing stringed instruments. These musicians meant nothing to her, but Sara was becoming progressively excited.

"I love bluegrass music," she said. "I wonder if Old Crow Medicine Show ever played here."

Robby laughed, pointing at the old photos. "I'd say these guys were way before Old Crow."

Amanda, still put off by the disagreement

regarding Mayberry Farm, felt even more like the odd man out. "Sara, I never knew you like old-time music."

Sara winked. "See there? I'm still a woman of mystery. You can't grow up in North Carolina and not develop a taste for the foot-stompin', banjo-pluckin' heritage of these here hills."

"Is that right?" Amanda was flabbergasted. Who knew Sara, with her Puerto Rican roots and serious devotion to female vocalists like Annie Lennox, would be a fan?

"Hey, I love it, too." Robby enthusiastically herded them across a parquetted wood dance floor to the first row at the foot of the stage. "I bet these local performers are the real deal."

Someone blinked the lights, signaling an impromptu start of the festivities, and eventually, a very tall blond guy with the rugged scruff of a new beard and tattered jeans scrambled onto the stage and adjusted the microphone. Apparently the master of ceremonies, the man introduced himself as Marty Roach and said, "Okay, who goes first?"

A trio took the stage, two middle-aged men and a girl who looked to be one of their daughters. Before they began, one of the men said, "This song is dedicated to our dear friend, Myron Landry, may he rest in peace."

Into the absolute silence, the men's guitars began a slow, classical rendition of *Danny Boy*. They were soon joined by the girl's violin, which cried like a clear-throated mourning dove. By the third stanza, an old man from the audience went up with a gawky teenage boy. The old man played the piano, and the young tenor sang so sweetly Amanda was almost moved to tears.

Indeed, when she glanced up at the tall moderator, she saw he was openly crying, head bowed. When he lifted his face, she felt she knew the man. Something about the set of his jaw, the curve of his full lips, and certainly his piercing blue eyes when he looked directly at her, seemed familiar. He seemed to recognize her, too, or perhaps it was only his curiosity about a newcomer.

When the song ended, there wasn't a dry eye in the house. The locals were obviously grieving the loss of their beloved commissioner, but they all willingly left the sorrow behind when Marty Roach cracked a joke about *Danny Boy* being an Irish tune, while most of those present were descended from Scots. His words cued a new quartet of pickers and strummers to strike up a Scottish reel, fiddlers taking the lead.

And so it went. Not far into the rollicking program, which included generational performers—kids, parents, grandparents—Amanda realized she had also become a fan. Someone had left an open guitar case on the floor, obviously for tips, so she decided to leave a few bucks on the way out.

Just when everyone was running out of steam, the doors at the rear of the theater swung open, and a gang of teenagers came laughing down the aisle. Their intrusion caused mixed reactions on the stage. The younger performers cheered, while Marty scowled and crossed his arms.

"Hey there, kids," he hollered into the mic. "We're almost done here."

"C'mon, dude, we respect the music. Let us join!" a guy with an impressive pair of dreadlocks draped forward over his shoulders hollered back.

Sara punched Amanda's arm. "Look, Lori's with

that bunch."

Amanda swiveled and saw Judd's daughter. She was hanging with a shorter, slightly plump African American girl with buzzcut hair and tattoo-covered arms. The other half dozen teens were white and male. She couldn't tell if the kids were out to make trouble or have fun.

Everyone was astonished when the gang, without benefit of accompaniment, began shagging, clogging, and heating up the dance floor. In response, the gawky boy who sang *Danny Boy* sat on the bench beside the old guy who played the piano and began playing something that sounded like a weird boogey version of Taylor Swift's *Shake It Off*. The old pianist joined in, as did several other young musicians with fiddles, an electric mandolin, and even a tambourine. Their music gave cover to the teenagers' antics.

Lori and her girlfriend performed a deliberately provocative grind, which Marty Roach found particularly offensive. Amanda looked on in horror as he came down off the stage and roughly grabbed Lori's shoulders. Amanda couldn't hear what the man said to Lori, but it clearly upset the girl. She jerked free of Marty's grip, took her girlfriend's hand, and defiantly left the theater. On her way out, she gave Marty the finger.

"What just happened?" Robby was stunned.

Sara hissed, "That jerk thought the kids were staging a hostile takeover. I'm going out to talk to Lori, make sure she's okay."

Before Amanda could protest, Sara bumped out the row and followed Lori. The other teenagers followed Sara, and eventually, most of the performers packed up their instruments and also left.

"I guess the party's over," Amanda told Robby,

who was still trying to make sense of the scene.

"Was that fun or a disaster?" he asked.

"I guess that depends who you ask." Amanda just wanted to get the hell out of there and rejoin Sara, but when she hurried toward the stage to drop her donation into the guitar case, Marty Roach approached and touched her arm. She again felt that odd tug of recognition. "Do I know you?"

He smiled and respectfully backed off a few paces. "First, I hope you enjoyed our jam tonight. It's always exciting to entertain a new audience. Next, no, you don't know me, but I know you."

By then, Robby had joined her and was openly staring at the man.

Marty said, "You are Amanda and Robert Rittenhouse, correct? It's a small town, you see, and I understand you're part owners of Mayberry Farm."

"How could you possibly know that?" Robby asked.

The man grinned, dug into his jeans, and pulled out two business cards. "Let's just say I have close ties to the Taylors. I also have a personal interest in the property."

She glanced at the card he'd given her, which said: *Apollo Partners Real Estate, Residential and Commercial.* It had the guy's name, *Martin Roach Jr.* "What kind of interest?"

"I want to buy it." He crossed his arms, stretched to his full, impressive height, and rocked confidently on his feet.

Robby bristled. "Well, you're out of luck, Mr. Roach. It's not for sale."

"You sure about that?" The grin remained frozen on his face.

"I am absolutely not selling," Robby insisted. He crumpled up his copy of the business card and tossed it into the guitar case.

Before the confrontation turned into a pissing contest, Amanda intervened. "Actually, Mr. Roach, *I* may be interested in selling. At least we can talk."

"Very sensible of you, Ms. Rittenhouse. My number is on the card, so please call anytime." Then, with one last stern look at Robby, he walked away, retrieved the cash from the guitar case, and disappeared through a door beside the stage.

As they exited, Amanda knew Robby was mad at her. "Hey, I didn't say I would sell, only that we'd talk."

He shrugged but didn't comment. Somehow, it had become a sore subject between them. Feeling bad about that, Amanda stepped into the cool night air and spotted Sara and Lori sitting on the same bench the three of them had occupied before the show. Spotlights above the Coca-Cola mural washed down across their two heads, bent close together in earnest conversation. When Sara looked up, her smile illuminated Amanda's heart, but Lori's expression was less welcoming.

The girl stood and confronted them. "You were talking to Marty Roach, weren't you?"

"Yeah, we were," Amanda admitted. "So who is he? He said he has close ties to your family."

Lori snorted contemptuously. "You could say that. He's Mama's twin brother, my asshole uncle."

Amanda could not have been more surprised had someone offered to sell her a bottle of Coke for five cents, as the mural advertised. But it did explain why Marty seemed familiar. He was a taller, skinnier replica of Ella, his twin sister. "Why do you dislike him so much?"

Her eyes full of hatred, she answered, "Are you kidding me? Because he's a fucking racist pig."

## Chapter Twenty-four

Mayberry Acres...

Judd had finally called Friday morning and invited them to the farm that afternoon for a tour and to discuss business. Driving there, Robby said, "Judd sounded nervous."

"Not as nervous as you are," Amanda retorted. Robby was getting anxious. He had been away from his law firm for almost two weeks and was scheduled to be back at work by the following Wednesday, which meant they'd need to make some decisions that weekend. Yet she and he had still not come to a meeting of the minds regarding the disposition of Mayberry Farm.

Lincoln Davis had not made it any easier.

"Linc was actually very generous," Sara said. She was stretched out on the backseat, her bare feet propped on a windowsill as she attempted to mediate the two siblings while watching the blue sky and green treetops glide by.

Robby had phoned Linc that morning. Once he got over the shock of his wife harboring a secret bank account, he took matters into his capable hands. He got in touch with Howard Hayes and explained his status as Viv's widower and executor of her estate. The lawyer then provided him with the name of her bank and the account number.

Efficient as he was, Linc had visited a bank branch that morning, filed all the relevant paperwork, withdrawn approximately seven thousand dollars still held there, and then closed the account. All that had been accomplished by noon.

"You're right, Sara, Linc was very generous," Amanda admitted. He had divided the money equally between her and Robby and already cut two checks. Hers was waiting back home in Mooresville, while Robby's was in the mail to his law office in Philly.

"So what's the problem?" Sara pressed. "Linc's leaving everything up to you and Robby."

"That *is* the problem," Robby whined. "Linc refused to get involved or even offer a suggestion. Now we're back at square one."

Amanda thought, yes, now we have to make the decision all by ourselves. She sensed Sara believed she was being selfish by not siding with Robby and allowing Judd to keep the farm at bargain basement rent. Maybe Sara was right. Or maybe Amanda needed an adult in the room to step up and tell her what to do. The very idea made her furious with herself.

"Look, guys, I'm reserving judgment until I hear what Judd has to say," she offered in her own defense. "How can we proceed until we've heard his side?"

They turned onto Judd's gravel road, and Robby said, "Well, get ready to hear him out then, Mandy, because he's standing in his driveway waiting for us."

Sara scrambled upright, pulled on her sandals, and was first to greet their host with a big hug. Amanda and Robby were more reticent, settling for a handshake with their cousin.

As Judd led them inside, Amanda noticed that Michael and Miguel, the M&M's, were not in the field.

Judd was freshly shaved, showered, and clothed, like he had not worked at all that day. Perhaps because of this momentous meeting, he'd given the guys a long weekend, and he'd already explained that Ella and the kids would not be there, supposedly because they were tied up with school activities.

He took them to the kitchen table and poured his famous sun tea. "I hear you've spoken with Howard Hayes," he said without preamble. "So you understand the rental agreement we've had over the years."

"Yes, Judd, we do," Robby solemnly responded. "We need to talk about all that."

Suddenly, Sara picked up her glass and walked to the sliders leading to the back deck. "You folks don't need me for this. I'll wait outside."

"You're welcome to stay, Sara," Judd said.

But Sara just smiled, waggled her fingers, and left. Amanda watched as she flopped into a lounge chair, propped her feet on the railing, and tilted her face to the sun. Sara, her special adult in the room, had deserted her.

"I know what we've been paying is ridiculously low." A sheen of perspiration appeared on Judd's dark forehead, which was furrowed with worry. "But honestly, it's all we can afford. I know Ella told you about our big dream of restoring the Yount homestead, but I gotta tell you—no matter how cheap the rent, that ain't happening."

Judd's strong jaw and chiseled cheekbones seemed sunken and vulnerable. Amanda felt cruel, but she had to ask, "So maybe it would be better for you and Ella to sell?"

His amber eyes narrowed and hardened. "No, Mandy, we won't sell. Even if we have to live in this ratty ranch house forever, even if I work the fields till my back breaks, we won't give in to the likes of March Investments."

Amanda and Robby looked at each other, not understanding. "What is March Investments?" she finally asked.

"You don't know? Didn't Howard Hayes tell you?" Judd's question was met by confused silence, so he said, "It's easier to show than tell."

The big man fetched a laptop from the red Formica counter and booted it up on the kitchen table, positioned so they both could see. Sitting between them, he sped through his passwords and performed a Google search. A glossy website for March Investments filled the screen. The impressive site represented a mega real estate corporation specializing in high-end commercial developments. The menu offered many pages for various projects, an investor's prospectus describing the company's successful trading history on the New York Stock Exchange, and an "about" page introducing the corporate officers—featuring the CEO, Kenneth Klein.

"Wow, this is a big operation!" Robby exclaimed.

"One of the biggest," Judd bitterly conceded. "It's based in Raleigh, and Kenny Klein grew up right here in Mount Airy. He was a couple of years ahead of me in high school. Obviously, he's moved on to greater things."

As Judd scrolled through the list of projects, Amanda recognized the names of some of the major suburban developments March Investments had built in the Lake Norman area. Her mom had sold some high-priced homes in several. "Are you saying March Investments wants *this farm*?" she asked incredulously.

"Afraid so, take a look." Judd clicked on a link, bringing up Mayberry Acres.

She and Robby scooted closer to see the details. Even with her limited knowledge, Amanda recognized the distinctive triangle of land bordered by two highways, with the country road at its base. The plot plan overlaid gray shapes indicating the current buildings. It included a proposed residential town house community with a golf course, swimming pool, and club house, with the old lake as a landscape feature. That community sprawled across the lower two-thirds of the triangle, including the area where Judd's fields and the rancher now stood. The upper third nestled in the peak of the triangle was to be a fancy shopping mall, anchored by a Whole Foods right where the Yount homestead now sat.

Robby was flabbergasted. "Oh, my God, no way!"

"Can the demographics really support this?"

"Kenny thinks so. Lately, retirees have been flocking here in droves, with nowhere upscale to live. Professionals who don't mind a long commute to Winston-Salem or Greensboro think Mount Airy might be a decent place to raise their kids."

"Like growing up inside *The Andy Griffith Show*," Amanda wryly commented, while copying the web address on a scrap of paper to show Sara later.

"Exactly." Judd was grim. "I can't tolerate the idea of our family farm under tons of concrete."

"I'm assuming March Investments is offering big money," Robby stated the obvious.

Judd frowned. "No one has approached me because the project hasn't been green-lighted by the commission. But I've heard rumors of up to five million for the land, but that's just the beginning for the investors. On top of that, there would be the profit from all the town house sales and commercial leases. Our nine-person planning board has tentatively approved it, but three of the five commissioners have nixed it. But now with Myron Landry dead, I'm screwed."

Amanda tried to wrap her head around the concept. "What do you mean?"

"Landry was a *no* vote," Judd explained. "My pathetic brother-in-law, Marty Roach, who is also a commissioner, is a *yes* vote. Knowing Marty, he will bribe, blackmail, or strongarm one of the two holdouts to his way of thinking."

She and Robby were astonished speechless. How was it possible that the man they had met at the jam was one of the commissioners who held the Taylor family's fate in his hands? It now seemed that Lori was not the only family member who despised Marty.

"We met Marty Roach last night at the Earle Theatre," she said. "He told us *he* wanted to buy Mayberry Farm."

Judd's laugh was more like a vicious bark. "That loser couldn't buy a doghouse, let alone our farm. I'm surprised he had the balls to approach you." He went on to explain that Marty, twice divorced, was burdened with alimony and child support. His company, Apollo Partners, was in the toilet and desperate for cash. "Every deal he touches goes belly-up, so forget you ever met him."

Judd's animus toward his brother-in-law betrayed the kind of family dysfunction Sara dealt with all the time. Lori had called her uncle "a racist pig," so Amanda figured part of Marty's problem might have to do with a black man marrying his twin sister. She wondered if she'd ever find out, but in the meantime, she said, "Judd, could Marty be hooked up with March Investments? Maybe they've enlisted him to pressure you, through Ella."

At first, he scoffed, gulping down the remainder of his tea. Then he thoughtfully massaged his jaw, the habit of a man unused to being clean-shaven. "Well, everyone in real estate knows Marty's reputation, so ordinarily, they wouldn't give him an umbrella in a shitstorm. But Kenny Klein, March's CEO, is well aware that I'm married to Ella. After all, we all grew up together. So I guess it's possible Kenny has at least spoken to Marty. They were together at Myron Landry's pool party."

Mentioning the pool party put Amanda on high alert. When she glanced at Robby, he too looked disturbed. Although they'd not discussed that high-profile death, it was the talk of the town. Robby had likely heard the gossip, just as she and Sara had, and he immediately proved her right.

"Judd," Robby began. "The lawyer, Mr. Hayes, was also at that party. He told me there's speculation that Commissioner Landry's death was not an accident."

Giving them a dark look, Judd rose abruptly and walked to the glass doors. She couldn't tell if he was gazing at Sara, who now appeared to be asleep in her chair, or simply watching a large hawk soaring above the distant treetops.

"Here's the deal, guys," Judd said at last. "Trying to keep an investigation under wraps in Mount Airy is like trying to hide a shark in a fishbowl. The sheriff thought it was better that way, to keep the natives calm until we had the evidence, but he was a fool." He paused and sighed. "But I told you the truth the night I missed dinner. Myron Landry was definitely murdered."

## Chapter Twenty-five

The Yount homestead...

They took it outside, Amanda and Robby following the dark storm cloud named Judd. Clearly, the man did not want to talk about Myron Landry's murder. Instead, he opened his hands and forced a smile. "Hey, I promised you the grand tour, and you're gonna get it." He gently touched Sara's shoulder. "Wake up, sunshine, and come on our adventure."

Unaware of Judd's disturbing confirmation of a murder, not to mention the brewing disputes over Mayberry Farm, Sara opened her green eyes gradually and gave a contented smile. "Wouldn't miss it for the world. Where are we going?"

"We'll cut through the field into the forest, then follow a path to the Yount homestead, where Mandy's Grandma used to live."

Mentioning Grandma deepened Amanda's unease. So far, they had not discussed her murder with Judd, who either lacked curiosity or didn't want to know. As they followed his long strides through the fallow pasture, smelling both sweet and sour, like rotting hay, she reminded herself that Judd likely had enough stress in his life—financial, professional, and personal. She took Sara's arm, holding her back several paces as the men moved on. In a whisper, she told her the bare bones about March Investments' plans for the land and Landry's murder.

Sara listened carefully as she walked and watched the hawk still soaring and hunting. "Something's wrong, Mandy. I don't like it that Vivian was killed and now Landry. I pray to God there's no connection."

Amanda stopped and gaped at her. "What on earth are you talking about? That's insane. Absolutely nothing connects them."

"Only Mayberry Farm." Sara's gaze shifted as she studied Amanda's face. "The property is potentially extremely valuable."

"Yes, but so what? Two weeks ago, we didn't even know it existed. What's wrong with you? You fell asleep on Judd's deck perfectly rational and woke up a conspiracy theorist." Sara looked to where the men had pulled far ahead and were now moving into the forest. "You're right. Maybe Judd slipped some haha juice into my tea, and I'm hallucinating. Sorry, babe, I didn't think this through."

Amanda laughed, but it wasn't quite funny. They sometimes joked about ayahuasca, a psychedelic substance from the Amazon. Sara swore some of her patients were haha users, but this crazy idea of connected murders was off the wall.

By then, Robby and Judd had disappeared. Even the hawk was gone. He had banked and vanished down into the trees. "We better catch up with the guys because you're freaking me out, Sara."

Running helped put the unpleasant thoughts behind her. When they reunited with the men, Amanda had all but forgotten. She marveled at the soaring trees that blocked out all but small shifting patterns of light on the fragrant, pine needle-strewn path. Judd knew where he was going, yet it appeared no one else had used the passage for years. The evergreens were tall and spindly, the hardwoods old and majestic. The effect was like walking through a ruined cathedral. Completely enchanted, Amanda wondered if Grandma had ever roamed these woods.

Her sandal caught on a fallen branch, but Sara was right behind to catch her. As she steadied Amanda on her feet, Sara gave her a sly, sweet kiss, proving the forest was magical. The silence was total, disrupted only by their footsteps and the occasional scurrying squirrel. "It's beautiful, isn't it, Sara?"

"*You* are beautiful, Mandy."

They cut the dewy-eyed banter when they got close to the guys and when they heard the faraway drone of highway traffic.

Judd explained, extending his arms and pointing. "That's Interstate 74 to the north and Interstate 77 to the west. The barn's over that away, and the homestead's dead ahead."

"Where's the lake?" Robby panted excitedly.

"It's hidden, a surprise," Judd teased.

"Can you fish in it?"

"Hell, it's so full of perch, catfish, and even bass that if you whistle, they'll jump right out of the water and land in your cooler."

Amanda could almost hear her brother's heart palpitating from his lifelong love affair with fishing. She also heard the traffic sounds growing louder and figured they were in the upper third of the triangle, where the Whole Foods would be built. With each step, she was less inclined to sell.

Suddenly, they were standing on an actual dirt road. Across from them, hiding behind a tangle of azalea and rhododendron bushes, stood the Yount homestead. As they picked their way down an overgrown pathway to the front porch, Amanda's own heart fluttered to finally see Grandma's childhood home. Her anticipation was almost childlike, an ancestor fantasy come true.

The steps and several floorboards were rickety when they stepped up into the shade, where an old porch swing and two sagging wicker chairs sat under a flyspeck blue ceiling. The paint peeled like strips of white skin from the walls and the dark green shutters were semi-detached, hanging like crooked dominoes at the long windows. The screen door was torn, and the house offered none of the Victorian grandeur of the Bee & Bee, from that same era, yet the two-storied wooden structure had a no-nonsense nobility she found even more attractive.

Judd used an old-fashioned skeleton key to enter into a small foyer with burgundy-striped wallpaper that smelled like aged newspapers. She saw a tall carved mahogany hall mirror and a wide, unadorned staircase leading upstairs. The parlor was off to the left, the dining room to the right, with the kitchen behind it. As they roamed through the spacious, largely empty rooms, she noticed that what had surely been vintage furnishings had been replaced with more recent, utilitarian pieces. It made her wonder about the antique slant top desk mentioned in the private letter Grandma left, the desk for which she had only one of the two keys.

"Hey, Judd, what happened to all of Grandma's furniture?" she asked.

"We stored most of that stuff out in the barn. It just wasn't practical for our family."

"May I see it someday?"

He chuckled. "Sure, but wear old clothes and bring a dust mask."

She moved on, admiring a rustic stone fireplace with its damp ashes smell, a cracked porcelain farm sink, and even an ancient ice box beside a more modern refrigerator.

"I've never seen one of those!" Sara opened the old box, while Judd explained how the blocks of ice were placed. Sara was also drawn to the mouldings and various architectural details that confirmed what Ella had told them: "The place has good bones."

"Any ghosts?" Robby asked. Seemingly, he was already bored with the tour.

Judd made a comical, scary face. "My daughter Jana likes to think so. Once when we came here to visit, she brought a candle to summon dead spirits in the back bedroom. Wanna go up and see?"

"Not unless Jana was successful." Robby yawned. "Hey, Judd, can you point me toward that lake? I'd prefer to continue my tour outdoors."

So as Amanda and Sara started upstairs, Judd led Robby out the back door. They heard him tell Robby, "Hang a right on the dirt road, go about a hundred yards, then cut left onto the path by the split oak tree."

When Judd joined them in the second bedroom, where Amanda and Sara were imagining how it would feel to wake up together in the four-poster bed with a faded floral canopy, Amanda asked, "Will Robby be safe on his own?"

Judd smiled. "Long as the copperhead snakes or the bears don't eat him."

## Chapter Twenty-six

### Picnic...

The next day, Saturday afternoon, Amanda and Sara parked in the Food Lion parking lot just off Pine Street. They were again on their way to Judd and Ella's house.

"I'm so sorry I couldn't make a decision yesterday," she told Sara for the umpteenth time. "But it seems like a catch-22, doesn't it? The Taylors can't afford to stay on the farm and remodel the old house like they want, they can't easily pay the rent, yet they refuse to sell."

Sara sighed. "Yes, I get all that. Maybe you can work out a compromise."

Amanda couldn't picture such a compromise, but she said, "That's why I need to talk to Ella before I decide anything." She had told Judd as much the day before, and gentleman that he was, he had invited them all to the farm for a picnic with the entire family.

"I'm glad we insisted on supplying some of the food. It was the least we could do after all the hospitality the Taylors have shown us." They entered the store, found a shopping cart, and started at the deli, where they chose large tubs of potato salad, macaroni salad, and coleslaw. "I don't know why it's so easy for Robby," Amanda continued to obsess. "He acts like he doesn't care what happens to Mayberry Farm."

Sara laughed. "He doesn't want to sell that fishing hole, now that he's seen it. It's Robby's personal Christmas gift, Easter candy, and Halloween treat rolled into one little lake."

It was true. Robby had brazenly asked Judd if he could spend the afternoon fishing there and then join them around six for the picnic. Judd had graciously agreed, so they were driving to the Taylors' in separate cars. At that moment, Amanda suspected her brother was already drowning worms at the end of lines from Grandpa Whitaker's antique rods, the ones Robby had inherited from Grandma.

Sara stopped at the bakery section for apple, cherry, and pumpkin pies. "Does Robby even know what bait to use?"

"Well, he should. He's consulted with everyone from Judd to that lawyer Hayes. He even asked that old guy with a head like a hard-boiled egg, the one who eats breakfast every morning at the Bee & Bee, and grouchy Lou, who serves us coffee. Robby said they all suggested something different, so my brother was determined to try everything except the chunks of expired chicken livers Lou recommended."

Robby had visited three tackle shops and returned with insect repellant, a dip net, a new backpack, and a Styrofoam bucket filled with creepy crawlies Amanda didn't care to know about. In short, pretty much everyone in Surry County knew Robert Rittenhouse would be fishing at the old Yount place that afternoon.

They added several packages of hot dog and hamburger rolls to their cart. Judd had told them that Ella would supply the meats and veggies, while he would do the grilling.

"Is that everything?" Sara asked.

"Yep, let's hit the road."

When they arrived at Judd's, they saw Robby's rental Ford already in the driveway, but Robby himself was long gone into the woods. No one answered when they rang the doorbell, so they jogged around back and found the three female Taylors cleaning the deck. Ella was polishing the grill, Lori was scrubbing the picnic table, while Jana was dancing to rap from a boom box as she swept the floor.

Amanda caught the hint of a smile when Lori spotted them, directed primarily at Sara, but just as quickly, her expression reverted to its perpetual pout. Ella called out a warm hello. Jana dropped her broom, then hugged and high-fived them.

"Girls, help the ladies with their groceries," Ella commanded.

Surprisingly, both kids instantly took over their armloads of white plastic Food Lion bags and headed for the kitchen. Sara stayed out, offering help to Ella, while Amanda followed inside. After asking the girls' permission, she rushed down the hallway to the bathroom. Since she'd not yet seen Judd, she knocked first, then went in and took care of urgent business. By the time she returned, the girls had already put the food away.

"Where's your father?" she asked them.

Jana grinned. "He's dressing for work."

"Yeah, Dad's ducking out on us again." Lori snarled. "I'll be splitting, too, as soon as Mom cuts me loose."

Seriously? Amanda thought. It was déjà vu all over again, a repeat of the night they'd first been invited to dinner.

"*You* are not going anywhere, young lady." The deep male voice boomed down the hallway, followed by Judd in full deputy uniform. "Lori, today you stay home and get to know your cousins, and I have an assignment for you."

Lori exhaled dramatically and rolled her eyes as her father reached up a long arm and yanked at a rope on the hallway ceiling. A set of attic stairs unfolded. "When you climb up, you will find three white boxes labeled *family photos*. Hand them down to Jana, and she'll put them in the kitchen."

"Shit, it's hot as hell up there!" Lori protested.

"Watch your mouth, girl," Judd warned. "Today, you do exactly as your mother says, or you're grounded for the rest of the weekend."

"If I stay home today, I'm already grounded for half the weekend," Lori muttered under her breath.

"I forgot you worked Saturdays," Amanda ventured as Judd unlocked a small safe, removed a holstered gun, and strapped it on.

He eyed her, then corrected her. "Actually, I'm *on call* most weekends, but I had already been assured that I was free and clear today. Otherwise, I never would have invited you, Mandy. It's not my intention to be the world's worst host."

"No problem." She felt somehow chastised and wondered if they should leave.

He noticed her uncertainty. "No worries, it's all good. Ella is used to my weird schedule, and everything's under control. I saw Robby. He's out at the lake and promised to be back here at six. I promise to be back at five, so I can fire up the grill."

"Yeah, I bet." Lori sneered.

Judd spun around and frowned at his eldest daughter. "Lose the attitude, Lori. Now you understand why law enforcement is the pits. What have I been telling you, damn it?"

Amanda wondered what the hell was going on.

Jana explained, "Lori thinks she wants to be a cop. Dad thinks it's a stupid idea."

Lori turned her back, unwilling to confirm or deny.

"Anyway," Judd continued, "we thought it would be fun for your cousin Mandy to see what her extended family looked like and to hear a little about their personalities."

"Oh, great, ancient history day," Lori said snidely.

"It's great indeed." Judd gave his youngest a friendly chuck on the chin. "Give Sara my apologies, and tell her I'll see her soon."

With that, Deputy Taylor turned and left.

## Chapter Twenty-seven

Family tree...

Much to Amanda's delight, instead of exploring the photos on the kitchen table, Ella herded them out to a gazebo hidden in a copse of willow oaks at the back of the property. Lori and Jana carried the boxes, Sara and she hauled a cooler of sodas and bottled water, while Ella brought snacks. A tiny stream trickled alongside the shaded structure, and songbirds chirped from the trees. After Ella warned them not to soil the old photos with moist fingers and potato chip grease, they stashed the food and drinks under the big round table, while Ella pointedly supplied a pile of paper napkins.

With a lesson plan in mind and in her school teacher's voice, Ella said, "We will start with the oldest pictures, then move on to the current."

"That sounds wonderful!" Sara actually clapped her hands.

Amanda was intrigued by her lover's obvious excitement, which seemingly eclipsed her own. She really liked Judd's family, but starting with Grandma's death, it felt like the introduction of Taylors into their lives had opened a Pandora's Box, and she wasn't sure how deeply she wanted to dig. So as Ella lifted out old photos curled like dried leaves, she looked up into the branches of the huge oak and decided, like it or not, this was her family tree.

Ella handed Amanda a half dozen shots to view and pass on. "Okay, these are the only surviving images of Thomas Taylor, Judd's grandfather. Since Vivian Davis died, I've studied these old pictures, some of which have dates and notations on the back. I've attempted to piece together a timeline and possible storyline about what happened between Thomas and Vivian way back then.

"We know that Thomas was an orphan boy who was raised by Mandy's great-great-aunt Alice Yount, the owner of Mayberry Farm. Ms. Yount loved the Negro child almost like a son. He lived in her house. She taught him how to run the farm and depended upon him to do so."

Amanda scrutinized the pictures of a smiling little African American boy with very dark skin and apparently boundless energy as he rode tractors, fed chickens, and milked cows in and around the barn. In two shots, he was dressed in his Sunday best, standing on the front porch of the Yount homestead.

"Who is that older woman sitting behind Thomas?" Sara had spotted a tiny black lady hunched in a rocker in the shadows.

Ella laughed. "That would be Miss Mayberry Johnson, Thomas's maternal grandmother. They say Ms. Yount named the farm after her."

"No way!" Lori piped up, showing her first flash of interest. "I always thought it was named after the TV show."

Even Amanda knew that was silly. "No, Lori, *The Andy Griffith Show* ran between the years of 1960 and1968, much later than the farm was established."

Ella added, "Some say Andy Griffith may have

named his fictitious town after this farm. After all, Andy grew up here and was likely familiar with Mayberry Farm."

"But why would a white lady like Ms. Yount name her place after a black woman like Miss Johnson?" Jana wondered.

"Good question," Sara muttered.

Ella seemed thoughtful. "Well, Judd says his great-great-grandma was named 'Mayberry' because her full lips were red as the berries of May. It could be Ms. Yount thought the name sounded pretty. But also, by all accounts, the mistress of Mayberry Farm was a liberal, fair-minded woman way before her time. Why else would she more or less adopt Thomas? Even more relevant, why would she tolerate what happened next, when Mandy's Grandmother Vivian, also an orphan, moved to the farm?"

Those around the table grew very still while Ella began to speculate. "I believe Thomas was only sixteen when he met Vivian, who was also sixteen. They fell in love or at least had a brief affair. Instead of becoming enraged when young Vivian got pregnant, Ms. Yount must have shown compassion and restraint because we know from the dates on the photos that Vivian was allowed to stay on the farm to have the baby. I'm sure Thomas was told to break off the relationship. Also from the photos, I know that around that time, Thomas and Mayberry moved out of the house to live in a double-wide trailer located on the property."

As "proof," Ella showed them a photo of Thomas and Mayberry standing in the rusty doorway of the trailer, looking unhappy about the situation. The photo was dated 1953.

"That doesn't sound very 'fair-minded' to me,"

Lori said.

Ella rolled her eyes. "You have no idea how enlightened that was, considering baby Andrew Taylor was born in 1954. Back then, Ms. Yount knew sexual relations between the races were morally reprehensible to most locals, and marriage was illegal. Yet she chose to shelter and protect the young lovers."

"It's romantic, like you and Daddy," Jana said.

"It's hardly like me and your daddy," Ella retorted. "No one gave us a hard time when we got married."

"Except Uncle Marty and your own mom, Grandma Elsa," Lori grumbled. "That bitch practically disowned you, Mom."

"Never mind that." Ella gave her a warning look. "Which just goes to show how advanced Ms. Yount was for her time."

"But what about our Great-Grandma Bessie, where does she come in?" Jana asked.

"Well, that's the next chapter, isn't it?" Ella paused while everyone chose something to drink and ate a few handfuls of snacks. They listened to water trickling over the rock and a crow cawing from the field, while a large cloud drifted over the sun. In the meantime, their hostess spread out the next group of photographs.

"Also in 1954, Thomas Taylor married a local black woman named Bessie. Before Vivian came along, the two had been childhood sweethearts. The couple adopted baby Andy, and Bessie was the only mama he ever knew."

Perusing the photos, Amanda saw Thomas and Bessie's wedding, then many shots of Andy growing up with his parents, becoming an extremely handsome, light-skinned young man. They all looked happy as they went about their daily lives. Occasionally, Amanda caught glimpses of white people on the farm, always in the distance. She saw Ms. Yount and a very youthful Vivian, with a long blond ponytail. Clearly, the Taylor family remained part of life on the farm but remained segregated until Vivian disappeared from the pictures.

Amanda had learned that her Grandma Vivian had departed North Carolina two years after giving birth. She went on to marry Grandpa Whitaker, their only child was Diana, who married Robert Rittenhouse, and Robby and Amanda were born. All that was old news.

She sensed the bittersweet aspect to it all and took Sara's hand as they passed the pictures. It could have turned out much worse, she decided. As the photos changed from black and white to color, Aunt Alice Yount was depicted more often with the Taylors. Old Grandma Mayberry disappeared, but eventually, a stunningly beautiful young black woman became part of the group.

"Who is that with Andy?" she asked Ella.

"Andy is about seventeen there, and that is Miss Mavis Judd, the love of Andy's life."

"Yea, Grandma Mavis!" Jana cheered. "She looks like a little girl there."

"Mavis is your grandma?" Sara wanted clarity.

Lori said, "She sure is. Mama Mavis is sixty-five now, and she lives down in Pilot Mountain. She is one woke woman."

"So Andy and Mavis got married?" Amanda asked.

"Yes, when they were only eighteen," Ella said. "Unfortunately, Andy shipped out to Vietnam the very next year."

"Grandpa Andy never even saw our daddy get born," Jana said.

Amanda felt shell-shocked as the story unfolded. She knew Judd was born in 1974, at the very end of the Vietnam conflict. If Andy never saw his son born, then he must have been drafted soon after Mavis got pregnant, and then been killed in action. It was a bitter irony.

"I wish I could have known Grandpa Andy," Jana said.

"Judd wishes he could have known his father," Ella noted.

Amanda wished she could have known Andy, too. He was Grandma Vivian's son and Amanda's great-uncle. "So Judd grew up without a father."

"More or less," Ella conceded. "Although old Thomas Taylor mentored his grandson and taught him everything about farming. His Mama Mavis, who never remarried, has always been a wonderful, supportive mom to Judd."

She and Sara were mesmerized by a photo of nineteen-year-old Andy Taylor in his Army uniform. He looked so proud, grinning ear to ear, while flanked by his bride, pretty Mavis, and his daddy, Thomas, on one side, and an elderly, equally proud Ms. Yount on the other. The young man in the picture did not know he was about to die. Amanda assumed he served bravely and wondered if Grandma Vivian knew her son was a war hero.

"Did my grandmother know about Andy?" she demanded.

Ella sighed. "Now that we know Vivian existed, Judd believes she knew most everything. He assumes

Ms. Yount kept her up to date. Judd remembers he got Christmas and birthday cards from 'some white lady from up north' the whole time he was growing up. Judd also remembers his Grandpa Thomas telling him that Andy also got the 'white lady' gifts and cards. They never knew Vivian's name or that they were related. Bessie and Mavis were the only grandmas in their lives."

Somehow, that revelation was even sadder to Amanda. Grandma Viv had been entirely divorced from an entire branch of her family. She hoped Grandma had wanted it that way, but more likely, she had no choice. Tracking the changes in her will, Grandma clearly wanted to anonymously contribute to the Taylors' well-being.

She peered up again at the majestic willow oak above the gazebo. When the cloud cover passed, the sun revealed that someone had sawn off one large limb that threatened the structure: *an entire branch divorced from her family tree.*

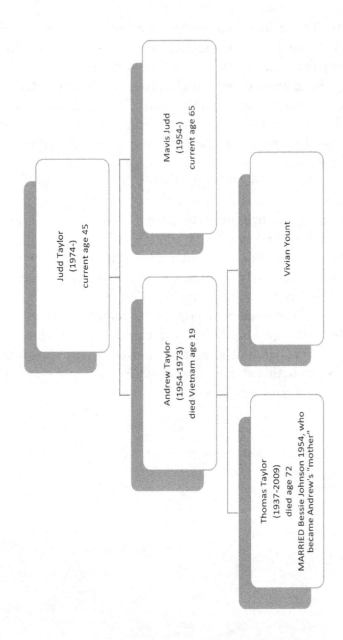

## Chapter Twenty-eight

The icing in the Oreo...

Ella glanced at her watch, then gathered the photos they had viewed and placed them back into the box marked *Taylor*. "Judd should be home soon, so if you'll excuse me, I'm heading back to the house to get ready. You stay here and look at the rest of the pictures."

"I'm coming with you. I want to help," Jana said, then skipped after her mother.

Amanda was alarmed by Ella's departure because she'd not yet discussed the farm and wanted to know if Ella had any ideas for a compromise, some way the Taylors could afford to stay on the land. She had hoped to get her alone, but the opportunity never seemed to present itself.

As she pondered this dilemma and Lori prepared to open the second box, labeled *Roach*, Sara suddenly said, "Lori, where did your father go today?"

Lori seemed to relish the change of topic. "I overheard him talking to his boss this morning, so I know Dad's gone to meet with the medical examiner in Raleigh. They finished the autopsy on Commissioner Landry, and I know he was murdered. Man, would I love to eavesdrop on that conversation."

"You want to hear the details of an autopsy?" Amanda was appalled.

"Sure, why not?"

Then Amanda recalled that the girl wanted to go into law enforcement. "So you really want to be a cop?"

"I want to be the sheriff or a chief. Even better, I'd like to hook up with the FBI, live someplace like Washington, D.C., get out of this hellhole."

Lori was both animated and adamant. If Judd truly wanted to discourage his daughter's choice of profession, he had an uphill battle.

"How far is Raleigh from here?" Sara asked.

"At least two hours. That's why Dad will never get home on time." Lori eyed Sara. "You're a shrink, right?"

"I am. I counsel at-risk kids and help parolees transition back into society."

"I bet you've seen it all. Do people, like, give you a hard time about being gay?"

Amanda sensed Lori attaching to Sara—hero worship, role model, or else she was just plain attracted to her. She noticed Lori closely watching how she and Sara interacted, especially when they touched or held hands. Amanda didn't mind. She liked the kid. But she couldn't help but wish Lori could meet their friend, Maya, an African American woman who had been a district attorney in Charlotte before moving to D.C. Maya's partner, Shar, had been elected to the U.S. Congress. Talk about role models!

"People always give you a hard time, Lori," Sara was saying. "Not just because you're a lesbian, but because you're a woman with power. You learn to blow it off, not let it get in your way. You'll be just fine."

Amanda began to fidget. All this bonding was

well and good, but she still needed to talk to Ella. "Hey, can we please look at the photos now?"

Lori snorted and roughly tossed the lid off the Roach box. "These are pictures from Mom's side of the family—the icing in the Oreo."

"What did you say?" Sara demanded.

"You know, say someone falls into a ravine and hurts himself. Then when he tries to get up, he breaks his leg. Breaking his leg is, like, 'the icing on the cake.' Like insult to injury? It's ironic right?"

Obviously, the girl was the daughter of an English teacher. "So what?" Amanda asked.

"So we Taylors are the chocolate brown cookies on the outside, the Roaches are the white icing inside, get it? They are the nasty part, the ironic insult."

Lori proceeded to dump out several picture albums for her show and tell. "This old book shows my Grandpa Martin Roach. Wait till you see all the pictures of him with my other grandpa, Andy Taylor!"

Amanda was genuinely shocked by the images of young Andy playing with a freckled white boy at Mayberry Farm. They did chores together, and apparently, Martin was a frequent guest at Ms. Yount's dinner table.

"They were best friends," Lori continued. "They even got drafted to Vietnam at the same time. Grandpa Martin came home from the war and lived a life, but Grandpa Andy died over there."

It was stunning that both Lori's grandfathers had worked at Mayberry Farm, gone to war together, and been best friends. It showcased the surprising frequency of interracial blending throughout the generations.

"The weird part was that Grandpa Andy, the black kid, was Grandpa Martin's boss," Lori said.

"Martin was Ms. Yount's hired hand, while Andy, the heir apparent, was the foreman."

Sara's eyes were jade green saucers. "That's amazing, Lori. The work relationship didn't seem to hurt their friendship."

"Not at all, but Martin knew he wouldn't stay at the farm forever. After the war, he went to Surry County Community College and later sold insurance in town. Had Andy lived, farming would have been his life. He loved the land just like my dad does."

Amanda studied the pictures of young Martin, a redheaded hayseed who seemed absolutely devoted to his black buddy. As much as Lori complained about the Roach family, at least at that stage of their history, racism wasn't an issue.

Sara must have been thinking along those same lines. "Lori, your Grandfather Martin seems like a decent man, so what's your problem with the Roaches?"

The girl slammed the early album shut and opened a new one. Her amber eyes flared, her features tensed, and she smashed an index finger onto the smug face of a white woman with heavy makeup and big, teased hair. "She's the problem. That's fucking Grandma Elsa, the bitch Martin married!"

Lori explained that Elsa was a country girl from the foothills, whose family tended to be members of the Ku Klux Klan. "I don't know what he was thinking when he married her, but that's when all the trouble started."

So that was when the white icing in the cookie turned sour, Amanda wryly surmised. She assumed that if Andy had still been alive at the time of Martin's marriage to Elsa, then Elsa would have ended that friendship. Yet Elsa's daughter, Ella, had married Judd

Taylor, and Ella seemed free of prejudice. "How does your mother feel about all this?" Amanda asked Lori.

Lori's full lips compressed into a thin line. By way of a partial answer, she showed them a photo of Judd and Ella's wedding. Ella's father, Martin, with a hint of gray in his red hair, stood awkwardly beside his daughter. With one hand placed protectively under her elbow, his smile was strained. Elsa with the big hair and Ella's twin brother, Marty, the man they'd met at the Earle Theatre, stood disapprovingly off to one side. A plump, sassy-looking older woman, whom Lori identified as Mama Mavis, Andy Taylor's widow, clung to Judd's arm beaming like a brown votive candle in an oversized floral muumuu. The bride and groom were happily focused on each other, but the dysfunctional family dynamics were obvious.

"Well, Mom tries to downplay this mess," Lori finally said. "It's not like she pretends we're one big happy family, but she does force everyone to get together for Christmas and birthdays. The last time I saw them all was at my big brother Micah's high school graduation. Grandma Elsa gave Micah tickets to a Panthers game, and Uncle Marty gave him a case of Coors Light. Problem was, Micah hates football and beer."

Sara had only one question. "Where is your Grandpa Martin now?"

Lori turned to a photo of an aging man with a severe sunburn sitting on a white sand beach. Palm trees waved from the shoreline behind him. "Grandpa divorced Elsa's ass years ago and moved to Florida. He was long gone before my parents got married."

Amanda wasn't sure she approved of a guy deserting his wife and young twins, but she said,

"That's too bad."

Lori shrugged. "Not really, he's better off. We all fly to Tampa for spring break and stay with him. It's chill. And Micah attends Rollins College, only an hour and a half away, so it's like a family reunion."

Amanda's head was swimming with too many names and images. She'd be lucky to remember any of these relatives by the following morning, but the family history was fascinating all the same. Now that she knew Lori and Jana, she wanted to meet Micah someday. And Mama Mavis seemed like a hoot.

But mainly, she worried about Uncle Marty, who had offered to buy Mayberry Farm. She knew from Judd that he was a twice-divorced loser desperate for money, and Marty's interests were in direct opposition to Judd's. It was almost impossible to reconcile that he and Ella were twins. They were like Gemini, the astrological symbol of good and evil, the dualities of light and dark. Just how dangerous was Marty?

## CHAPTER 29
*Autopsy...*

By the time they carried the boxes up to the house, Judd had returned. He was in the bedroom changing out of his uniform.

Lori took the opportunity to pull a fast one. "Mom, I've been good. I've hung around all day, but now can I go to Lily's party? She planned it ages ago, and how would it look if I didn't come?"

They were all standing in the kitchen. Ella put down the knife she was using to peel tomatoes. "What did your father tell you?"

"He said I'd be grounded all weekend if I left."

Ella frowned and considered, while Amanda wondered who Lily was. She supposed she was Lori's girlfriend, the pretty, plump young woman with buzzed cut hair and tattoos. They had been together at the Earle Theatre. She hoped Ella would cut Lori some slack.

"Your father and I are equal partners," Ella continued. "So we'll split the difference on this one. You can go to Lily's if you're home before midnight."

"Thanks, Mom!" Lori hugged her mother and then surprised Amanda by hugging her and Sara, as well. With that, she was out the door before Ella could change her mind or Judd could overrule.

While Jana was hunched over a bowl, obliviously stringing beans, Ella opened the fridge. "Do you ladies want wine, beer, or something alcohol-free?"

Sara quickly opted for the blushing rosé wine Ella was drinking, while Amanda asked for a Miller Lite and Jana took a Dr. Pepper.

Ella said, "Lily's a sweet girl. She looks punk and tough, but she's really quite steady and sentimental. She's good for Lori."

Amanda and Sara exchanged glances. They had compared notes about their high school days. Sara's traditional Puerto Rican parents had eventually accepted her sexual orientation, but Amanda had been too scared to tell her folks the truth. She had known instinctively that her conservative lawyer father, Robert Rittenhouse, would be disapproving, and she had only confided in Mom five years ago, when they were reunited after many years and after she'd met Sara. Mom had been compassionate and supportive, proving that Amanda's fears had been unfounded. So it felt good to hear Ella encouraging Lori. It was a brave new world.

Ella told the two of them to go out and relax on the deck, while she and Jana prepared the veggies. So they did, both taking comfortable chairs and propping their feet on the railing, with a peaceful view of the fields, forest, and the grove with the hidden gazebo.

"You have an extraordinary family, babe," Sara said with a crooked smile. "You could write a novel about the saga of Vivian and Thomas, their star-crossed love affair, and their motley progeny."

"No kidding. And what about those crazy Roaches? Can you believe Martin Roach was best friends with Grandma's illegitimate son, Andy Taylor? Then Martin's kids, Marty and Ella, are like twins from two different wombs. Even if I wrote that novel, no one would believe it."

"Yeah, wait till Diana hears, it'll blow her mind."

Indeed, ever since she began her adventure in Mount Airy, Amanda had been in constant touch with her mother, keeping her up to date nightly. She wished Mom could be there to savor the complex flavors of their unique new family soup. And while at first Mom had been resistant to embracing Grandma's shadow family, she was now quite curious and longed to join in. Unfortunately, Mom's supervisor had suddenly taken ill, leaving Mom responsible for shepherding her real estate team to a convention in Las Vegas next week. Most agents would love that job, but it was anathema to her mother, who would just as soon let "what happens in Vegas" happen without her.

Sara said, "I wonder if Robby is catching any fish."

"I wonder why the hell Robby's not here yet." Amanda checked her watch; it was almost six. She was secretly pissed he had skipped out on the family history lesson, which was not only fascinating, but also stuff he needed to know.

"He'll be here soon enough," Judd said as he joined them on the deck. "As soon as I fire up this grill, he'll smell the charcoal and come running. Fishing is hungry work."

"Hi, Judd." Amanda smiled at her cousin, who wore white shorts and an improbable pink polo shirt. His big brown feet were boxed in Crocs slip-ons that resembled old Swiss cheese. With a frosted beer in one hand, he juggled a group of grilling utensils in the other. "We missed you today," she added.

"Missed you guys, too. I'm sure you had more fun than I did." Certainly, Judd's defeated posture and furrowed brow were in direct contrast to his colorful attire.

"I can imagine that considering autopsy results are no picnic," Sara said.

"How did you know?" Judd tensed, then relaxed. "Never mind. I'm sure Lori told you. That girl listens in and snoops around whenever police work is involved."

"Sure she does." Sara winked. "She wants to follow in her daddy's footsteps. So tell us what you found out."

Sara's question was brazen, but Amanda was dying to know the answer.

He frowned. "You realize this is official business, right? Why should I tell you anything about Myron Landry's autopsy?"

"You know we'll find out eventually. Nothing stays secret long in this little town, and if the newspapers don't tell us, Lori will."

"Besides, we're family," Amanda argued.

Judd sighed as he balled up paper and lined the stainless steel bowl of the grill. He dumped some coals onto the paper, squirted a little lighter fluid and then ignited the pile with an electronic barbecue wand.

"You realize Grandma Viv was murdered, right?" Amanda prompted. "We never talked about that, either."

Judd seemed chastised. "Yes, I know, and I'm sorry. But her lawyer, Mecklin Adams, told me about the circumstances of Vivian's death the first time he called. Then, of course, I called Detective John Winston in Mooresville for the full picture. Officer to officer, Winston admitted they'd seemingly hit a dead end. Don't think I haven't been keeping up, Mandy. I call Winston daily, and his lack of progress is a damn shame."

"So we all want some answers," Sara gently pressed. "Don't you think two murders related to Mayberry Farm is suspicious?"

Judd gaped at Sara. "Why would you say such a thing? There is no relationship. Vivian died in a botched burglary, while Commissioner Landry could have been killed for any number of reasons."

"But you said Landry was the swing vote standing in the way of the development's approval. You said Mayberry Acres was potentially worth millions, so a lot of money is at stake if the project moves forward," Amanda pointed out. "Grandma owned the land, Landry opposed development. They both stood in the way."

Judd stood back from the fire and crossed his muscled arms. "You girls are crazy, you know that? Landry had enemies. Several of them attended his pool party. Your theory is way off base."

"Did those enemies have multimillion-dollar reasons to kill him?" Sara stood her ground.

Judd's laugh was bitter. "People kill for love or money, right? Well, in Landry's case, the motive was love. There were at least two men, maybe one woman, at that party who were sleeping with Landry's wife. The beautiful, unfaithful, oversexed Mrs. Landry was most likely the cause of her husband's demise. Some jealous lover decided he didn't want to share her. Is that good enough for you?"

His angry outburst startled them both. Amanda wished she had never mentioned Sara's bizarre conspiracy theory and felt like a fool.

"Besides, Vivian was hit from behind with a golf club, or so the theory goes. Landry's murder was far more sophisticated."

They waited while he fiddled with a long fork, poking the coals. Finally, he dropped into a chair, took a long gulp of beer, and said, "Okay, here's the deal. Someone sneaked up and injected a massive dose of Tributame into his neck. That deadly cocktail of embutramide, chloroquine, and lidocaine stopped his heart. Poor guy was dead before he hit the water and had a chance to drown. Is that specific enough for you ladies?"

Sara's eyes were shifting rapidly back and forth, a sure sign she was processing data. Amanda, on the other hand, had no idea what he was talking about. "What kind of drug is that?"

"You could say Myron Landry was euthanized," Judd grumbled.

"Yes!" Sara put it together. "It's like pentobarbital, what they use to put animals to sleep."

As always, Amanda was impressed by her lover's command of all things pharmaceutical. As a psychiatrist, Sara had a medical degree and a license to prescribe.

Judd also regarded Sara with newfound respect. "You're right, and Landry was given a dose big enough to kill a horse—literally."

"My God, who would have access to such a dangerous drug?" Amanda asked them.

"Veterinarians, of course," Sara said. "Were there any at the party?"

"If only..." Judd shook his head. "But everyone around here owns pets, farm animals, or even horses. So everyone knows a vet or is related to a vet or sleeps with a vet. What I'm trying to say is folks have access."

While Amanda's brain ticked through the

difficulties of obtaining such a drug, which was surely kept under lock and key, Ella and Jana stepped onto the deck with a tray of uncooked hot dogs and hamburgers, packages of buns, covered vegetable dishes, and the salads she and Sara had provided.

Ella said, "Where's your brother, Mandy? We're about ready to eat."

"I don't know. Robby is usually prompt." She looked out at the field and forest, willing the tardy one to return from his day of fishing. Just then, she heard three muffled retorts—*pop, pop, pop*—and a flock of crows squawked into the sky off above the trees where the old homestead would be. "What was that? A car backfiring out on the highway?"

"Sounded more like firecrackers," Sara said.

But Judd was on his feet, moving fast. "Those weren't cars or firecrackers, they were gunshots!"

## CHAPTER 30
*The split oak tree...*

"What's happening?" Amanda said as she and Sara leaped from their chairs and Judd ran toward the garage.

"Where's Daddy going?" Jana's dark eyes were round as black olives centered in tiny white plates as she took Ella's hand.

"Do you allow hunters on your land?" Sara demanded.

"No, never!" Ella exclaimed. "Judd forbids it. He's posted signs all around the perimeter. We sometimes get poachers in deer season, though, but that's months away, in autumn."

"Is Robby in trouble?" Amanda cried.

Clearly, the others shared her panic. Sara already had her phone in hand. "Should I call 911?"

"The closest help is already here," Ella said. "Judd can respond before anyone else can come the distance. Besides, his vehicle is one of the few that can quickly cross the terrain."

Right on cue, Judd opened the garage door with a remote. Seconds later, he backed out in a contraption that looked to Amanda like something out of a teenage boy's video game. The black and gold vehicle had four deep-tread tires on springs, roll bars, a cow-catcher, and a short platform on the back. "What is that?" She gasped.

Ella groaned. "It's Judd's favorite toy, a Ranger XP 1000, UTV, or utility terrain vehicle. It'll go most anywhere on the farm. He and the M&M's play with it every chance they get."

"So it seats three?" Amanda concluded.

"Sure, if you don't mind your pelvic bone being hammered up your spine."

"We're going with him." Sara was not asking permission, only delivering a statement. She had also called 911, in spite of Ella's assertion that Judd's rapid response would suffice. Sara had informed the operator of shots being fired at Mayberry Farm, and unlike the other locals they'd encountered, the operator knew Judd and promised to send sheriff's deputies to the location.

Amanda beat her to the Ranger and climbed in beside Judd as the vehicle moved.

"You can't come, Mandy!" he barked.

"The hell I can't!"

Sara swung up into the backseat as it picked up speed. By then, Ella and Jana had joined the chorus forbidding them to go. Sara lifted a long canvas case out of her way to sit down. "What is this, Judd?"

"Don't mess with that, and fasten your seat belts, damn it."

Amanda figured it contained a rifle and was grateful for its presence. As much as she tried to tell herself that the gunshots had nothing to do with Robby, the fact remained that her brother was late, which was out of character.

As Judd steered through the rutted field, she looked back at Sara, who was hanging on to the roll bars for dear life. The shredded clouds in the clear blue sky tilted and jiggled at unnatural angles. When he veered into the woods, bumping mercilessly over logs and mowing down brush without losing speed, Amanda understood what Ella had meant about pelvic bones, spines, and hammers. More disturbing was the nausea rising like bile in the back of her throat as her stomach did flip-flops.

She recognized the spot where Sara had so tenderly kissed her the other day, but instead of the trees and light seeming like a holy cathedral, today the forest was an unholy hell as she worried about Robby.

"Are you okay, babe?" Sara reached out, and her hand was a jogging claw on Amanda's shoulder. Her words came out like a skipping record.

"Not really. You?"

Sara didn't even try to answer as Judd swung suddenly to the right. It seemed the vehicle would flip, but it righted itself as it came down hard on the dirt road.

By the time they roared past the old Yount homestead, leaving clouds of choking dust in their wake, Amanda was nauseated and dizzy. Soon Judd cut a hard left at "the split oak tree" he had earlier described to Robby as a landmark to the lake. The once majestic oak looked like the hand of God, in the form of a lightning bolt, had come down like an ax from the heavens and severed the tree in half. Now it looked like two bleached skeletons shunning each other.

"Hang on!" Judd warned as the ground beneath their tires changed to marshy mush. The UTV wobbled like a drunken sailor, spinning mud back onto their clothes and faces.

"Are we almost there?" Amanda yelled over the racket.

Instead of answering, Judd started calling out

Robby's name, again and again. Amanda and Sara joined in, fully hoping to see Robby emerge from the overgrowth, wondering what all the fuss was about.

Suddenly, the lake was dead ahead, lying peacefully in a ring of swaying green reeds like a big blue eye, staring at the sky. Judd abruptly cut the engine. The Ranger rattled a few gasps, and then went still, leaving them in a silence disturbed only by the now-familiar growl of distant traffic.

"Where is he?" Amanda whispered.

Judd lifted his dark hand and jabbed his index finger at both their faces. "I'm getting out now to look around. You stay put in the vehicle, you hear me?"

They must have looked defiant because he repeated the warning even louder, then added, "If you so much as unfasten your seat belts, I'll shoot you myself."

To emphasize his intent, Judd removed a wicked-looking long gun from its canvas case and a handful of shells from an attached pouch. He placed the butt of the stock on his left hip and secured the stock under his arm, upside down. They watched him slide the shells in one by one, then pump the slide backward, ready to fire. "This is a shotgun, ladies. If there's a bad guy out there, he'll think twice. So I ask you again, did you hear me tell you to stay put?"

They both nodded. He then started slogging toward the lake, splashing like a whale.

Sara whispered wryly, "That bad guy will sure as hell hear him coming."

Amanda was too busy holding her breath to respond as Judd disappeared behind a stand of wild blackberry bushes and angled off toward a different part of the lake. When she could no longer hear him splashing, she said, "Let's go!"

She didn't need to ask twice. In seconds, they were knee deep in water and weeds that tickled their shins like snakes. The bottom muck sucked at their feet with each step, yet they made far less noise than Judd. Rounding the bend, they discovered a tributary pool with a narrow, sandy beach under an umbrella of weeping willow trees. Sunlight sparkled through the gently waving fronds, leaving rippling shadows on the shore.

First they saw Judd's crouching back. He had propped his shotgun on an outcropping of rocks as he gaped at an out-of-place scatter of color on the sand—a striped towel, a blue and red Philadelphia Phillies ball cap, and an upended white ice cooler, which had spilled its contents of dead minnows onto the beach. Judd was also inspecting a bundle of camouflage green rags, which Amanda soon realized was a person stretched out prone, his head face-down and dangerously close to the lapping waves.

The scream broke from her throat and shattered the silence. It echoed off the willow trunks and ricocheted into the woods because the bundle of rags was Robby.

And he was not moving.

## CHAPTER 31
*Divine intervention...*

"I already called 911," Judd shouted as they ran toward him.

"So did I," Sara screamed back.

"Yeah, I know. They told me."

While Sara and Judd hollered at each other about who had called for help, Amanda dropped to her knees beside Robby. She felt Sara's hands on her arms, pulling her backward, and Judd's outstretched arms, attempting to restrict her access. "Hey, he's *my* brother. Let me touch him!"

"Give Robby space, Mandy. Let me help." Sara took charge, holding her fingertips to his limp wrist and to the base of his neck, seeking a pulse. Judd did not block Sara. "He's alive but unconscious. I can't tell what happened to him."

Robby was lying face-down, dangerously close to the water. "We have to move him." Judd gently ran his long arms under Robby's body, like a human forklift, then shifted him out of harm's way. Apparently when Robby fell, his knees had buckled, leaving his legs bent beneath him at odd angles. "Help me straighten out his legs, will you, Sara?"

Sara considered the medical pros and cons. She slid her hands over Robby's hips, thighs, and shins before deciding. "Okay, we can do that. The extension will help him breathe."

"He's not breathing?" Amanda tried to control her panic as they eased her brother's legs out straight and propped him slightly on one side.

"His breathing is labored but steady," Sara assured her. "It seems like something is constricting his lungs. I don't get it."

Amanda was suspended in hyper reality as they worked on Robby. She felt wet sand soaking her knees. She startled at every sound coming from the forest and fancied she could smell, even taste, the thin trickle of blood leaking from her brother's back when Judd cut off his backpack with a pocketknife. "Why is he bleeding?" she cried.

"Question is, why isn't he dead?" Judd's voice was grim. "Take a look at this."

While Sara carefully eased up the loose fabric of Robby's T-shirt to inspect the wound, Judd showed Amanda the backpack. She recognized it as the brand new one he'd purchased for this day of fishing. It was constructed of dark green canvas with a closure flap.

Judd said, "Robby must have been bending over when the bullet hit him because the flap had fallen open."

"What bullet?" Amanda shrieked.

"Calm down and look at this, Mandy," Judd commanded. "Because the flap was hanging open, the bullet penetrated the fabric beneath it and trashed the stuff inside." First Judd poked his finger through a charred, ragged hole in the green canvas, then dumped out a shredded paper bag containing an exploded sub sandwich, two shattered plastic water bottles, and finally a flat steel box with an enormous dent in its lid. "This steel box saved Robby's life," he finished with a dramatic flourish and handed the box to Amanda.

"What is that?" Sara looked up from her efforts at first aid.

Amanda was incredulous. "That's Grandpa Whitaker's old tackle box. Robby inherited it from Grandma." The bullet's impact had creased and jammed the hinged lid, but she managed to pry it open. The box was about an inch deep, a foot long, and six inches wide, with little steel partitions inside for each colorful lure. The baits toward one end of the box had been damaged and had shed flakes of paint, but otherwise, the makeshift bulletproof vest was intact and had served its purpose. "Thank you, Grandpa!" She lifted her face to the heavens.

At that moment, Robby stirred. His eyes fluttered open, and he moaned. "Grandpa?"

Unable to contain herself, Amanda pushed Sara aside and held Robby's face in her hands. "Can you hear me?"

He blinked and shifted. "Mandy? What are you doing here?"

Blinded by tears of joy, she touched his lips. "Don't talk, Robby. You were shot, but you'll be okay."

"Shot? Someone shot me in the back? It hurts like hell!"

"I'm sure it does," Sara interjected, also through tears. "You're gonna have the mother of all bruises between your shoulder blades. The bruise will be about a foot long and six inches wide. The corner of the steel box broke your skin, but that's not too bad. Basically, you had the wind knocked out of you, and I'll wager you have at least one cracked rib."

"What box?" Robby was struggling. He tried to sit upright, screamed in pain, then flopped back down into the fetal position. "I was getting ready to leave," he whimpered. "I put on my backpack and stood up to go. That's the last I remember."

"Well, someone didn't want you to go." Judd growled. He lurched to his feet and began to pace. "It looks like the bastard got off three rounds. The first one killed your bait cooler, the second one chipped that rock over there, and the last one got you. Good thing that asshole was a lousy shot."

"He tried to kill me?"

"I suspect he thought he *had* killed you."

Judd's statement hung between them, heavy with malignant portent. They stared at one another in disbelief, not only that such an attempt had been made, but also that some sort of divine intervention had spared Robby.

"But why?" Robby croaked through parched lips.

No one had an answer.

"The shooter's not still around, is he?" Sara's eyes were suddenly stretched wide in fear.

"I'd say he's long gone." Judd peered up into the trees across the lake and pointed. "I'm sure ballistics will determine he took his shots from up there."

Amanda squinted into the sun just beginning its descent in the west. She followed Judd's finger to where a rustic wooden platform hung crookedly suspended between two pine trees. "Is that a treehouse?"

Judd slowly shook his head. "Nope, that's Grandpa Thomas's old deer blind. They say Ms. Yount never approved of Thomas hunting, but then she never said no when he put venison on the table."

Amanda had never heard of a "deer blind," but common sense told her such an insidiously concealed crow's nest was a perfect place to hide, then shoot Bambi when he came out of the forest for an innocent drink from the lake. "I'm surprised it's still here."

Judd hung his head. "I've been meaning to tear it down but just never got around to it. I'm so sorry, Robby."

Sara was still apprehensive. "So where did the shooter go? We didn't see any sign of him on our wild ride in, so how did he get past us?"

"He didn't get past us." Judd again pointed west. "He headed that way, toward the highway. There's a pull-off on Interstate 74, where you can hide a car behind some trees and scramble up a steep hillside to get here. The poachers use it, and so did this cowardly piece of crap."

"So you think the shooter escaped down the hill and drove away?" Sara asked.

"I'm sure he did. Unless he had a UTV like mine, it's the only way. In fact, that's where the emergency response will come for Robby. The patrol units and ambulance will pull off and wait for me there."

"If the hill is that steep, how will the ambulance get up?" Robby asked in a weak, raspy voice.

"They can't get up, so I'm taking you down, dude." Judd's tone reeked of false bravado. "Did you ever ride in a Ranger XP 1000, Robby?"

## CHAPTER 32
*Evidence...*

After some complex maneuvering, they got Robby arranged in the backseat of Judd's UTV. The vehicle carried a first aid kit, so Sara covered Robby's small wound with a patchwork of plastic bandages and cushioned his ribs with the striped beach towel. Combining the two rear seat belts, they strapped him in place for the steep descent to the highway. By the time Robby was secured and ready to go, they heard sirens in the distance and knew the troops had arrived.

"How steep is this hill?" Robby asked nervously.

"Steep but not too bumpy," Judd reassured him. "You'll be fine."

"What about us?" Amanda asked.

"You two can hang out here till the officers and the crime techs arrive. I'll tell them the gist of what occurred, but you can fill in the blanks. Just stay the hell out of their way."

"What will you do, Judd?" Sara demanded.

"I'm going to the hospital with Robby, then arrange for a flatbed to haul my Ranger home on real pavement. Eventually, I'll get myself home for that picnic we promised you."

Amanda was beyond upset that she couldn't accompany Robby to the hospital, but there wasn't room for them all in the UTV, and neither she nor Sara could drive the thing. "How do Sara and I get home?"

"I'm sure you know the walking path by now,

but if you feel like flirting a little, I promise one of the deputies will give you a lift." He grinned, then started his vehicle. Moments later, they had driven around to the other side of the lake and disappeared into the woods.

Completely at a loss, Amanda took Sara's hand. "Can you believe this?"

"It's unreal. Should we gather up Robby's stuff to take with us?"

"I'm not sure we should touch anything," Amanda said through her tears. The sobs she'd been holding back came in gut-wrenching spasms.

Sara took her into her arms, held her tight, and stroked her back. She tucked her head under Amanda's chin and whispered, "Robby will be all right. That's all that matters."

They were holding each other when the first responders burst from the forest. Amanda broke free, composed herself, and counted four men in gray uniforms with gold Surry County badges like Judd's. They approached cautiously, yet no one had drawn a gun. The one in charge, a lanky older guy with thick gray hair and a big droopy mustache, introduced himself, but Amanda immediately forgot his name.

"Deputy Taylor explained what happened here," he said. "Can you tell me in your own words?"

And so it began. One guy took notes, including their names, their reasons for visiting Mount Airy, their relationship to the victim, and so forth. Since they weren't eyewitnesses to the attack, Amanda assumed they weren't much help.

A third man strung yellow tape enclosing a huge swath of territory, including part of the lake, the deer blind, and the forest as far as the eye could see. "What's the point?" she grumbled to Sara. "Who's going to invade the scene out here in the wilderness? Bears? Wolves?"

"You never know. They might find something useful—cigarette butts, footprints, some real evidence."

The guy with the big mustache said, "Does your brother have any enemies in this neck of the woods?"

"My brother's only been in 'this neck of the woods' six days, Officer. He hasn't had time to make enemies." She wasn't about to stray into an explanation of their conspiracy theory relating Grandma's death to Commissioner Landry's murder to now possibly the attempt on Robby's life. Making that third jump to Robby sent chills from her neck to her tailbone. Besides, Judd had already pooh-poohed their ideas. If this country sheriff was curious, let him and Judd connect any dots.

"I've got an intact bullet, boss!" the fourth man called as he pulled on latex gloves and dug something from the sand around Robby's destroyed cooler. "It's in good shape, so we could make a match if only we could find the damned gun."

"What kind of bullet?"

The man dropped it into a little plastic baggie. "Looks to be a .35 Remington. Odds are it came from a Marlin Model 336."

The boss looked mournfully at Amanda and Sara. "Too bad. Everyone and his brother own a 336. Around here, that rifle is *numero uno* for shooting white tail."

She watched while the same fourth man found a mashed bullet that had ricocheted off the rock, and the officer out near the deer blind discovered the three shell casings. She hoped these bits of evidence would help, but she feared they would not.

Amanda and Sara stood off to one side for another half hour while the sun began to set and the woods got darker. "Can we go now?" she bluntly requested.

The boss seemed to have forgotten them. He raised his bushy gray eyebrows. "So I hear you're headed back to the Taylors. Do you gals have a flashlight?"

"We know our way through the woods," Sara informed him. Apparently, she would rather walk than flirt for a ride.

Amanda agreed. "Yes, we'll be fine. Can we take Robby's stuff with us?"

The officer in charge refused to release Robby's ball cap or rod, promising, however, that her brother would get his items in due time, after they'd been fingerprinted. Next he walked to the edge of the water and pulled out something on a long stringer. "I reckon you can have this, though. Looks like your brother caught himself a nice little keeper bass."

They gaped in horror at the fat, pearly scaled fish hanging very much dead at the end of the string. "Is it still safe to eat it?" Amanda said.

"Hell, yes! He kept it cold in the lake. If you get it home and stick it in the fridge, it'll make a tasty meal."

The very idea filled her with revulsion, but Amanda figured the fish might go a long way toward lifting Robby's spirits when he eventually returned from the hospital. "Can we do this?" she asked Sara.

"Why not?" Sara took the first turn carrying the thing.

It got heavier and heavier as they stumbled through the darkening trees. The slimy burden bumped against their legs all the way home.

CHAPTER 33
*A long day...*

Two floodlights from the corners of Judd's deck glanced eerily across the clods of dirt and ash-colored stubble as they approached, making Amanda feel like she was walking across a surreal, bombed-out wasteland or perhaps the surface of the moon. Sara had called ahead on her cell, telling Ella what had happened out at the lake, but of course, Ella already knew because Judd had also called. So they were expected, so was the fish, and Ella and Jana were waiting.

Jana held out a plastic grocery bag and screwed up her nose. "Drop it in here. Mom says we'll put it in the garage fridge for now."

They happily relinquished the bass, which Jana hustled away, holding it at arm's length.

Ella used her arms to enclose them in a heartfelt hug. "I am so sorry about Robby. Why on earth would somebody shoot at him?"

Amanda hoped she was wrong about the answer, but he had been vocalizing all over town about his determination not to sell the farm. He'd blabbed to Marty Roach at the theater, to lawyer Hayes, to everyone at the Bee & Bee, and God knew who else. If the would-be assassin had designs on the land, the attack might be explainable.

"Judd said it was no accident," Ella continued. "He said someone wouldn't take three shots before discovering his target wasn't really a deer." She paused and regarded them with sympathy. "But why am I going on like this? You both must be exhausted. I am so, so sorry."

As she led them into the house, Amanda noticed someone had lowered the lid of the barbecue grill, extinguishing the charcoal fire, and all the meats and veggies had disappeared. Inside the kitchen, Ella poured them steaming cups of coffee, set out milk and sugar, and kept talking:

"Judd called from the hospital. Robby's going to be fine. The doc confirmed two cracked ribs, but since they don't tape ribs anymore, all they did was bandage the small wound on his back and give him a couple of Tylenol. He'll be bruised and sore as hell but otherwise fully functional."

"He was lucky," Sara said grimly. "But maybe I should counsel him for PTSD. It's not every day someone tries to kill you."

Amanda agreed with Sara's dark view. How could anyone be "lucky" when they'd been shot and left for dead? So far, Andy Griffith's Mayberry had not been the welcoming, idyllic fantasy as seen on TV. She was ready to pack up her loved ones and head home yesterday.

Jana came in and produced a plate of cookies to go with the coffee. She was clearly curious, had obviously heard about Robby, but seemed reluctant to talk about the scary event. Instead, she was determined to play the adult hostess. "We can eat when the men come home," she said. "Mom and I put all the food away, but we can take it out and get it cooking in a jiffy."

While Amanda smiled at the girl's eagerness to

please, she heard the crunch of heavy tires on gravel. "Are they here already?"

Apparently not, because Ella remained seated and Cob the dog didn't bother to lift his boxy head from his pillow. Ella said, "No, that'll be the flatbed truck bringing Judd's Ranger. Don't bother to get up. The guys from the station know the drill. They'll get it into the garage."

They sipped strong, hot coffee and listened to the men shouting to one another, maneuvering the vehicles, and evidently accomplishing their mission. Soon the electronic door rattled down, and the men left.

"I've been thinking," Ella then continued, "that Robby should spend the night here with us. Judd says he's really tired, and the sheriff will want to debrief him again in the morning. It just makes sense for him to stay put instead of driving back and forth to the hotel."

"Yeah, I've already changed the sheets in Lori's room, and she can bunk with me like she did before Micah left for college," Jana said.

Amanda glanced at Sara, who shrugged uneasily. The coffee burned like battery acid in her stomach, and she did not want to give Robby up when she'd almost lost him—not even into the care of the kind Taylors. "I don't know..." she stalled. "It's very generous, but Robby wouldn't want to be a bother."

"It'll be fun," Jana insisted. "Let's ask him when he gets here. I'll make pancakes for breakfast, then if Daddy skins Robby's nasty fish, maybe Mom will fry it up for dinner."

"No, I don't think so," Amanda began, but Sara cut her off with a stern look and subtle shake of the head. *What was that about?*

"Good idea," Sara injected. "Let Robby decide for himself."

Before Amanda could argue, old Cob pricked his ears, whined, and bolted for the front door. This time, his master really was home. The door flew open, the dog jumped up, and Judd shoved him away.

"Down, boy!" he commanded as he helped a very pale Robby into the room.

Amanda ran to her brother, intending to squeeze him, but stopped just in time as she remembered his hurt ribs. She kissed him instead, and Robby responded with a grin that was more of a grimace.

"Easy, Mandy!" he begged. "Just lead me to an easy chair and get me a beer."

"Get it yourself, hotshot," Sara teased as she planted a second kiss on Robby's cheek. "Haven't you caused enough trouble for one day?"

Robby tried to laugh but coughed instead as everyone helped him get seated. "Can you rustle up some food to go with that beer?"

With that request, Ella and Jana went into high hostess gear. Jana hauled out the food, while Ella fired up the grill. In the meantime, with tears of joy in their eyes, Amanda and Sara studied Robby.

"We were worried sick," Amanda confessed.

"Robby, what the hell happened?" Sara wondered. "Do you remember anything?"

But Robby held up a shaky hand. "I don't want to talk about it. I already told them everything I know, which is nothing. Can't we just drop it for now?"

Judd nodded in agreement. "It's been a long day. I could use a cold beer, too." When he walked to the fridge, Amanda noticed Judd was limping slightly.

When he returned with four frosty brews and offered them all around, she and Sara did not say no.

Soon it became clear that the men would not discuss the shooting, so the women filled them in on what had happened at the crime scene, including the discovery of the bullets. They told how the character with the big mustache had handled things.

Judd laughed. "That would be my boss, Sheriff Bill. He looks like the actor Sam Elliott and acts like he's starring in a Western movie, but he's a good cop."

"Good to know," Sara muttered.

Amanda wondered if Judd remembered any of what she and Sara had told him before, about their theories regarding motive. Clearly, it wasn't the time to bring it up. She also noted that Robby was eager to spend the night at the Taylors'. He readily accepted when asked, which caused her to feel a sense of loss because she wouldn't be the one coddling and tending to her wounded brother.

Since the night had turned cold, Ella served the picnic in the kitchen to all but Robby, who took his on a tray while seated in his easy chair. He was half asleep before dessert, so everyone bid him good night, and then Jana took him to his bedroom.

Before her midnight curfew, Lori returned from Lily's party and was shocked to see them all just finishing dinner. "What's happening?" she chirped.

"It's a long story." Ella sighed.

"And guess what, Lori, we're bunking together tonight," Jana smugly told her sister.

While Judd slowly and patiently brought his eldest daughter, the would-be cop, up to speed, his deep voice lulled Amanda to a near stupor of exhaustion. She watched Ella cut one of the pies they had purchased at the Food Lion that morning. It seemed a lifetime ago. Amanda signaled Sara that they needed to depart without dessert. They quickly said their goodbyes and promised to return for Robby the next day.

"He'll be busy with Sheriff Bill till afternoon. You two might as well sleep in," Judd said.

"We'll take care of Robby," Ella assured them.

Once they were in the Miata, Amanda took her lover's hand. "How come you thought it was such a good idea for Robby to stay the night with the Taylors?"

Sara squeezed her fingers. "Someone tried to kill your brother today, and now he's safe with an armed deputy. Think of it as protective custody."

## CHAPTER 34
*Family...*

They pledged not to discuss the violence once they returned to the Bee & Bee that night, but rather promised to concentrate solely on each other. This resolution of love, not war, took them to the king bed where they tangled, played, and took turns.

Sara's full lips brushed the contours of Amanda's face, explored the delicate shells of her ears, nibbling the lobes. She moved to her mouth and probed with her teasing tongue. Never breaking rhythm, she found the pulsing hollow at the base of her throat, then down to the small soft mounds of her breasts, to circle and nip each tender tip until Amanda arched with need and guided her lower. The long strands of Sara's hair feathered the moist skin of Amanda's belly, while her lips and tongue invaded her hot core, to explore and palpate the tender folds until Amanda begged for release—again and again—until Sara replaced tongue with practiced fingers and brought Amanda convulsing over the edge.

Laughing, crying, and gasping for air, Amanda held her tight, with Sara's full breasts cradled between her knees and Sara's head resting on her thigh. When their hearts stopped racing and they were able to breathe, she eased Sara over onto her back and slid her long body on top. Initially, she pinned Sara's hands above her head, determined to return the sweet favor in kind. Although Amanda's lovemaking was a variation on the same theme, her style was more athletic and direct, her long fingers insistent and somewhat rough, as Sara preferred. She was the heavy metal to Sara's slow bolero, which often brought Sara to a fast, hard climax, which she also preferred.

Their coupling was a perfect symphony, with just enough consistency to anticipate, just enough variety to surprise and delight.

When it was over, with quiet replacing the excesses and expletives of pleasure, their minds often roamed onto different paths. Sometimes they shared a passing thought, hope, or fear, but that night, the silence extended as they returned to their individual identities, each becoming her own unique half of the whole.

Amanda's drowsy images explored the nature of family, which had become suddenly complex over the past two weeks. It was a difficult jigsaw puzzle assembling from the Rittenhouse remnants of childhood—her loving mom Diana, her distant father Robert, her older brother Robby, her nurturing grandparents Vivian and Will Whitaker. The puzzle had expanded five years ago to include her stepfather, Trout, who was more supportive than her biological dad had ever been. She gained a soul stepsister, Ginny, as well as Ginny's strong husband, Trev, and kids Lissa and baby Thomas—not to mention Grandma's new husband, Linc.

As she sank deeper into the dream, the jigsaw pieces multiplied and even race-shifted to Judd and Ella, and their kids, Lori and Jana. Then came all the exotic ancestors staring from faded photographs—Thomas, Andrew, and the rest. These new faces remained blurred, not yet clearly formed, but so intriguing. While other faces, like Robby's, dormant for many years, now came into clear focus, dazzling her with redeemed love for which she was deeply grateful.

Turning onto her side, she encountered Sara's warm body, her knees drawn up and her lips parted in sleep. Amanda draped her arm across, cupping Sara's breast, and spooned against her. In that blessed moment, she understood that Sara was perhaps her most precious family member, linked not by blood, but by love.

She breathed a sigh of contentment, remembering Judd had encouraged them to "sleep in," with no need to confront the evils of the wakeful world until much later that day. The brocade drapes of their hotel room swayed gently, the window cracked open to the pre-dawn April Sunday. She gloried in the rich scent of Sara's skin, the soft tickle of her hair on her face, and then the phone rang.

Totally disoriented, she recognized the lilting bossa nova beat as coming from Sara's Android. Since Sara was dead to the world, she groaned and decided to let it go to voicemail. Unfortunately, the music brought her lover awake and revving into high gear. She scrambled from Amanda's embrace, folded over the edge of the bed, and began frantically searching the floor for the pocket of her discarded jeans.

"Let it go!" Amanda pleaded.

"You know I can't do that, Mandy," Sara answered huskily. She switched on the bedside light, blinding Amanda and revealing the red digital dials of the clock, which said it was only six thirty.

Amanda covered her eyes with a pillow, and her emotions plummeted into the basement. Too often they had been awakened by such calls, and considering the nature of Sara's life as a counselor, they were never good news. When the conversation ended, she peeked at Sara's creased brow and tense mouth.

"What this time?"

Sara pinched the bridge of her nose. "A patient is in trouble."

"What kind of trouble?"

"I'm so sorry, a trans boy tried to OD. I have to return to Charlotte today."

## CHAPTER 35
*Double betrayal...*

Later that afternoon, when Sara delivered her to the Taylors to reunite with Robby, Amanda knew she was beaten. No amount of pleading had changed Sara's mind because in her world, clients were family, too. The plan was to drop Amanda off, then drive directly to the city.

"It may not take too long to get my patient squared away," Sara said. "With any luck, I'll be back here by Wednesday."

"I understand." And Amanda did understand, at least intellectually, but emotionally was a different story. With the imprint of their lovemaking still on her skin, Sara's sudden departure, leaving her to cope with the aftermath of violence and all it might imply, felt like a betrayal. "Can you at least come inside and say goodbye to everyone?"

"Very briefly, but then I gotta go, babe

They were all around the kitchen table eating a special Sunday dinner of Robby's bass, baked potatoes, and leftover salads. Robby was puffed with a fisherman's pride. "Stay and eat with us, Sara," he urged.

"I'd love to, but I can't." She hugged them all, with a lingering kiss for Amanda, and then she left.

"She'll be back, right?" Lori inquired wistfully.

"So she says." Amanda took a seat and began to eat. The batter-fried bass was surprisingly tasty. Taking care to remove the few thin, translucent bones, she savored the flavors and determined to enjoy herself. "So how did it go with Sheriff Bill this morning?"

"May I be excused, Mom?" Jana, clearly bored with the subject, got permission to leave the table, cut a slice of cherry pie, and went to her room.

"Jana wants to play stupid video games," Lori said. "She's at that age."

Robby pushed away his plate. "I don't want to talk about Sheriff Bill."

Ignoring him, Judd helped himself to seconds. "Well, I can tell you that Bill is covering all the bases. He's checking the list of folks who have registered Marlin 336 rifles in the county. We know from some footprints found up near the deer blind that the shooter wore a size twelve muck boot. From the tread, the boot might have been a Fieldblazer. They sell locally for about a hundred bucks a pop."

Lori scoffed. "Yeah, but what if the gun wasn't registered in Surry County? Maybe never registered at all? So what if the guy had big feet? How many of those dudes do we have tromping around the county? *You* wear size twelve, Dad."

"You're right. A motive would help." Judd gave Amanda a grudging nod of approval. "I'm beginning to think you and Sara might be on to something. Maybe the attack did have something to do with the Mayberry land."

"I don't want to talk about it," Robby repeated, a look of disgust on his face "All I know is someone tried to kill me, and if it has to do with this property, I want nothing more to do with it."

Amanda studied her brother. He had a nasty bruise on his forehead, he sat hunched on the edge of his chair to protect his back, and the fork trembled in his hand. "What are you trying to say?"

He frowned. "I say I'm washing my hands of the whole mess. I don't care what happens to Mayberry Farm. I don't need the damned money. You can sell it or keep it. Doesn't matter to me, but you and Judd decide. It's on you now."

Ella, who had been uncommonly silent, said, "Judd and Robby struck a deal, Mandy. We gave Robby a check for one thousand dollars to cover the May rent. That buys us another month, but after that, it's up to you."

Robby added, "I've already written you a check for five hundred. Just let me know what you guys decide."

Amanda was dumbstruck. They had cut her out of the loop and left her holding the bag—both clichés applied. She could refuse to sell and make Judd happy or strike up a bargain with Apollo Partners, March Investments, or some other buyer, and the Taylors would despise her. She confronted Robby. "Just like that, you up and walk away?"

"Just like that." He smiled and left the table, moving to his easy chair in the living room.

She followed him. "So you're going home?"

"Yep, I'm leaving tomorrow."

She sank into the sofa directly across from him and tried to manage her anger. "But how can you drive all that way with two cracked ribs?"

"He's not driving. I'm taking him to Raleigh-Durham International Airport tomorrow morning," Judd said as he joined them on the couch. "He already has reservations."

Her anger rapidly morphed to panic. "But you

had round-trip reservations from Charlotte, and what about your rental car?"

"Reservations can be broken, right? And I'm leaving the car for you. Now that Sara's split, you'll be needing wheels. Then, as soon as Sheriff Bill returns my fishing rod, you can take it, along with the books I inherited from Grandma, home with you to Mooresville. I'll pick all that stuff up in the fall when I come for another visit."

She'd been gut-punched. When she looked to the kitchen for support, Ella and Lori were quietly doing dishes, staying well out of it. "So let me get this straight. You're leaving tomorrow, I get the Ford Fusion, everyone's happy, and how do I get back to the hotel tonight?"

"I can answer that." Lori strode into the room, a pink dish towel draped around her neck like a boa scarf. "You take the car, and *I'll* drive Robby to the airport. Dad, you'll let me use your truck, right? That way, you and the M&M's can clear that back field like you planned."

"Okay by me." Judd shrugged.

Lori continued, "I've got you covered, Mandy. You can move in with us tomorrow. I'm already bunking in Jana's room, so mine will be free. I'll even change Robby's dirty sheets. It'll be fun."

They seemed to have it all figured out. Amanda said, "Don't you have school tomorrow, Lori?"

"Nope, it's a teacher's work day, so the kids are off."

"It's perfect, Mandy," Ella piled on from the kitchen. "Why should you pay to stay at the Bee & Bee when you can stay with family for free?"

Cornered, Amanda considered her options.

When Sara returned to Mount Airy, they'd have to rebook the hotel—*if* Sara returned. She glared at Robby. It was official. Sara was gone, he was leaving, and she'd fallen prey to a double betrayal.

## CHAPTER 36
*The dark side...*

As Amanda drove the Focus to the Bee & Bee that night, she realized that tomorrow, Monday, would be a landmark—exactly two weeks since she walked into Grandma's town house and found her dead at the bottom of the stairs.

When she entered her lonely room, where Lois had changed the sheets, she realized the bed no longer smelled like Sara. So Amanda felt cold and empty until Sara's phone call much later:

"My patient is still on the hospital's watch list," Sara said. "I want to hang around till they release him, so I'm planning to return to Mount Airy on Thursday."

But Amanda knew from hard experience not to count on anything when Sara's patients were in jeopardy. Then, when she brought Sara up to date regarding Robby's defection and desertion, Sara ominously said, "You know what that means. If our theory of the case is correct, that leaves only you and Judd standing in the killer's way. You better watch your back."

A less-than-comforting thought. She knew Sara was desperately worried about her safety, but what could Sara do about it? She was in Charlotte. Robby was also gone, and so, too, were the Taylors when Amanda arrived at their rancher the following afternoon and pushed through the unlocked screen door to an empty house.

"Anybody home?" She wandered through the eerily quiet space, with family photos staring at her from dark walls, and soon she saw Lori lounging on the back deck. Lori wore earbuds as she tapped her feet and sang along to rap music, then jumped nearly out of her skin when Amanda touched her shoulder.

She pulled out the earbuds. "Shit! You tryin' to give me a heart attack, white girl?"

Amanda laughed, dropped into a chair beside Lori, and tilted her face to the warm sun. "Did you get Robby to the airport all right?"

"No worries, mate. He's in Philly by now."

"So how come you're not off with Lily?"

"How come you're not off with Sara?" Lori shot back. "Truth be told, we're not exclusive. Besides, I'd rather hang here with you."

The glint in Lori's amber eyes made Amanda slightly nervous. She and Sara were "exclusive," and no way was she interested in teenagers. "So what's happening?"

Lori's glint became conspiratorial. "Well, Jana's with her friends, and our parents are working, so we have the house to ourselves."

Lori's suggestive tone was becoming more troublesome by the minute, but Amanda kept silent, hoping the girl would explain herself.

"Are you up for a little snooping, Mandy?"

*What on earth?* At least Lori's intentions seemed to have nothing to do with sex, which was a relief, but Amanda couldn't understand why Lori took her by the wrist and hustled her down the bedroom hallway. They passed the kids' rooms and entered Judd and Ella's master. "What are you up to?"

Lori pointed. "Dad's study is over there. So is his computer. I know his password, so I can access all the information about Commissioner Landry's murder."

The space was larger than expected, with the couple's king bed, dressers, and walk-in closet located on the front wall, while a well-equipped office, with twin personal workspaces facing each other, ran along the back. The middle wall, backing to the garage, was lined with floor-to-ceiling bookshelves. Most of the titles were English and American literature—Ella's—with a high shelf devoted to Judd's case files. The colorful, slightly cluttered space smelled vaguely of Ella's floral cologne.

"No way, Lori. I'm not doing this." Amanda felt every inch like the home invader she was. "Besides, I saw your father's truck in the driveway, so he can't be far away."

"But he *is* far away. He took Michael and Miguel on the Ranger to work one of the back fields. No one will be home till suppertime. Aren't you curious?"

She was curious, all right. Lori, with her passion for all things law enforcement, plus the instincts of a sneak thief, was the perfect co-conspirator. "It's wrong," Amanda protested without conviction.

"So let's do it!" Lori pulled up her father's black leather desk chair and indicated that Amanda should take her mother's—which she did, shamelessly. Then she watched in guilty silence while Lori got the monitor up and running. Her long, milk chocolate fingers flew across the keyboard, and in no time, she had opened the Landry file. "Dad calls this a *murder book*. There's only one other in his files, and that homicide was two years ago."

"He lets you look at this stuff?"

"Not really." Lori scrolled through a table of contents and opened a section called *autopsy results.* "Check it out. You already know Commissioner Landry was killed by an injection of the drug they use to euthanize animals. Bet the medical examiner found very little water in his lungs, which shows he was dead before he hit the pool."

Unfortunately, the file included postmortem photos of Landry, and although Lori didn't seem to think he looked bad at all since there were no physical wounds or signs of obvious trauma, Amanda was horrified. She had seen a picture of the smiling, rather ordinary-looking, middle-aged Landry in his obituary. These shots detailed a slack, soulless death mask, void of personality or even an echo of life.

"I'm not enjoying this, Lori."

"Squeamish, are we?" the girl teased. "Good thing you don't want to be a cop. But Sara told me you like playing detective from time to time."

"Is that a fact?" *What else had Sara told her?*

"So I bet you'll be interested in this." She clicked on a list called *attendees.* "Recognize any names?"

The page seemed to group the partygoers in relationship to one another—businessmen with their associates, husbands with wives, etc. "I recognize your uncle, Marty Roach. Who's that with him?"

"That's his partner, Lonny Appleton. Those losers started the Apollo real estate company together. They're the same age, talk the same bullshit, and treat women like personal possessions. Lonny's been divorced three times, not just two like my asshole uncle."

Amanda studied Lonny's picture. He actually looked a lot like Marty—same weight, height, coloring, and attitude. Only where Marty was scruffy-looking, like a bad boy musician, Lonny was groomed and polished like a star salesman. His blond crew cut and tightly knotted tie radiated success. "Does Lonny have any financial problems like Marty?"

"Who the hell knows? His five kids all dress well and flash expensive gear. His youngest daughter, Cherry, is Jana's best friend. Go figure."

Amanda wondered if Lonny was as desperate for cash as Marty. Obviously, the men would share the goal of acquiring Mayberry Farm. If the kids had nice threads and bling, perhaps it was one of Lonny's ex-wives who supplied the money. Filing that question away, she looked down the list. "I recognize this name Howard Hayes. He's the local lawyer, right?" Amanda pointed to an elderly, heavy-jowled man in a bow tie.

"Yeah, Mr. Hayes has been around forever. He even knew Great-Grandpa Thomas back when your grandma was banging him. My dad pays him rent each month."

Amanda bit back a knee-jerk urge to scold Lori for characterizing Grandma Viv as "banging" someone. But after all, Lori didn't know or love these dead relatives and likely meant no disrespect.

Hayes, of course, was the lawyer Robby had met several times, which was neither here nor there. She next placed a finger on an extremely suave fellow who looked like a Wall Street executive, with perfectly styled hair and an expensive suit. "This name, Kenneth Klein, rings a bell."

"He's the CEO of March Investments," Lori said. "Supposed to be hot shit, like, small town boy makes the big time. He was a senior when Dad was a sophomore. Dad hates his guts, but I think he's just jealous."

Amanda suspected Lori knew nothing about March Investments' desire to buy Mayberry Farm or how Kenneth Klein was itching to boot her and her family out on their keisters.

Beneath Klein's photo were two other associates from March Investments, who looked equally savvy and successful. Then came the five elected commissioners, including Marty again, the victim Landry, two other men, and a woman. The nine-member planning board was in attendance, as was the mayor of Mount Airy, who seemed to pattern himself after Andy Griffith.

Near the bottom of the list, she recognized another face, the dapper egghead from breakfasts at the Bee & Bee. "What do you know about this guy Max Eagle?"

"Nothing, really. I see him around town, and I know he's a rich widower with a horse farm. He even ran for mayor once, but he lost."

Interesting. So including spouses of attendees, Amanda counted two dozen people, one of whom was likely the murderer. She also noted the file was a JPEG, and Judd had added his own notes before scanning it into his computer. He had drawn little frowny faces beside Marty Roach and two of the commissioners, likely those who would approve Mayberry Acres. He had also noted some relevant professions beside names, including two veterinarians and three people who sold fishing bait at their establishments. He had also marked hunters with a little gun symbol. So clearly, Judd was connecting the dots between this crime and the attempt on Robby's life.

"Lori, can you print me a copy of this list?" Even as she spoke, Amanda knew the request had pushed her over the dark side. She would now be an official thief of classified data.

The girl high-fived her. "I already sent it to the printer and made one for myself. This means we're partners, right?"

## CHAPTER 37
*Apollo Partners...*

Amanda had no intention of working with Lori as amateur sleuths. Luckily, she never had to put the girl down with a hard "no" because the whole family left for work or school Tuesday morning before Amanda was fully awake. From the privacy of Lori's room, she listened to the shower sounds, breakfast chatter, and Ella's departure with the girls. She heard the M&M's arrive and leave with Judd for another day of planting in the back acres. Once everyone was gone, she emerged for coffee and toast on the back deck and to call Sara.

"What's up, babe?" Sara answered in her too-busy-to-talk voice.

Amanda told her about the stolen attendees list and all the clues it provided.

"Stay out of it, Mandy. Let Judd handle it, you hear?"

How many times had she heard such advice from Sara? Often enough that Amanda knew to ignore it and follow her own lights. Sara also reported that her patient was out of crisis and scheduled to leave the hospital, but Sara's return to Mount Airy would still be delayed until Thursday. After some hurried sweet talk, she signed off with Sara to call Mom in Vegas and Robby in Philly. Both were fine but too busy to talk.

So Amanda was left to her own devices with a

new day waiting to be painted like a freshly primed canvas. She had some creative ideas, conceived during the night, so she dressed in the only non-casual clothes she had packed—beige linen pantsuit, crisp pale blue blouse, and unscuffed sandals—and went into town.

Robby's rental Focus had GPS, so she entered the address for Apollo Partners and drove into the bustling tourist district, which was becoming familiar. She jockeyed for parking and finally found a space in the lot behind the Earle Theatre. The office turned out to be on the second floor of a green brick building called Main Oak Emporium, which was largely abandoned but for a restaurant called The Loaded Goat. She climbed the steps to a dark and dusty hallway, and her palms were sweaty when she knocked.

From within, someone turned off country/western music, and moments later, a man in shirtsleeves and jeans answered the door. She recognized him immediately as Marty Roach's partner.

"Mr. Appleton? I'm Amanda Rittenhouse. May I come in?"

His Nordic face seemed panicky, and he stuttered, "Call me L-Lonny, please. I'll clear a chair for you."

The first thing she noticed was the man—tall, slim, athletic, blond, and blue-eyed—could have been her twin. The second was the clutter of magazines, CDs, DVDs, and a full-length clothes rack with what looked to be an entire wardrobe in Lonny's size.

"Are you living in your office, Lonny?"

He blushed. "It's only temporary. In between wives, you know?"

It sounded like a joke but didn't seem to be a laughing matter. She saw no kitchen or bathroom, and judging by the third thing she noticed—the smell of onions and cooking grease and fast food wrappers strewn everywhere—he was living on takeout. She had seen a public restroom out in the hall and assumed Lonny put it to good use, but the fact that he didn't rent an apartment or even a room between marriages indicated he might be as broke as his partner, Marty.

Amanda waited while he cleared a straight-backed chair of old newspapers, then they both took seats. "I'm here to talk about Mayberry Farm. Should I wait until Marty Roach can join us?"

He actually seemed more nervous than she was but got his emotions under control. "No, I can handle it. In fact, I'm thrilled to discuss the property. Marty's not coming in today anyway." He paused and grinned. "He's nursing a hangover from one of his gigs last night."

She was surprised Lonny had offered this bit of unsolicited information, which was unfavorable to his partner and caused her to wonder if Marty had a drinking problem. She said, "I'm thinking about selling my share and my brother's."

That got his attention. He sat up straighter, took a fresh legal pad from a desk drawer, and picked up a pen. "I thought your brother was dead set against selling. At least that's what Marty told me."

"Robby changed his mind, left the decision in my hands." If nothing else, that statement might get her and Robby off the kill list, if there was such a thing, and if Apollo Partners was involved.

"Well, that's very good news, Ms. Rittenhouse. What did you have in mind?"

"Question is, what do *you* have in mind? Let's talk money."

For the next half hour, she listened to his sales

pitch. Lonny knew she was dealing with only two-thirds of a deck, but he seemed willing, for the time being, to set aside the obstacle of Judd Taylor. What Lonny did not know was that she was only bluffing, not necessarily interested in selling. She was fishing for figures, trying to determine what was at stake and who the power players were.

Lonny said, "You'll be happy to know the board of commissioners held their bi-monthly meeting last night and approved the project. Marty and another guy on the board said *yes* to Mayberry Acres, but the mayor had to step in and break the tie. So we got our way in the end."

This was terrible news for Judd, and no doubt, he'd be aware of it by the time they all gathered at the dinner table. As she listened to Lonny, she discovered Apollo Partners was offering two million dollars, which broke down to about ten thousand per acre. When she did not respond, the price went up in five thousand-dollar increments per acre until Lonny stopped talking and stared at her.

"Will I get a better price from March Investments?" she asked.

The question got him stuttering again, "M-March Investments is working with us. I'm sure they'll agree to any terms we come up with."

"But they are the developers. They get the land, the town houses, and the shopping center. How do *you* get paid?"

He hemmed and hawed some more, then mumbled something about a commission and a percentage of future earnings. While she suspected that Apollo Partners would come out with significant cash, they were not in charge.

"Maybe I should just cut out the middleman," she said.

His sunny features turned stormy. "I would not recommend it, Amanda," he said, pointedly switching to her first name. "Kenneth Klein and his gang are the big league, and they sometimes play rough. Look what happened to your brother."

"What do you know about my brother?" she snapped.

"Apparently, he changed his mind about selling pretty quick after someone shot at him. And if the sheriff keeps pushing that incident as an accident, just like he did with Myron Landry's death, no one's gonna believe old Bill."

"Are you threatening me, Lonny?"

"God, no!" He spread his big hands in a gesture of innocence. "Just sayin'. Kenny generally gets what he wants, and he's not to be trusted."

"And you are?"

"Hell, yes! Think of it this way. My partner, Marty, is Judd's brother-in-law. We're practically family, so we have your back."

She rose abruptly and shook his hand. "Let me think about this and get back to you." As she scurried out the door, she saw the red-faced Lonny take out his phone. Was he calling Marty or Kenneth Klein?"

She closed the door and hurried down the stairs. *Trust these guys? About as far as I can throw them.*

CHAPTER 38
*The Loaded Goat...*

At the bottom of the stairs, Amanda's pulse raced, and she was faint from her brief encounter with Lonny Appleton. She needed to sit and compose herself, so she entered The Loaded Goat restaurant, with a logo of a cartoon goat smoking two red sticks of lit dynamite. It was supposed to be a pub and grill, and she figured a cold beer might just keep her from exploding.

She was ushered to a round oak table near a window facing the street. The packed space had exposed brick walls, a suspended metal grid of lighting hung from high, warehouse-like ceilings, and the obligatory TVs anchored on all the walls. One screen was looping a vintage episode from *The Andy Griffith Show* featuring Jimmy, the dynamite-eating goat bent on destruction: "A goat filled with dynamite? What are we gonna do, Andy?" asked the distraught Barney Fife.

Amanda ordered not a beer, but a Mayberry Margarita and an appetizer of four fried green tomatoes with ranch dressing and pimento cheese. What had she been thinking, confronting Appleton without a plan or exact purpose? What had she achieved, other than stirring up trouble by postulating an elaborate bluff about selling the land? She practiced deep breathing before taking the first spicy sip of her drink and then stared out at the busy street.

At that moment, a man stopped on the other

side of the window, squinted, and peered directly at her. Lonny Appleton had followed her down. His narrowed blue eyes registered surprise, recognition, and something akin to hostility as he seated himself on a sidewalk bench on the other side of the glass and crossed his long legs, apparently settling in to intimidate her. He took out his cellphone and made a call.

The waiter served the fried green tomatoes, and her stomach churned. If Lonny had something to say, why not come inside and face her like a man?

Amanda decided two could play that game. Turning her face away, she took a first bite and pretended to enjoy it, but as the minutes ticked by and Lonny did not move, her mouth dried up and she could not eat. She looked around for a back entrance, so she could pay, escape to the parking lot, and drive away without incident. Seeing none, she was considering hiding in the women's restroom when a black Lincoln Town Car pulled to the curb, prompting Lonny to stand up and wave.

Had he simply been waiting for a ride? Her heart pounded in her ears as another tall, very elegant man stepped from the backseat of the limo. He said a few words to his chauffeur, then motioned to Lonny to climb into the car, which Lonny obediently did. As the stranger stood to his full height, buttoned his suit coat, and straightened his tie, Amanda realized she was looking at none other than Kenneth Klein, CEO of March Investments, and he was moving into the restaurant, heading right to her table as his ride pulled away.

"Hello, Amanda. Mind if I join you?" Without waiting for permission, Klein unbuttoned his jacket and sat. "How fortunate to find you in the right place at the right time."

She swallowed hard, moistening her mouth enough to speak. "I suspect Lonny Appleton told you I was here."

He shrugged his broad shoulders and pinned her with his Pierce Brosnan gaze. The man did look like the actor, but he was older than Pierce had been as James Bond. She was certain most women would swoon at Klein's manly presence, but she was immune.

"Yes, Lonny informed me of your conversation, so I'm here to follow up." His voice was smooth as maple syrup as he took an e-cigarette from his breast pocket. He inserted it between his lips, took a puff, held, and inhaled.

"Hey, I don't think vaping is allowed in restaurants," Amanda objected as a sweet, fruity smell floated between them.

"You are wrong, it's perfectly legal in North Carolina."

She could warn him that e-cigs were hazardous to his health, but she didn't give a flying fig about his well-being. "What do you want, Mr. Klein?"

He smiled slightly, holding the tube in his long, manicured fingers, then took another puff before answering, "No deal." He exhaled.

"I beg your pardon?"

His eyes were black ice. "Two-thirds of Mayberry Farm is useless to us. We need all or nothing. Please tell your cousin Judd to get with the program because time is money. We want to break ground this summer, and with each passing week, we'll offer less to purchase the land."

The man was a pathetic narcissist. "Give me a

break. You can't force people to sell."

He blinked back a flash of anger. "You're a feisty one, aren't you? Have you ever heard of eminent domain? Surry County can take private property for public use, and I promise they'll pay less than we would."

"Why would the county do that?" But she already knew the answer from hanging around her Realtor mom. She'd seen it happen in Mooresville, land stolen for pennies from farmers for highway projects. Clearly, the Mayberry Acres development would create jobs and prosperity for Mount Airy.

He continued, "If push comes to shove, I'll suggest it to the planning board. They're already salivating like Pavlov's dog to change the zoning and start building."

Was he bluffing? She didn't know the nine members of the board, the same ones who attended Landry's pool party. Would they all approve such a land grab? Or would Klein encounter some resistance, as he had with the five commissioners?

"There are no guarantees," she said. "Why should I believe the planners will go along with you?"

He laughed, tucked the e-cig back into his breast pocket, and stood. He took a twenty from his wallet and lay it on the table. "Lunch is on me." He yawned and walked away but said over his shoulder on the way out, "The commissioners went along with me in the end, didn't they? Don't forget what happened to Myron Landry."

## CHAPTER 39
*Suppertime...*

Suppertime at the Taylors was a disaster. Michael and Miguel had brought Judd home from the back fields with a broken arm and the following explanation: "His bad leg gave out, and he slipped backward over a rock ledge. We got him home on the Ranger, transferred him to his truck, and took him straight to the emergency room."

"You're getting too old for that kind of work," Ella admonished Judd as she passed the homemade chili.

"The hell I am." Judd was grouchy and mean. Insult to injury, he'd broken his left arm, and he was a leftie.

"Mom's right. You should let the M&M's do the heavy work," Jana said.

"Yeah, Dad, why don't you sell the stupid farm?" Lori piled on, surprising Amanda, who had steered clear of the family argument.

Until then, Amanda had not known how the girls felt about the land, but during dinner, she discovered that neither wanted to go to the community college, like their parents. Jana was interested in the arts—fashion, music, and even dance—majors unavailable locally. Lori was determined to chase her dream of joining the FBI and wanted to study as close as possible to the nation's capital.

Neither child had inherited a love of the land or sentimentality for the old Yount homestead, so unless Micah, the son she had never met, was interested in Mayberry Farm, that devotion would end with Judd's generation. Micah had gone away to college on a scholarship, and just paying his room and board had depleted the Taylors' savings, so sending the girls off seemed an impossibility unless...

Maybe Amanda's bluff of selling two-thirds could work for the family. What if Judd and Ella could retain the portion including the old house and relocate his organic farming business to those acres? It would mean giving up the fields surrounding the rancher, but could Judd live with that sacrifice? Maybe she and Robby could loan the family enough from the sale of their two-thirds that the Taylors could remodel the homestead, prepare the new acreage for farming, and help pay the girls' tuition? It was a lot of "what ifs," but a distinct possibility had Kenneth Klein not shot it dead with his "No deal."

So she did not mention it.

"I hear through the grapevine that some bigshots are offering lots of money for the farm," Lori said as she passed the salad.

"Me too. Everyone at school is talking about it," Jana agreed.

Judd growled and dropped a spoonful of chili on his sling. Ella told the children not to pester their father. Amanda knew the kids did not exist in a bubble, folks would talk, and a family conference could not be delayed much longer.

The meal ended soon thereafter. Jana went to her room to do homework, Ella and Lori cleared and washed dishes, refusing Amanda's offer of help, so

Amanda retired to the living room with Judd.

"How are you feeling?" she asked once they were settled.

"Stupid. How 'bout you?"

"I feel stupid, too." In a whisper, she told him everything about her confrontations with Appleton and Klein. She held nothing back.

For a full minute, he just studied her, his tired eyes shifting back and forth. "Maybe you were even stupider than I was."

"Could be." When she realized he wasn't about to absolve her, she said, "I was only trying to help."

"I know, but like they say, it's dumb to poke a hornet's nest." He paused, pulled some pills from a baggie in his pocket, and swallowed them with the rest of his beer.

"You shouldn't mix pain meds with alcohol."

"Are you my mother? These are aspirin."

They sat in miserable silence until Judd said, "I have news. Sheriff Bill told me that some of those hornets you've been aggravating own Marlin 336 rifles—Uncle Marty, Lonny Appleton, and Kenneth Klein. Plus three other guys on that list of attendees you and Lori stole from my computer."

Her gut turned inside out. "How did you know?"

He sighed. "Aw, shit. I didn't know *you* were guilty until this very moment. Ella was straightening up the girls' room and found Lori's copy sticking out of a textbook. I haven't punished Lori yet because Ella says I can't ground her for the rest of her natural life. But what should I do with you?"

God, Amanda could not imagine a proper punishment for herself. Should he kick her out of the house, disown her as a cousin, or send her to jail? "I'm truly sorry, Judd. How can I make it up to you?"

"Butt out of my business."

Justified but harsh. He had every right to be furious, but in truth, it was her business, too. Plus, the way he had wheedled a confession out of her demonstrated a superior interrogation technique. Maybe Judd should give up the farm and become a full-time detective.

"Point taken, Judd, but since those suspects own Marlin hunting rifles, can't you get a search warrant? They could have motives and possibly shot at Robby."

"We can't go to a judge with that. We'd need to demonstrate just cause to get a warrant, and we have nothing in the way of proof."

At least he was using the pronoun "we," so he recognized her as a stakeholder. "Can't you check their alibis for the time period when Robby went fishing last Saturday?"

"I'm not sure I'm ready to tip them off by playing that hand."

"Is it better to wait until someone takes a shot at you or me?"

He gazed down at the hand dangling helplessly from his sling and pretended not to hear her. Either he thought she was crazy or refused to entertain the possibility that they were in danger.

The silence between them deepened, became downright oppressive, until Jana literally danced into the room. She wore white tights, a blue leotard, and a pink tutu. She pointed a soft ballet slipper, spun, then graciously curtsied.

"Check out my recital costume!"

"I thought you were doing homework," Ella called from the kitchen.

Judd laughed and clapped his knee with his one good hand, but Amanda could not breathe. She was riveted to Jana's flat little chest and the ballerina pin fastened there. It was about an inch long, encrusted with fake diamonds, and had a little blue skirt that swiveled.

"Can you come closer, Jana?" She gasped. "I want to look at your pretty pin."

When the child approached and Amanda fingered the antique piece, she recognized it as from a distant dream, including the tiny pit where one diamond was missing from the hem of the skirt. She viscerally recalled how it felt to pin the jewelry to her own leotard all those years ago and then to store it away in Grandma's magic box.

"Where did you get this?"

She looked guiltily to her father. "Cherry gave it to me. Is that all right?"

"Cherry is Lonny Appleton's daughter," Judd explained. "It's not a problem. She's Jana's best friend."

"Yeah, but it was Uncle Marty who gave Cherry the pin. She didn't like it, thinks ballet is for sissies, so she gave it to me."

Amanda felt the blood drain from her head, and for the second time that day, she felt faint. When Jana danced away to show off to Ella, Amanda leaned to Judd and whispered, "I think you can get a search warrant now."

CHAPTER 40
*Deeds and wills...*

Once Jana had danced back into her room and Lori had left the house to meet up with Lily, the evening unraveled when Amanda explained the significance of the ballerina pin.

"Are you sure it's the same pin you had as a child?" Judd demanded.

"One hundred percent. One rhinestone is missing from just the right place. It was in Grandma's jewelry box, the one I call the magic box. The killer stole it!"

Judd rose from his chair and spat out a string of curses, which brought Ella rushing into the living room. "What's wrong with you, Judd?"

"It's not me, it's your fucked-up brother. Marty's really stepped in it this time."

Judd got redder, and Ella got paler as Judd explained the pin's chain of custody from Grandma to her killer to Cherry Appleton and finally to Jana. "Jesus Christ, Ella, don't you get it? It's possible that Marty killed Mandy's grandma, who just happened to be my grandma, too."

As the drama escalated, Amanda felt compassion for the couple. If Marty Roach was guilty, the scope of the tragedy was Shakespearian—twin brother of wife kills husband's grandmother—it could tear the family apart. To defuse the situation, she said, "Judd, you should call Detective John Winston in Mooresville.

He has my inventory of the items I recall being in Grandma's jewelry box. I promise that ballerina pin is on the list, but could there be a different explanation?"

"Yes, there must be a different explanation." Ella seized upon the hope. "Maybe someone gave the pin to Marty. Besides, why on earth would my brother hurt Vivian, a total stranger?"

Amanda could think of a million reasons, and they all had dollar signs. Yet Marty did not strike her as a mastermind with the intellect to plan or execute the break-in at Grandma's. Yet more and more, the spate of violence seemed directly connected to Mayberry Farm.

"Why did Grandma have to die?" Amanda mused aloud. "If someone wanted Judd to inherit his share of the land, they just had to wait it out. She was an old lady."

"Maybe he couldn't wait," Judd said darkly. "Certainly, March Investments won't wait forever. If the deal doesn't pan out soon, Kenny Klein will simply move on."

Ella shrieked, "You're *both* crazy! You're talking about *my brother*. Shame on you!" With that, Ella stomped down the hallway, entered the master bedroom, and slammed the door.

Judd hung his head and fingered his broken arm. "I need to contact Sheriff Bill. With a little luck, he can call the local judge before the old man goes to bed. I don't expect we can go there tonight, but I'd like to search Marty's home first thing in the morning."

"I'm so sorry."

"It's not your fault, Mandy, and I pray we're wrong about all this. Because if Marty is guilty, I'm a dead man. Ella will kill me."

Later that night, when the family was asleep, Amanda called Sara and told her all the news. "It was horrible seeing Judd and Ella fight that way. Sometimes I wish I'd never inherited this wretched farm."

"You and me both, babe."

"I wish you could come tomorrow, Sara. It's May 1, our special day, and we should be together." It wasn't an anniversary or anybody's birthday, but to them, it symbolized the first day of spring, and they always celebrated.

"I'd love to come dance around the Maypole with you, but I just can't leave. I have a better idea, though. You come home. Right now. I don't like you in the middle of that mess."

The concept was tempting. She could drive to Mooresville and be sharing Thai food with Sara by dinnertime, safe in the intimacy of their condo. She had done her bit, met the family, but also stirred up trouble. Unfortunately, the fate of the farm remained unsettled, and she had to see that through.

"I need to find out if Marty did it. In some respects, it doesn't make sense. If this is all about the farm, then yes, Grandma had to die to get the ball rolling, but why kill her in her town house? Why go to all the trouble of a rental car, fake ID, the golf game—all that subterfuge when he could have arranged a simpler 'accident' or approach her when she was alone, away from home?"

"Let the cops handle it."

"Why would he come to her house?"

"I don't know, but if he did it, maybe he'll explain himself. Marty does resemble the perp in the golf course security tape—same build and coloring."

"Yes, but that guy was clean shaven and had

short hair, didn't he?"

"True, but whiskers grow fast, and he was wearing a ball cap. Marty could have altered his looks that day."

Sara had a point, but Amanda was bothered by some little detail just out of reach, and it involved Grandma's town house—the way it looked the day she died. It seemed related to motive. "Sara, land titles are public records. Anyone could go to the Surry County Courthouse or online to see who owns what, right?"

Sara considered the question. "That's right. Mecklin Adams told us Viv had changed the deed over the years to first include Thomas, who was replaced by Andrew, who was finally replaced by Judd—the three generations of Taylor men. She added Robby, then you, so that eventually Judd, Robby, and you each owned twenty percent, while Viv retained forty percent."

"Where are you going with this?"

"So all these deed changes would have been recorded over the years, likely by the Mount Airy lawyer Howard Hayes."

Amanda still didn't see the significance. "Yes, but so what?"

"Listen, Mandy, anyone could see the *deeds* but not Viv's *will*. That's the point. No one could know what would become of Vivian's forty percent share until she died. If a bad guy was concerned about the eventual distribution of her controlling share, he would have to see the final draft of her last will and testament."

"Yes, and because Grandma hired Mecklin Adams to draw up her final will, then unlike the deeds, it was not prepared by Howard Hayes. Theoretically, no one in Mount Airy knew what that will stipulated."

Sara laughed. "You got it. The bad guys could see

the deed but not the will."

"Not even Linc knew what was in that document," Amanda finished as the proverbial light bulb finally clicked on in her brain.

CHAPTER 41
*Follow her hunch...*

Amanda did not tell Sara about the memory lighting up her brain because Sara would think she was bonkers. Instead, she nursed that memory through the night and called Linc in the morning to tell him about the ballerina pin and the search warrant being executed on Marty. She was eager to give the family something concrete because she and Robby had been less than truthful to date. They had mutually agreed not to tell Mom, nor anybody else back home, about the attempt on Robby's life. It would only upset them, and what could they do long distance anyway?

Turned out Linc already knew most everything because Detective Winston had updated him. "I didn't tell your mother about Robby, though. After all, he's okay and back at work, so why worry Diana out in Vegas? But you should have told me yesterday about this search warrant."

Apparently, Winston had given Linc no false hope that his wife's killer would be apprehended anytime soon, and Amanda didn't want to get out ahead of her skis, either. All she knew was that on the day Grandma died, she and Mom had followed Winston up the stairs in Grandma's town house. When they reached the landing the couple used as a home office, the detective had asked, "Do you see anything odd up here?" All Amanda saw was that one drawer of a tall metal filing cabinet was slightly pulled out from flush. She had reflexively closed that drawer, returning the space to the perfect order Grandma preferred.

"Linc, where did you find Grandma's will?" she abruptly asked.

He hesitated, thought about it, and finally said, "Actually, I had a devil of a time locating it. You know how organized Vivian was, but she had misfiled the document. Instead of putting it with our important personal papers in the bottom drawer, it was in the top drawer under 'W' with the water company stuff."

Amanda's synapses fired double-time. It had been the top drawer she had shoved back into place that day. Had the killer broken in to find Grandma's new will? Had he stupidly misfiled it? The possibility was a longshot.

Linc demanded, "Why do you want to know? It seems to me that Vivian's will has brought a load of trouble down on this family."

She couldn't argue with that. "Do you happen to know if Mecklin Adams told Howard Hayes about the new will?"

"Not that it's any of your business, but the answer is likely *yes*. Mecklin would have told Hayes that a new document existed, if only to prevent any confusion about which instrument took precedence in the event of Viv's death." She heard both the emotion and impatience in Linc's voice as he continued, "But under no circumstances would Mecklin have told Hayes the *contents* of that new will. Such a revelation would be a complete breach of his professional ethics."

That was what she needed to know. Linc's answer confirmed that any party interested in Grandma's new will could only get that information from Grandma herself or from somehow seeing the document itself. But how would the killer even know a new will existed?

Amanda intended to find out and follow her hunch. So after some small talk with Linc, who was about to depart for Paris with Grandma's ashes, she said goodbye and set the GPS in the rental Focus for a new address: the law offices of Howard Hayes.

## CHAPTER 42
*All her prime suspects...*

Amanda found Howard Hayes's office on South Main, not far from the Bee & Bee. Unlike the musty office of Apollo Partners, Hayes's digs smelled of old money and expensive cigars. It offered high-quality mahogany furniture and a snooty, blue-haired receptionist who functioned as the lawyer's ancient watchdog. The elderly advocate himself was ensconced behind an oversized antique desk, sleeves rolled up, apparently too busy to make much time for the likes of Amanda.

"I already met with your brother twice," he complained in a gravelly bass voice. "Robby seemed to be a nice young man. Pity what happened to him."

"Any idea why someone would take a potshot at my brother?"

He shook his heavy jowls and scowled from beneath bushy white eyebrows. "I heard it was an accident."

Sensing hostility, she sat across from him, without being invited, and jumped in feet first. She sketched out her suspicions about Mayberry Farm as the catalyst for violence against her grandmother, Robby, and Commissioner Landry. Not giving away details, like the clue of the ballerina pin, she presented a case for the property as motive. She then remarked upon Hayes's unique position as the land's legal guardian through the years.

As Hayes listened, his rheumy eyes, nearly colorless, blinked incessantly behind thick lenses. He fingered a cigar but did not light it. When she finished, he said, "My, my, you have an active imagination, young lady. Have you considered writing fiction?"

Her palms became sweaty as she twisted her hands in her lap. "You must admit there's a lot of money at stake, sir."

He coughed up a phlegmy laugh. "That is God's own truth. I don't know what Vivian was thinking when she passed the ball to those Taylors. I guess your grandma made a little mistake when she was young, but she could have put it behind her. Those people don't think like you and me."

Amanda was appalled. It was all she could do to keep herself from screaming at the old bigot. His remarks could only be interpreted as raw racism, and she wondered how successfully the man had disguised it while accepting checks from the Taylors month after month. Likely, he thought of them as tenant farmers, not stakeholders, and resented the fact that Judd was a player.

Yet she had a mission and kept her cool. "So did anyone ask you about Grandma's will? Please answer me directly, Mr. Hayes."

He laughed again. "Now don't be climbing on your high horse, missy. Fact is, Mayberry Farm has been nothing but a pain in my keister ever since March Investments took an interest. It would be quicker to tell you who has not been pumping me for information than who has."

He proceeded to describe the folks who had asked, directly or indirectly, about whether Vivian had left a will. The list included Apollo Partners. Marty and Lonny had visited Hayes's office together. Kenneth Klein had called, as had two commissioners and three members from the planning board. Even the egghead from breakfasts at the Bee & Bee, Max Eagle, had quizzed Hayes over lunch.

"Max and I have been friends for years, golf buddies, and he owns many shares of March Investments stock. But I told Max the same as I told the others—nothing, nada, zippo. I confirmed that Vivian Davis had indeed made a new will without my help, and I didn't have a clue what was in it."

She stared at him, disgusted by his attitude and stymied by his answer. Seemingly, all her prime suspects had questioned Hayes to no avail, yet somehow the killer seemed to have known in advance of Grandma's death how she intended to bequeath the land. Amanda believed this because by the time she arrived in Mount Airy, all the interested parties already knew the inheritance was a three-way split. She doubted Judd would have passed on this information after Mecklin called and told him he was an heir.

"Mr. Hayes, Mecklin Adams sent you a FedEx containing a copy of Grandma's will to give to Judd. Did you peek at it?"

"I most certainly did not."

She wasn't sure she believed him, but Hayes's answer played to her theory of the bad guys seeking and viewing the document at Grandma's town house. This would explain the break-in but did not prove the killer's identity.

But Judd would soon know.

Later that afternoon, when Amanda returned to the Taylors' and found Judd's truck parked in the driveway, she felt certain the ballerina pin would have nailed the murderer, and she couldn't wait to find out. But when she burst into the living room, she found Judd and Ella seated side by side on the couch. The room was semi-dark as no one had bothered to turn on the lights. Judd hung his head with his good arm wrapped around his wife's shoulder as Ella sobbed, her face buried in her hands.

Amanda approached slowly. "What's wrong? Did you execute the search warrant? Did you talk to Marty?"

Judd's voice was barely audible. "Yeah, we did the search, all right."

Ella lifted her tear-ravaged eyes. "They found Marty. He was dead. He killed himself!"

## CHAPTER 43
*A suicide note...*

Amanda was dumbstruck in the face of their misery and couldn't find words. Instead, she sank into the nearest chair and tried to catch her breath. Not in a million years would she have anticipated this turn of events.

"I am so sorry." She breathed at last. "What happened?"

But Ella was having none of it. She balled her small hands into fists and began beating Judd's chest. "It's the stupid land, and I'm sick to death of it!" Sparks flew from her blue eyes. "It's not true, Judd. My brother would never..." she shrieked, then jumped to her feet.

"Calm down, honey," he wearily begged.

Yet his plea was lost on Ella, who turned her back. She fled down the hallway and locked herself in the master bedroom.

Amanda was at a loss. One minute, Ella had seemed fragile as a wounded bird; the next, she was angry as a viper. Amanda wondered how she would have felt had she actually lost Robby that day at the lake. No doubt, she would have been equally manic and depressed.

She listened to Judd's heavy breathing and watched him massage the salt and pepper stubble on his jaw as the weak available light glistened on the smooth brown contour of his shaven head. She had no idea how to comfort him.

He cleared his throat. "Marty left a note."

Amanda held her peace.

"It was a suicide note," Judd continued hoarsely, "and a confession."

As she waited, blood pumped and flowed from her swollen brain as she anticipated his next words.

"Marty killed our grandmother," he choked. "But he claims it was an accident." He handed her what appeared to be a Xerox copy of the note.

Striving not to be too obtrusive, Amanda quietly switched on a table light so she could read. It was handwritten in shaky block letters, as though the author feared his cursive script would be illegible.

"Is this Marty's handwriting?" she whispered.

"Yes, I'm afraid so."

The message was short and to the point: *I never meant to kill Mrs. Davis. She wasn't supposed to be there. I am so sorry. Please forgive me.* It was signed *Martin Roach Jr.*

"That's it?" Amanda gasped.

"That's all he wrote, but we found much more." Judd dried his eyes with the back of his good hand, then squeezed the bridge of his nose, as if warding off a massive headache. "Marty had been drinking. Judging by the number of empty whiskey bottles, he was well on his way to being drunk when he pulled the trigger."

Judd explained his brother-in-law had put a pistol in his mouth and died instantly. His words planted a horrible image in Amanda's mind as she imagined the carnage. She also recalled Lonny Appleton telling her when she visited the Apollo Partners office yesterday that Marty had not come to work because he was "nursing a hangover" after one of his gigs. "When did

Marty die?"

"Just guessing, but I'd say he'd been dead at least twenty-four hours."

Judd then told her that he and Sheriff Bill had found what appeared to be Grandma's jewelry box, a fake driver's license with the name Ralph Morgan beside Marty's picture, and also a Marlin 336 rifle like the one used to shoot Robby.

Amanda was astounded. "Judd, *Ralph Morgan* was the name the guy at the golf club used the day Grandma died! Also, Detective Winston said the same name was used when the guy rented a car."

"Yeah, I remember. I wouldn't have thought Marty had the skill or ability to come up with such a sophisticated plan. But hey, I guess I never really knew the man."

The blood pulsing in her brain slowed enough for her to wonder if Marty had had help with the scheme. She also realized the evidence was damned conclusive. Grandma's "magic box" was the coup de gras. Only the killer could possess it.

Judd, clearly beaten to the bone, said, "We won't have an approximate time of death until the ME finishes with the body, and we won't know if Marty's rifle was used on Robby until the ballistics experts match it with the bullet and casings we found at the lake. But it looks bad. I'm sorry, Amanda."

She nodded weakly, though Judd had nothing to apologize for. It wasn't his fault, it was a family tragedy. She wondered if he and Ella would ever recover from it.

"Did they find Grandma's diamond engagement ring?" she asked.

"Not yet, but the crew will be there all night. If it's

there, they'll get it." Judd shifted on the sofa and then dropped his head between his knees for a moment. When he looked up, his eyes appeared haunted. "I can't reconcile it. The proof is all there, but Ella will never believe Marty was capable of murder. It's true I disliked the man, but I never figured him for a cold-blooded killer. I wish I could believe it was really an accident."

Amanda was neither emotionally nor intellectually ready to forgive Marty, but she was in possession of one relevant fact that might ease Judd's pain. She remembered it vividly. It was the day of Grandma's funeral. Dr. Patel, Grandma's endocrinologist, had approached them with a bizarre story about how a man claiming to be Linc had called his office to inquire as to the time of Grandma's appointment for the day she died. The receptionist told the imposter, whom Amanda now assumed was Marty, that Grandma's appointment was for ten. Then at the last minute, Grandma had changed it to eleven, which left her at home during Marty's fatal visit. That call had taken place several weeks before the murder, giving the killer time to make a plan.

She explained this to Judd. "So it's possible, even likely, that Marty didn't expect Grandma to be there. He planned to be in and out with no one getting hurt."

She saw a glimmer of hope in Judd's expression that maybe, just maybe, Ella's brother was not the total monster they imagined. "So maybe Vivian surprised him and he overreacted."

Amanda shrugged, unwilling to give Marty that big a pass. After all, there had also been the attempt on Robby's life, and who had assassinated Commissioner Landry? They had no direct linkage to those two attacks yet, but Amanda suspected they soon would. In fact, her throat hurt from suggesting even a small exoneration for Marty, but it seemed to have helped Judd.

More importantly, an "accident" scenario for Grandma's murder might allow Ella to remember her brother without revulsion. Sara had told her about some of her clients who suffered the shame of a violent crime in their families. That shame, or blame, often destroyed the innocent family members, and Amanda didn't want that for the Taylors.

It was then she remembered the girls. "Judd, do Lori and Jana know?"

He expelled a long, shuddering sigh. "Not yet. They both had after-school projects. God help us all when they get home. I'm afraid Ella doesn't have the strength to tell them, so I guess I'll have to do it."

"I guess you will." Her heart broke for him.

## CHAPTER 44
*Bates Motel...*

Amanda longed to escape the oppressive atmosphere of the Taylors' living room, but Judd beat her to it. He climbed wearily upright, muttered something unintelligible, and attempted a smile. He then limped away to comfort his wife, and Amanda burst out the front door to freedom.

She gulped the fresh air and fingered the car keys in her pocket. She longed to jump into the Focus and drive straight home to her condo and the safety of Sara's arms, fast as the law would allow, not looking back. At the same time, she saw a cloud of dust moving fast down the gravel road in her direction. She prayed the approaching car contained neither Lori nor Jana, for she refused to be the one to tell them that their uncle Marty, who just committed suicide, had also murdered their great-grandmother.

As her fevered brain calculated how to sidestep the issue and put the responsibility on Judd, she noticed something familiar about the vehicle. The small red convertible sports car was driven by none other than her beloved Sara. *Oh, my God!*

The Miata stopped on a dime, and Amanda yanked open the driver's door. "What are you doing here? You're a day early!"

Her lover's full lips twitched up in a smile. "Aren't you glad to see me?"

"You have no idea."

"It's May Day, babe. Did you think I'd let you celebrate alone, without our favorite Thai food?" Sara patted the passenger seat occupied by a large white takeout bag giving off tantalizing odors.

"How did you get away from your patient?"

"He was coping much better, so I hit the road and called the Bee & Bee to reserve our old room. Lois was delighted to oblige."

Amanda was torn. She knew it was only polite to invite Sara inside to say hello to the Taylors, but she said, "Judd and Ella are holed up in their bedroom. Lots of bad stuff has happened. Can we just leave right now?"

Sara gave her a quizzical look, then moved the bag to the floor and patted the seat. "Hop in."

"But what about the Focus and my stuff? All my clothes are inside Judd's house."

Sara cut her green eyes suggestively. "You won't need your clothes tonight. Leave a note, and we'll pick them up tomorrow."

The note was an excellent idea because when she sneaked back into the rancher, Amanda heard unhappy sounds coming from behind the closed door of the master bedroom. She scribbled a quick explanation with one of Jana's colored markers on a loose sheet of paper and left it on the kitchen counter. She did not relax until she was arm to arm with Sara as she pulled out of the driveway.

Sara caught her mood immediately. "What's wrong, Mandy?"

Even talking nonstop over the next few miles, Amanda barely had time to explain the full, horrific scope of the past days' events, but when she finished and Sara parked at the Bee & Bee, Sara was no longer smiling.

"Jesus, Mary, and Joseph!" Sara cursed. "I am so very sorry. I should have been here for you."

Sara, a lapsed Catholic, never used religious blasphemies unless extremely upset. "It's okay. You're here now." Amanda leaned over and gave her a grateful kiss.

They checked into their former room, which held some very good memories. Sara unpacked rum and tonic to go with dinner, then put the tonic and takeout bag into the mini fridge provided. "Can we lie down for a little while before we eat? I'm exhausted."

They snuggled on top of the quilt, fully clothed, for some much-needed mutual comfort mixed with a few tears. Finally, as the sun began to set beyond the brocade drapes, they realized they were hungry and their Thai food beckoned.

Amanda said, "Lois has a big microwave down in the kitchen. I'm sure she wouldn't mind if we use it to heat up our supper."

It felt odd sneaking down the grand staircase when the lobby was virtually empty. The other guests were seemingly either out at restaurants or in for the night. They heard muted television sounds coming from behind the closed doors of Lois's quarters, while the ornate Victorian foyer and reception desk seemed ominous in the dim light.

"I feel like we're in a scene *from The Addams Family*," Sara whispered.

"What's that?"

"C'mon, Mandy, it's an old sitcom about a family of spooks."

"Never heard of it."

"Yeah, you never heard of *The Andy Griffith* show, either."

As they slipped into the dark kitchen and turned on the lights, Amanda realized Sara truly was an aficionada of 1950s and '60s television. It was one of the many quirky trivia talents she loved about her. The only old movie Amanda could recall that applied to their current situation was Hitchcock's *Psycho*, and when the lights revealed an oversized collection of evil-looking kitchen knives mounted on the wall, she easily imagined herself at the Bates Motel.

"Here we go…" Sara found the microwave and began inserting the little white cardboard food boxes

"Wait!" Amanda cautioned. "If those boxes have those skinny metal handles, they'll spark when you nuke them."

"Nope, we're good to go. Can you find a couple of plates and some silverware?"

Amanda started rooting through the tall cupboards. "Yeah, and maybe I'll find us a couple of crystal goblets for our drinks."

"Hey, what the hell are you doing?" A tall, stork-like man appeared from nowhere, screaming at them. He lurched forward, brandishing a raised baseball bat. His beady eyes glowed like hot coals under bushy brows.

Amanda and Sara screamed in return and defensively raised their hands to fend off the blows. In the process, Amanda dropped a plate, which shattered on the ceramic tile floor.

"Hell's bells!" the man roared and kept coming.

In a flash, Amanda realized he was not Norman Bates, but only grouchy old Lou, the distant relative Lois employed. "Stop! Don't you recognize us? We're

Sara and Amanda, guests at this hotel."

"Cool it, Lou," Sara commanded in her shrink voice. "We were just heating up our dinner. Is that a problem?"

He deflated before their eyes: shoulders sinking, bat lowering, he gazed mournfully at the floor. "You broke one of Lois's favorite plates."

Sara continued calmly, "Yes, sorry, we'll pay for it."

Still breathing shallow and fast, he narrowed his eyes. "Aren't you the girls been stayin' at that teacher Ella Taylor's place?"

Amanda braced herself. "I have, yes."

He puffed out his bird-like chest. "Then I guess you heard the news. Her brother done killed himself."

## CHAPTER 45
*It's over...*

Predictably, breakfast hour at Bee & Bee was buzzing with speculation about Marty Roach's death. Maybe Amanda was paranoid, but the dapper egghead Max Eagle and all the other patrons seemed to know she was somehow connected to the tragedy and gave her a wide berth. Only Lois hovered at their table, fluttering her plump hands and expressing sympathy by assuring her that she need not pay for the plate she'd broken the night before. In truth, she seemed to be fishing for juicy details not yet provided in the scanty coverage in *The Mount Airy News*.

"Look, I only met Marty once," Amanda told Lois. "It's not like we're related or anything."

"No, but I've heard that Judd is your cousin, and family is family."

Grouchy Lou appeared. "Ask me, no good comes from mixing the races."

"No one asked you," Lois snapped, then sent him on his way. "Like I told you before, Lou's head is stuck back in the previous century. I apologize for his behavior, both today and last night."

"No problem." Amanda just wanted Lois to go away.

But her hostess was determined. "Seriously, some folks think Mount Airy is like Andy Griffith's Mayberry, and they believe that was a perfect world.

It wasn't."

"How so?" Sara's ears pricked.

"I had this conversation with Judd years ago. Did you ever notice how the fictional Mayberry in the TV show never included black people?"

Sara, the vintage TV expert, said, "Yeah, that's right. Except wasn't there one episode where an African American football coach came to town?"

"Exactly. One episode out of two hundred forty-nine. And I guarantee you our town then, and now, had a large, active African American community. It's beyond me how some people then, and now, think America is greater when certain people are out of sight and mind."

"It's pathetic," Sara said. "How did Judd feel about the show?"

"I suppose Judd approved of the upbeat life lessons and sense of decency in the show, but for that other, somewhat racist exclusion, he hated it. So do I."

Amanda butt in. "But, Lois, you named your hotel after Aunt Bee."

"Yes, I'm a hypocrite but also a businesswoman."

With that, she walked off.

※※※※

Amanda had no desire to return to the Taylors', but they had no choice. She knew the family would be in the throes of a very complex grief, but she had to retrieve her possessions. While Sara drove, they rehashed the implications of Marty's suicide. It was pretty clear he had killed Grandma and likely shot at Robby—less clear he'd been responsible for Commissioner Landry's murder. Amanda had shared the list of attendees at Landry's pool party, the one she and Lori had stolen from Judd, and Sara thought it included several prime suspects who should not be summarily eliminated.

Sara said, "It looks like Marty was guilty on all counts, but who knows?"

"I agree. His suicide note only takes responsibility for Grandma's death."

"True, but possibly he only felt *guilty* about that one because in a roundabout way, Vivian was family."

Amanda was also not convinced that argument held water because she wasn't certain Marty even knew Grandma was Judd's grandmother when he broke into her town house. "I don't think anybody was aware of the family relationship until Grandma's will revealed it."

"So what? Marty found out later, just like everybody else. That's when the guilt started gnawing at him. A delayed reaction. It happens."

They turned onto the gravel approach to the Taylors', and Amanda said, "Maybe, but did Marty go to the town house to find the will? Was he capable of making such a complex plan, complete with a fake driver's license and address? What happened to Grandma's diamond engagement ring? We don't know the answers to any of those questions."

"No, and maybe we never will."

"But if Marty was behind it all, the two murders and the attempt on Robby, then it's over."

Sara sighed. "Yes, that would be true. It's over."

## CHAPTER 46
*It's not over...*

They found the house deserted, except for Ella and Lori. Mother and daughter were on the back deck watching some storm clouds roll in. They were drinking wine in silence.

"Hey, Lori, are you old enough to drink?" Amanda teased.

"She is not," Ella answered for Lori. "She's supposed to be twenty-one, but she's only sixteen. Yet today she gets a pass, that's my decision."

Sara eyed the bottle of fine Italian rosé. "Hey, do we get a pass, too?"

Ella replied wearily, "Sure, pull up a seat and take a Dixie cup. Judd's out with the sheriff, and we gave Michael and Miguel the day off. I'm taking a week's vacation and allowing the girls to skip school, as well."

"Where's Jana?" Amanda asked.

Lori said, "She's playing with her friend Cherry. Mr. Appleton, Uncle Marty's partner, convinced his ex to give Cherry the day off, too. I guess we all know how shitty it would feel to have all the other kids staring at us, asking stupid questions."

"Yeah, right." Amanda recalled how awkward it had been for her when, as a teenager, her parents got divorced. All the kids at school had wanted lurid details, and a suicide in the family was even more gossip-worthy.

She and Sara each poured a dollop of wine into a waxed paper cup and took a sip.

Sara finally said, "I am so sorry for your loss of Marty. Mandy told me what happened."

Lori grumbled something incoherent, while Ella broke into tears and said, "It's horrible! I can't stand it! And I refuse to believe it for one second."

"Mom's upset. She's sad and ashamed. We all are," Lori said.

Amanda looked from one to another and saw a grieving sister in deep denial and a rebellious teen without a clue how to deal with a tragedy of this magnitude. Lori had expressed hatred for her uncle, calling him a loser and a racist, but at the same time, she was sure Lori never wished him dead. Likely, she was feeling a measure of guilt. "I understand, Lori," she said, knowing the comment was woefully inadequate.

"How can you possibly understand?" Ella refilled her cup. "My brother was a mess. I concede he made a terrible mistake, and it's true I'm ashamed. But he wasn't a monster. Yet I don't expect you to forgive him, and I don't blame you."

Ella was right. Amanda would never forgive him. But she also knew Ella desperately needed a way to forgive herself.

"Marty was no saint," Ella continued, "but he could be generous. He even let Lonny Appleton, his slob of a business partner, live with him awhile in his little apartment. Marty had a kind heart."

Sara said, "It doesn't feel like it now, but it will get better."

Amanda thought, Seriously? Is that the best Sara the shrink can offer?

Lori said, "Uncle Marty did it, but he was too

stupid to plan it."

The comment caused Ella to snatch Lori's cup away from her. "You've had enough, young lady. Maybe you should keep your opinions to yourself."

"Maybe I should *be* by myself." With that, the girl slid off the picnic bench, turned her back, and stalked into the house—but not before Amanda saw tears in her eyes.

Ella said, "I'm sorry. Lori doesn't know what to do with her grief."

"It's impossible for everyone right now," Sara stated the obvious and poured more wine for herself and Amanda. "Lori will find her way. She'll talk with Lily, then other friends, and get over the initial shock. In a few days, maybe she'll help make arrangements for Marty's funeral. Are you planning a service?"

Sara's question seemed to refocus Ella. Drying her eyes with a paper napkin, she looked off into the gray clouds and began talking about her family. She had called her father, Martin Sr., who was retired in Tampa, Florida, and spoken with her estranged mother, Elsa, who was local. As Ella mentioned the names, Amanda recalled their stories: Martin had been the redheaded, colorblind best friend of Andrew Taylor, Grandma's illegitimate son. As boys, they had worked together at Mayberry Farm and gone off to Vietnam together. Andrew had died in the war, Martin came home to marry Elsa, the country girl with ties to the KKK, and that had been when the racial division began.

Ella continued, "Dad will be flying up from Florida and bringing our son, Micah, with him to attend the service. Mother will be there, naturally, and I pray everyone gets along."

"So we'll get to meet Micah," Sara said

enthusiastically.

Ella smiled. "Yes, it will be good to see him, and he's eager to meet you all."

Amanda recalled that Micah went to Rollins College, near his grandpa. She did want to meet him but refused to attend a funeral for the man who killed her grandmother.

Ella said, "Best of all, Mama Mavis will be there. If you remember, Andrew Taylor married Mavis just before he left for Vietnam, when Mavis was pregnant with Judd. My girls adore their grandma Mavis, the merry widow."

Amanda had seen a photo of Mama Mavis taken at Judd and Ella's wedding—a sassy little woman in a big floral muumuu.

"My brother will be buried in Mount Pilot, in a cemetery where all the Roaches are interred. It's not far from Mama Mavis's old farm, so she's offered to have a reception for us there."

The family connections were intriguing, but Amanda wanted no part of it. "Sara, don't we have to leave before Marty's funeral?"

Sara gave her an odd look, then shrugged. "Up to you. I'm flexible."

Amanda frowned as a wall of rain poured from a dark cloud bank across the wide field. It moved toward them like a gray sheet dragging across the ground.

Ella cocked her head to one side. "Oh, I hear Judd coming." She rose and moved toward the door into the house. "You best come inside before you get soaked."

Only then did Amanda hear tires on gravel. Moments later, Judd parked his truck and strode toward the front door, all dressed up in his deputy's uniform.

Amanda eyed the wine and asked Ella, "Is it okay if we stay out and finish this bottle? We'll be in before the rain hits."

"No problem." Ella disappeared into the kitchen.

Amanda wanted Sara to get with her program of leaving town before the funeral, but before she could make her case, Judd came out onto the deck.

He placed his hands on Sara's shoulders and kissed the top of her head. "It's good to have you back, Sara. I missed you, but Mandy missed you more." He slid in beside them on the bench, took the bottle, and poured the rest for himself. "Sorry, but I need this more than you do. Jesus, what a day."

Sara smiled. "Good to see you, too, Judd. What's going on?"

"Well, I'm sure Mandy told you about our nightmare, but it just keeps getting worse."

Amanda put her hand on his forearm. "Do we really want to hear this?"

"No, I guess not. We had some contradictions at the scene of Marty's suicide, and I can't make sense of them."

"Can you tell us?" Sara asked.

"Inconsistencies. First, there's the problem of Marty's Marlin 336 rifle. Ballistics concluded it was the same gun used to shoot Robby. It had been carefully cleaned since it was fired, but we found not one fingerprint on it."

Amanda was confused. "Wouldn't Marty want to eliminate fingerprints from a weapon used in a crime?"

Judd sighed. "He would have to wear very thin gloves to perform such a delicate and thorough cleaning, and even then, it would be cumbersome and require patience Marty did not normally possess. Also, no cleaning solvent, lubricant, bore brush, patches, or cleaning rod were found anywhere in Marty's apartment."

"So maybe he cleaned the rifle elsewhere?"

"Marty didn't think that way. It was his gun, in his place, where else would the cleaning supplies be?"

Amanda couldn't answer that one. "Anything else?"

"Yes, Marty definitely wrote the note. He used a pistol registered in his name to kill himself, and there was nothing suspicious about the positioning of his hand to mouth to the trajectory of the bullet, so he definitely did the deed. But I'm worried about the boots…"

Judd reminded them about the footprints found under the deer blind at the lake where Robby was shot. From the tread, they knew the prints were made by a size twelve muck boot, possibly a brand called Fieldblazer. "We did find a pair of size twelve muck boots at Marty's, and they were covered with mud consistent with that at the lake."

Amanda exclaimed, "Then he did it. He shot Robby!"

Judd mournfully shook his head and rubbed his broken arm. "Problem is, Marty wore a size ten."

"What does it mean?" Sara demanded.

"It means it's not over," Amanda finished sadly.

## CHAPTER 47
*Busted...*

"So who owned the muck boots?" Sara asked late that night, after they made love while listening to rain pelting the tin roof of the Bee & Bee.

They had been over it again and again. Judd had told them Sheriff Bill considered the case closed with regard to Grandma and Robby and believed Commissioner Landry's murder was unrelated. The sheriff still thought Landry was killed by one of his wife's many jealous lovers—some cunning guy or gal who wanted the wife all to themselves.

Judd was unconvinced, Sara was doubtful, and Amanda was absolutely certain there was another guilty person out there somewhere getting away with murder.

"I have an idea," Amanda said.

※※※※

"It's a terrible idea," Sara insisted the next morning when they parked the Focus in the lot behind the Earle Theatre.

"We'll have a friendly chat with Lonny. What's wrong with that?"

As they made their way up the alley between buildings, trying to avoid puddles, they longed for an umbrella as wind whipped and rain drenched their clothes. The small scattering of tourists roaming Main Street seemed wet but determined to enjoy "Mayberry" regardless of weather.

They crossed the street to the green brick Main Oak Emporium and wandered into The Loaded Goat restaurant to catch their breath. Only a few of the round oak tables were occupied, and even the TVs seemed muted.

"Can't we sit down and have a coffee first?" Sara pleaded. "Or one of those Mayberry Margaritas you told me about?"

"Not now, Sara. I see the waiter who served me the other day. I'd like to ask him a few quick questions."

The college-aged boy in black pants and white shirt looked bored shitless. Once he got over his disappointment at not being allowed to seat them, he said to Amanda, "Weren't you here earlier this week? You were eating with that rich asshole who was vaping."

"Yeah, that was me, but I wasn't *with* the asshole, I was waiting for Lonny Appleton, the real estate guy with the office upstairs."

The kid snorted. "He's an asshole, too."

She laughed. "You know him then?"

"Sure, he eats here most every day, and he's a lousy tipper."

"Has he been in today?"

The boy, whose nametag said "Benjamin," screwed up his face. "Haven't you heard? His partner, Mr. Roach, the other lousy tipper, offed himself. Mr. Appleton came down for lunch all bent out of shape. He told me he was leaving town for a vacation—the beach, I think. He said he needed to get over the shock or some such thing."

Sara lifted her eyebrows in surprise. "Did Mr. Appleton say how long he'd be gone?"

Benjamin fixed on Sara's breast. "One week? Maybe he'll be back in a couple of days." He frowned. "What's it to you?"

Sara, who was used to men not looking her in the eye, but rather focusing slightly lower on her anatomy, avoided the question and winked. "Thank you, Benjamin. You've been a great help." She gave him a small tip.

Amanda would have stiffed him.

Out in the hall, Sara said, "So that's that. Let's get on with our day."

"Wait. We know Marty and Lonny were best friends, business partners with the same goals. They knew each other inside out, and Lonny had access. He even lived with Marty for a while. Can't we just go up and knock on his door? Make sure he's really gone?"

"What's the point?"

"Just humor me, okay?" Amanda was already climbing, and Sara followed reluctantly.

The hallway outside Lonny's office was still dark and dusty, but Amanda saw no light seeping out from under the closed door and heard no country/western music coming from inside. "He's not here, Sara. Do you mind practicing your special skills on this lock?"

"What the hell are you suggesting? Do you want to get us arrested?"

Amanda smiled beguilingly. Years ago, a convicted burglar on parole had shared the secrets of the trade with Sara. As his counselor, she pretended to be uninterested, but in fact, she had paid attention. On several occasions, she had awed Amanda with her dexterous fingers, and she always carried a small set of lock picks in her purse.

"Pretty please? You're so good at it. We can be in and out in a couple of minutes."

The standoff lasted one full minute, Amanda begging—Sara resisting. Finally, knowing she was beaten and unable to pass up a challenge, Sara got to her knees and took out her picks.

"Piece of cake!" Sara hooted when the tumblers fell into place and Lonny's door swung open. "This is your last chance, Mandy. One step inside and we're breaking and entering. It's a Class H felony punishable by up to twenty-five months in jail."

"Too late now." Amanda was already inside. Lonny's "home between wives" was no more attractive than before—same clutter, same smell of onions and cooking grease, same fast food wrappers everywhere.

Sara quietly closed the door. "What are we looking for?"

"How about we start with shoes?" Bypassing Lonny's grungy desk, she made for the long rack of clothes beyond. Sliding the hangers back and forth, she saw a couple of rumpled business suits and heavy winter coats. Missing were casual wear and T-shirts. "I guess he really is on vacation."

"Not necessarily. That's secondhand information, and why should we trust Benjamin the waiter?" Sara dropped to her knees and took out a tiny flashlight which, along with a panic whistle, she always carried on her keychain. She illuminated a pile of shoes under the rack. "I don't see any boots."

In the meantime, Amanda squatted down to sort through Lonny's shoes, looking for markings. Suddenly, she held up a loafer and squealed in triumph. "It's size twelve! Lonny wears size twelve. Those were his muck boots they found at Marty's."

"That's a big leap of faith," Sara grumbled. "Do you really believe Lonny tried to frame Marty for shooting at Robby?"

"Why not? How easy would it be? He 'borrows' Marty's gun, attempts to kill Robby, cleans the gun of trace, then returns it, along with the incriminating boots, to Marty's place."

"Wouldn't Marty notice the gun was missing or wonder where the boots came from?"

"If Marty drank as much as they say, I suspect he wouldn't notice much of anything."

"But why would Lonny betray his partner?" Sara wondered.

"What if Marty had become a liability? What if guilt over Grandma's death was inclining Marty to go to the police? If Lonny helped plan the break-in, then a confession from Marty would incriminate him, as well."

"That's a lot of 'what ifs.'"

"Yes, Sara, but the partners shared the same financial distress and were both desperate to land the Mayberry Farm deal. Lonny could not afford a fuck-up on the team."

"Jesus, Mandy, to hear you talk, you'd think Lonny also faked Marty's suicide."

The comment knocked the wind from Amanda's sails. She stopped sorting through the shoes, rocked back onto her butt, and looked up from the floor. "Oh, no, I didn't mean that at all."

"Okay, then, show me some proof."

"Let's keep looking."

Sara helped Amanda to her feet, then walked to the desk and began rifling through Lonny's drawers.

Amanda searched a tower of battered metal file cabinets, then a pile of white cardboard storage boxes seemingly stuffed with personal memorabilia. "Wait, what's this?"

The box stank of oil and contained all the paraphernalia Judd had mentioned as necessary to clean a gun, including a plastic bag filled with greasy cotton balls and a dirtied pair of thin latex gloves. "Is this what I think it is?"

Sara was already kneeling at her side. She shined her flashlight on a small, heavy box within labeled *.35 Remington cartridges.* "Are these bullets?"

"Yeah, I think they are." Amanda took out her phone and Googled. "No way! Those cartridges are recommended for the Marlin 336 rifle, the gun found at Marty's, the gun used to shoot Robby."

"Didn't Judd tell you that Lonny also had such a rifle registered in his name?" Sara cautioned.

"I don't see any guns in here, do you?"

Neither woman seriously believed Lonny would have taken a hunting rifle with him on vacation.

"Now what?" Sara said nervously.

"Now we get the hell outta Dodge."

They relocked the door, hoping they had left the office as they had found it, and scampered down the stairs.

"We left our fingerprints everywhere," Sara said.

"So what is Lonny gonna do? Call the cops if he suspects a break-in? I don't think so."

They were feeling home free until they reached the bottom of the stairs and bumped into Benjamin taking a break. He was whispering into his cellphone but quickly pocketed it and raised his eyebrows at them. "You again. Were you just up in Mr. Appleton's office? God, I hope you two aren't dating that asshole."

"No, we are not," Sara coldly replied as they attempted to push past him.

"So do you guys have a key to his apartment?" Benjamin pressed.

Amanda said, "Yes, we do, but it's none of your business."

He crossed his long arms and grinned. "So you're not dating him, but you have a key. What's the story?"

Amanda noticed that he was again ogling Sara's breasts, and she was furious. "Look, we're his cousins, you little punk. Does that work for you?"

"Okay, so that explains it." Benjamin chuckled, finally allowing them to pass. "I'll be sure to tell Mr. Appleton when he comes home that his cousins were here. What are your names? Better yet, can I have your phone numbers?"

By then, even Sara had lost her famous cool. Without a word, she pushed Benjamin aside, and they exited into the rain. "Shit, *cousins*?" She gasped.

"Yeah, busted," Amanda agreed.

## CHAPTER 48
*Landing on the moon...*

"We can't tell Judd what we've done," Sara insisted.

"He should know what we found in Lonny's office. "What's he gonna do, throw us in jail for twenty-five months?"

As they rushed across Main Street, the rain suddenly stopped and the wind died down. Sara paused in the alleyway leading to the parking lot. "Clearly, we need to think this through. I'm starving. Maybe some food and coffee would help us think straight."

They couldn't return to The Loaded Goat, where Benjamin still lingered in the doorway watching them, so they scurried up the block to Snappy Lunch. Thanks to the weather, there was no wait line, and they were seated immediately. After ordering two famous pork sandwiches, fries, and coffee, they took turns visiting the restroom to pat down their soaked hair and dry their arms and faces with paper towels.

Once settled with their food, Amanda said, "What do you think?"

Sara nibbled thoughtfully on a fry. "Well, the gun-cleaning kit, the cartridges, and the size twelve shoes are compelling but hardly smoking guns—pardon the pun. If we took that evidence to Judd, he'd laugh his head off before locking us up."

Hard as it was to believe, Amanda realized those

items could likely be found in many North Carolina homes and were hardly proof of guilt. "So our little adventure was a waste of time?"

"Like robbing a bank with no money. If caught, we'd do the time, yet discovered no crime."

"That's cute, Sara. Now what?"

"Honestly? I don't think there's much left for us to do in Mount Airy. You've already decided to go with the flow regarding the sale of the land. You told me neither of Judd's girls care about the farm. In fact, they'd appreciate having the money for college."

"Yes, and after Marty's suicide, Ella claimed she wanted nothing more to do with the land, though she was upset at the time." Amanda felt deflated. "So it seems Judd is the only holdout on selling."

"It's a Taylor family matter now," Sara said. "And if you really want to avoid Marty's funeral, then we should pack up and go home right away."

As Amanda digested Sara's words, she looked across the heads of the other diners to the small window at the street, located directly above the cooking grill. She saw the sun had come out and was shining like a rainbow on the steamy glass. Normally, the sight would have lifted her spirits, yet at that moment, it made her sad. So much violence, death, and destruction. Yet what had been accomplished? Surely, Grandma would not have wanted this. She had been a woman of strong will, whose last will had shaken the world she left behind.

"You could be right. I'll have to think about leaving, but first we'd need to say a proper goodbye to everybody."

Sara joined her in looking at the sunshine. "Okay, but it's turned out to be a beautiful day. Are there any sights left to see in Mayberry? Any tourist stone left unturned?"

Amanda could think of only one.

※ ※ ※ ※

They had some trouble finding "The Rock" but eventually followed East Pine Street to a turnoff called Quarry Trail. Unfortunately, the short stretch of pavement was partially blocked by a steel arm with a warning sign saying: *Temporarily Closed for Renovations.*

Amanda stopped but left the Focus's engine running. "Shit! Robby enjoyed this place. He visited when we first got to town and said it was like landing on the moon. I really wanted to see it."

Sara studied her lovingly, then laid a hand on her arm. "I'm sorry, Mandy. This has been a day of disappointments, hasn't it?"

"They say it's the world's largest open-face granite quarry. They say the astronauts could see it from outer space."

"Is that a fact?" Sara cocked her head to one side, an impish expression on her face. "I see the gate is not exactly closed, and we could easily drive through for a quick peek. If they really wanted to keep folks out, they'd lock it, right?"

Amanda looked up hopefully. "It wouldn't be the worst thing we've done today."

"Ain't that the truth? So let's go!"

Amanda steered cautiously around the barrier, then drove along a short industrial road graced by a few struggling trees. It terminated at a parking lot outside a three-storied building with "North Carolina Granite Corporation" carved above the entry. The structure, like several other smaller ones on site, was constructed of white granite blocks surely mined from this quarry. More blocks formed a waist-high retaining wall with a grassy park beyond. The place was deserted, not a car or person in sight.

Amanda complained, "We can't see a thing from here."

"Nothing but a sandbox filled with powder." Sara lifted one foot and pointed to her sandal. "Looks like talcum."

"Yuck, that stuff that causes ovarian cancer?"

Sara shrugged. "That's not proven, but I bet the miners wear face masks. I'd hate to breathe this junk all day long."

They wandered downhill to yet another gate. This one was chain-link and locked to drive-through traffic, but apparently, the quarry itself was just beyond and over a rise. Another sign with a directional arrow pointing right promised a scenic walk and an observation lookout. That path was available by foot.

Amanda hesitated. "Should we do this?"

Sara gave her a look. "Hey, since when did you get squeamish about trespassing? You're the outlaw today, and we're on a roll. I say we go for it."

"Besides, we're all alone, so no one will ever know."

They sneaked onto the path, rounded a bend, and suddenly saw the huge white expanse of quarry stretched out before them as far as the eye could see. A drop-off ranging from ten to twenty-some feet fell away beside the path, where scraggly bits of brush fought for survival in the crevices. This was not a deep canyon, as Amanda had expected, but rather an endless, rugged field that appeared to be covered by snow. Or maybe it looked more like a littered beach. Clearly, the rock surface had been scraped or gouged out to access the granite.

The landscape was strewn with giant blocks set at random angles in piles, or solo. Amanda saw exposed walls marching like fortresses and ancient ruins, battlements, and moats. Yellow steel buildings stood in the far distance along with work trucks, some railroad tracks, and a stream bordering one side. "Holy shit!"

"No kidding," Sara agreed. "It's not one of the Seven Wonders, but it's impressive all the same. I can't get my head around it. I can't tell if it goes for miles or forever."

"Let's keep walking, and maybe we'll get a better perspective."

The path was slippery from the rain, and the moisture caused the granite dust to cling to their shoes. They held on to each other in particularly treacherous spots because toppling down the embankment was not a good option.

"Are we having fun yet?" Sara had decided that no matter which bend they rounded, the perspective was no better—only an endless white, jagged wasteland.

"Robby loves this kind of stuff. At one time, he wanted to be a geologist, but it doesn't rock *my* world. We can head back whenever you want to."

They reversed course immediately. As they retraced their steps, the silence was absolute but for the clatter of a miniature landslide sending pebbles scattering down the hillside around the corner ahead. "Wonder what caused that?" Amanda said.

"Maybe a dog followed us."

"Hope it's a friendly dog."

They rounded the corner and saw not a canine, but rather a human figure backlit by the sun. The glare was such that they could not see a face, only that the silhouette was tall and male.

"Hello?" Amanda called out tentatively. Suddenly, she was feeling very vulnerable.

"Hello?" the man called back. "I never expected to run into my *cousins* out here in the middle of nowhere."

## CHAPTER 49
*Deep shit...*

The blood drained from Amanda's head, leaving her faint as she clung to Sara and gaped at Lonny Appleton. Today her blond look-alike wore jeans, mountain boots she knew to be size twelve, and a camouflage combat jacket with his right hand buried ominously in its pocket.

"I thought you were on vacation." She gasped.

Sara had never met the man, but she knew as soon as he called them "cousins" that they were in deep shit. "Hello, Mr. Appleton, I'm Sara Orlando," she managed to calmly introduce herself.

"I know who you are. My daughter Cherry told me there were two dykes hanging out with Judd Taylor. But you had my pal Benjamin fooled. He was panting like a lovesick puppy when he described you on the phone."

So Benjamin the waiter was a traitor. Amanda wanted to wring his scrawny neck. "He told us you were vacationing at the beach. He also said you were a lousy tipper."

Appleton threw back his head and laughed. "I may be a lousy tripper, but Benji's my buddy. He doesn't complain when I slip him a couple of twenties each month to keep an eye on my office. Seems like today that investment paid off."

Amanda recalled the waiter watching from the

doorway as they walked to Snappy for lunch. No doubt he called Appleton right away and told him about the office break-in. The kid would have known where they parked, so all Appleton had to do, since he was obviously in town, was drive to the lot and wait for them.

"You followed us here," she accused.

He shrugged and stepped a few paces closer on the sloping path.

Sara froze, and her breathing accelerated. They were two against one. Appleton was bigger and stronger and occupied the higher ground on a very treacherous playing field. While he plainly wasn't carrying the Marlin 336 rifle that seemed to be missing from his office, Sara was desperately worried about what might be concealed in his pocket.

"So did you two lesbians find anything of interest when you broke into my place?" His pale skin was blotchy red across his cheekbones, and his mouth had narrowed to a thin slit.

At such close quarters, Amanda smelled sour sweat oozing from his pores. To say she was intimidated was an understatement. She was terrified. So was Sara. Her fingernails bit into Amanda's forearm, and she was trembling. But knowing Sara, she would stand her ground. No point trying to bluff.

Sara said, "Well, Lonny, we found your gun-cleaning kit and suspicious cartridges. We also took note of your shoe size, same size as the muck boots found at Marty's apartment. We decided you did a mighty fine job of framing your partner for shooting Robby."

His reaction was swift and violent. Pushing between them, Appleton grabbed Sara's shoulder with his left hand, causing Amanda to topple backward onto her butt. She landed in a pile of rubble on the safe side of the path, away from the drop-off.

He spat words into Sara's face. "You're a smartass, aren't you?"

Although Amanda saw fear in her eyes, Sara said, "It doesn't take a genius, Lonny. Did you kill Marty, too? Or fake his suicide?"

Was Sara trying to get them both killed? As Amanda struggled upright, she realized Appleton was walking Sara closer to the edge.

He said, "You're not as smart as you think, bitch. It didn't take much to convince that loser to put himself out of his misery. Marty was a pussy. He was so torn up with guilt that a pointedly worded suggestion did the trick."

Amanda was frantic. The man was openly confessing. Surely, he would not allow them to escape this godforsaken place alive. In the meantime, Sara was doing something weird with her eyes—rolling them off to the left, while making little shoving gestures with the hand unobstructed by Appleton's grip. Dear God in heaven, did she expect Amanda to push him off the cliff?

Amanda had always been fast and athletic in a basic way, but Sara was skilled in the martial arts and was much more nimble and strategic. So Amanda could not come up with any move that would not endanger them both.

Unfortunately, Appleton took the decision out of their hands. Still gripping Sara's shoulder, he gave a quick shove, throwing her off balance. Amanda screamed when Sara fell backward, hands flailing like a disoriented bird hoping to fly. At the same time, Sara cocked one knee and struck out, hooking Appleton with her leg. He teetered momentarily, latched on to the airborne Sara, and they both went over the edge.

Still screaming, Amanda lunged forward onto her hands and knees. She reached out, desperate to grab some part of Sara's body to stop the freefall, but it was too late. Still joined together, the two hit the steep slope of the embankment and began to roll. At one point, Appleton's heavy body bulldozed over Sara, who cried out in pain. Amanda was sure his weight had cracked or broken at least one rib, and in a visceral, sympathetic response, her own chest constricted, and her screams became sobs.

Halfway down, the two collided with a bramble bush, which split them apart. Appleton rolled left, Sara rolled right, both grasping for anything to hold on to, both failing. At the same time, Amanda found her wits and looked for a way to follow them down without imperiling her own footing. The choices were few. She spotted a place about thirty yards back on the path where the crest dipped closer to the valley floor, where she could conceivably inch her way down to assist. She began running in that direction as fast as she safely coul

"Sara, Sara, Sara!" She hadn't been aware of calling out her name, expending precious lung power, but she couldn't help it.

"No, Mandy! Please stop!" Suddenly, Sara shouted up to her.

Startled, Amanda halted long enough to see that Sara had ceased rolling and was standing on her feet. She was frantically waving her arms. She had landed on a smooth rock ledge, much like a high, curving wall. Appleton was still careening downhill toward a shallow, mucky pool.

"Mandy, listen to me! We need to split up. Please run back to the car and call for help."

Still stunned, Amanda could hardly believe her beloved had survived. Yet Sara seemed unhurt and in possession of her faculties. "I'm not leaving you, Sara. I'm coming down."

"No, run now, Mandy!"

Just then, Appleton hit bottom about twenty feet beyond and below Sara's perch. He picked himself up shakily from the mud, bent over at the waist, dropped his head, and shook it several times. When he stood erect, he paused, ran a hand across his eyes, and then squinted up in search of his prey. When he saw Sara, his contorted expression could only be described as homicidal rage.

Sara saw it, too, and instinctively ducked behind one of several large blocks spaced out at equal intervals along the top of the wall.

Appleton limped forward, reached into his pocket, and pulled out the handgun Amanda had long anticipated. He fiddled with the safety and took aim.

Both women screamed when he fired. The shot echoed like an explosion. It ricocheted off Sara's granite barrier and echoed across the wasteland.

"Get going, Mandy!" Sara begged, this time with an urgency that defied argument.

To emphasize the urgency, Appleton spun around and set his sights on Amanda. He roared and pulled the trigger. The bullet hit an outcropping at her feet, sending a rock splinter speeding at her face. It struck her forehead inches from her right eye.

The pain was less concerning than the blood, which poured down, blinding her. Amanda dropped to her belly, hopefully presenting less of a target. She searched her jacket pocket and retrieved the man-sized handkerchief she habitually carried. She folded it diagonally and knotted it tightly around her head, stopping the flow. Only then did she realize Sara was calling to her in sheer panic.

"I'm all right, Sara!" she shouted as she assessed their situation. On one hand, Sara had some good cover and the advantage of height. Appleton had no easy access to her without mountain climbing equipment. On the other hand, Amanda was a sitting duck. Unfortunately, they had left their purses behind in the car, and their cellphones were in their purses. Fortunately, Amanda had been driving, so she had the keys. If she kept low, she figured she had a fifty/fifty chance of making it to the parking lot without a bullet in her back.

"I'm going, Sara!" she shouted into the void. "Hang in there, and I'll be back. I promise."

With that, she started running bent over on all fours—toes and fingertips—as fast as a human primate could travel.

## CHAPTER 50
*Battle stations...*

Sara flattened her back against her rock barrier, then slid down to a seated position, gasping for air. Her hands and knees were skinned bloody, and her injured ribs burned with each breath. The bastard! First he'd crushed her, then he'd shot to kill. And now he was laughing.

At least Mandy had escaped around a bend on the path and was out of his line of fire. Sara couldn't tell if the blood she'd seen on Mandy's face was from a direct hit or from flying rubble, but it broke her heart.

It also inspired a pure, primal urge to kill Lonny Appleton. Forcing herself to regulate her breathing from the shallow strokes that caused less pain to deeper intakes that allowed blood to flow to her brain, she then took stock of her situation.

So what was he laughing about? For the moment, she felt safe. From what she remembered about landing, her ledge was high and impossible for Appleton to scale from where he had fallen. She wasn't sure how the land lay right there at quarry bottom, and it was suicidal to peek around the corner of her granite block to find out.

She could see her ledge was at least ten feet wide and curved like a semicircle for several hundred yards. It had large blocks, like the one behind which she was hiding, spaced along at regular intervals. Bizarrely, it resembled the battle stations topping medieval castles, from behind which defending archers shot their fiery arrows. Ordinarily, that image would be comical, but she was personally under siege and increasingly desperate to understand why her enemy was laughing.

He was also moving. Judging by the stumbling sound of his boots, Appleton was making his way along the base of her ledge toward an unseen destination. What could he see that she could not? Conceivably, if he was watching his step instead of focusing on her, she could scamper between the blocks before he could get off a shot.

Holding her breath, Sara sprinted to the next barrier. Surprised, Appleton looked up, aimed, but did not fire. Instead, he picked up his pace. Unfortunately, she'd been unable to determine where he was going in such a hurry, yet she had sensed a gradual uphill angle to his progress. This implied the height of her level ledge would gradually shorten, making his ascent easier.

She scampered behind the next barrier for confirmation. This time, the asshole didn't even look up but rather started running. God help her. Was she advancing in the wrong direction, right into his arms? Retreating to escape was impossible, for there was no way she could climb up the way she fell down.

Sara had to see more. Dropping to her stomach, she crawled to the edge, exposing as little of herself as possible. Looking down, she finally saw the ladder, and her heart seemed to stop. It was propped against the face of the cliff several yards away, and Appleton was climbing.

Crabbing backward in sheer panic, Sara knew she had to make a decision—either freeze in place and wait for a bullet or jump. The ladder was against the outer curve of the wall, so the inner curve was the only logical way to go. Once up, he could either jump after her, risking injury, or retreat down the ladder again. In that case, he would have to run all the way to the end of the wall and around to follow her. If he chose that option, she might have time to find cover.

Of course, he had a third option, which was much more troubling. Assuming she jumped off the inner curve, he could remain on top and shoot, his bullets traveling faster than either one of them could hope to. At the moment, however, he was climbing, both hands occupied, so Sara boldly stood to scan the terrain. She immediately saw a wedge-like gravel slide tapering down from the inner curve. Beyond that, man-sized granite chunks randomly dotted the field.

Without hesitation, she took the plunge. She leaped onto the wedge, sandals hitting gravel, and stumbled down the incline. Her foot got stuck, twisting her ankle, but somehow, she made it down just as Appleton's head crested the ledge and he climbed aboard.

He spotted her instantly, braced his feet, and took aim. Sara dove at the nearest chunk, arms extended, hands and knees landing on unforgiving rock. She crawled toward the shelter followed by a spray of bullets, then rolled behind to safety.

In a matter of seconds, Appleton would follow her down the gravel wedge. They would play cat and mouse around the rocks until, advantaged by uninjured ribs and a long arm terminating in a gun, Appleton would catch her.

Just then, she heard distant sirens. She also heard tires advancing fast on one of the quarry's work roads.

The vehicle was kicking up a white cloud of dust and heading in her direction. So the troops were coming. Too late, she feared.

Lungs burning and ankle throbbing, she dragged herself around the corner of her chunk to avoid his approach. The car was almost upon them. It was some sort of a white vehicle completely disguised by its dust cloud. Surely, Appleton would not shoot her with a witness so close at hand.

But he was crazy! Her assessment was not a professional diagnosis but rather a gut certainty as her pursuer stepped into full view. He was breathing hard, his bloodshot eyes glaring through a white mask of powder. Indeed, the huge, menacing figure was covered in white, like the abominable snowman, she thought absurdly. He extended his right arm, steadied his wrist with his left hand, and Sara prepared to die.

The car door slammed, and someone screamed, "Drop the gun, Appleton, or I'll shoot your fucking head off!"

Mandy? Had Sara died and gone to heaven? There was no other explanation.

Yet the woman, definitely Amanda, strode closer with a long rifle braced to her shoulder, its sights trained on Appleton's forehead. "Did you hear me, fucker? Drop it!"

Sara sensed the instant when Appleton gave up. His eyes blinked uncontrollably, he cursed, groaned, and then placed his weapon on the ground. Sara crab-walked across the rubble and grabbed it.

Blinded by primal rage, she pointed it at his heart. "I'm going to kill you!" She meant it.

"No, Sara!" Amanda tossed the rifle aside, beyond Appleton's reach, and ran to her side. She gently took the gun away and guarded their prisoner as the sirens drew closer. "It's okay. This time, it's really over."

## CHAPTER 51
*The full dilemma...*

Sheriff Bill responded in person. In addition to his unit, two more patrol cars and an ambulance screeched to a halt at their feet. All officers rushed them, weapons drawn.

"What took you so long?" Amanda gasped as one man pinned her, while his partner wrenched Appleton's gun from her hand.

At the same time, someone cuffed Appleton, and Sara climbed shakily to her feet.

"What the hell happened here?" the sheriff barked.

"These women attacked me," Appleton whined. "First they broke into my office, then they followed me here and threatened me with that rifle."

"Bullshit." Sara rolled her eyes at the long gun lying in the dust. "Jesus, Mandy, where did you get that thing?"

Amanda laughed while she too submitted to handcuffs. "Would you believe it's one of the antique rifles Robby inherited from Grandma? It was still stashed in the rental car, and I figured it might come in handy."

A deputy gingerly picked up the rifle, frowning as he inspected it. "Check it out, Bill. This old thing belongs in a museum. It's not loaded, it's rusty, and it hasn't been fired in years." The officers passed the weapon around, while Appleton groaned, realizing he was the victim of Amanda's bold bluff.

Sara yelped when they pulled her wrists together and cuffed them. "Hey, I'm one of the good guys!"

Amanda snapped. "Can't you see she needs an ambulance, not restraints?"

"It looks like you could use some medical attention, too, Ms. Rittenhouse," Sheriff Bill said.

"You remember me?"

"I remember both of you ladies from that day at the lake when your brother got shot."

Amanda winced when a young female paramedic removed her makeshift bandage and cleaned her head wound with antiseptic.

Sara hopped forward on her one good foot and confronted the sheriff. "About that day at the lake... Mr. Appleton fired those shots. He tried to kill Robby, didn't you, Lonny?"

Appleton's mouth dropped open in feigned disbelief. "Why, that's just plain foolish, Bill. We all know, sad as the truth may be, my partner, Marty Roach, went after that boy. I should sue this woman for slander."

Amanda suggested the officers should search Appleton's office to confirm their accusation. She was about to itemize the proof they'd discovered there when Sara gave her a warning look and shook her head.

The sheriff scowled. "So you *did* break into Lonny's office?"

"We most certainly did not," Sara insisted. "I work for the Charlotte Judiciary. As an officer of the court, I would never do such a thing."

Only then did Amanda understand the full dilemma. Should Sara be indicted, let alone convicted of breaking and entering, she would most certainly lose her job. Worse, the whole B&E caper had been Amanda's idea. Sara's life could be ruined, and it would be all her fault.

Appleton said, "There's a witness, Bill. Benjamin from The Loaded Goat will testify as to what they did, and I guarantee their fingerprints will be all over my stuff."

Amanda couldn't believe Appleton really wanted a search because the authorities would turn up the same incriminating evidence they had. But whether he was bluffing or not, she and Sara were losing ground. Lonny Appleton was Mount Airy born and bred. If not a pillar of the community, he was also not a stranger, as they were. "He shot at us! He tried to kill us today!" she cried.

Appleton chuckled. "Hey, did you see *me* holding any gun? The bitch was threatening me. You saw it with your own eyes, Bill."

When the sheriff looked at her again, she saw no compassion.

"Is this your gun, ma'am?"

"No!" Amanda and Sara said at once.

"Well, it ain't mine," Appleton drawled.

Clearly, they had reached an impasse. Sara pointed at Amanda's wound. "Look, did Amanda shoot herself? Use your common sense."

The EMS nurse said, "This woman wasn't hit by a bullet, boss. Looks like she might could've fallen and hurt herself."

Amanda groaned. *Whatever happened to female solidarity?* She played the one winning card she had left. "I'm Judd Taylor's cousin. Could someone please call him? He can vouch for us."

"He's on his way," Sheriff Bill said. "My deputy already phoned him. We figured he'd want to know what kind of trouble you've stirred up this time."

It seemed, in addition to everything else, they would be charged with trespassing in the granite quarry in defiance of the warning signs. Indeed, when Amanda called 911, the operator, who knew the quarry was closed for renovations, scolded Amanda for being there before getting help. One could argue the delay forced Amanda to crash through a chained gate, damaging the Focus, to get to Sara. Now she prayed Robby had purchased collision insurance when he rented it.

"Okay, everybody, listen up. We'll sort this out down at the station," Sheriff Bill said with finality.

They tucked Appleton into a patrol car but allowed Sara and Amanda to ride in the ambulance. As they were getting ready to pull out, Judd arrived in his truck looking angry and not at all sympathetic to their plight. Apparently, he'd been briefed along the way.

"What happened to you two? It looks like you've been rolling around in a flour bin," he said without a trace of humor.

Both talking at once, they told him their side of the story. Amanda concluded, "So you know we would *never* break into Mr. Appleton's office."

"Is that right? Aren't you the same woman who, along with my delinquent daughter, broke into my private computer and printed out sensitive information?"

What could she say?

Sara spoke up. "So, Judd, how long will they keep us down at the station house?"

He narrowed his amber eyes and massaged his

jaw with a big brown hand. "Personally, I'm hoping they lock you up and throw away the key."

## CHAPTER 52
*Diamond engagement ring...*

They did not rot in jail. Instead, they made a devil's bargain with Judd. Although he did not believe in their innocence any more than he believed in the Easter Bunny, he agreed to dissuade Bill from dusting Appleton's office for their prints so long as they left town by Monday, which gave them only the remainder of the weekend in Mount Airy.

"Fine by me," Sara grumbled as she eased onto their bed at the Bee & Bee. "We were going to leave anyway, right?"

"Right."

Amanda felt Sara's pain. After hours at the station house, they spent another hour at the hospital. Before the medical staff could examine their injuries, they were hustled into showers to wash off the layers of white granite goo. They found Sara had two cracked ribs and a badly sprained ankle, while the cut on Amanda's forehead required five stitches. The final indignity was being driven to the hotel by a one-handed Judd with his broken arm. They rode wearing revealing hospital gowns, while their filthy clothes traveled in a garbage bag in the bed of the truck.

Amanda lay on the bed beside Sara. It was early Saturday morning, and neither had been able to sleep. "Will Judd ever forgive us?"

Sara smirked. "Hey, Judd would have charged us

if he didn't have that ace up his sleeve."

"The muck boots, right?"

"Absolutely. I think Lonny was already confessing to shooting Robby by the time they sent us to the hospital."

Turned out the authorities had never fully bought into the theory that Marty Roach masterminded the break-in at Grandma's and also shot Robby. Judd had taken it upon himself to bag the boots and get them to forensics, where the techs found Appleton's prints all over them. They also determined the composition of the mud on their soles precisely matched the unique soil at the lake where Robby was attacked.

Sara said, "It's lucky Lonny got sloppy that one time with the boots."

"It's lucky Lonny was a lousy shot." For Robby's sake, and for their sakes at the quarry, Amanda was grateful that Appleton was no kind of a marksman. "Do you think that connection Appleton made with the forger will pay off?"

"Not our problem." Sara dragged a pillow under her sore ribs and closed her eyes.

"Still, I wish they could prove something definitive."

Judd had also told them that a shady local informant, with expertise in forging documents, had recently been arrested for a minor offense. As part of a plea deal, he confessed to forging a fake driver's license in the name of "Ralph Morgan," the same name used by the "golfer" who broke into Grandma's. Possibly the guy who paid for the fake was Lonny Appleton. Sheriff Bill expected the forger would remember that detail if they exonerated him for the minor offense.

"Sara, I still think Marty killed Grandma, but I'd

love to see Appleton nailed as the mastermind. I'd be willing to bet he called Grandma's doctor to find out the date and time of her appointment. Do you think Dr. Patel's receptionist would recognize Appleton's voice?"

But Sara was already asleep.

Amanda pulled the quilt up over Sara, then lay down fully dressed to worry some more. There were still too many loose ends, like why was Commissioner Landry murdered and who did it? Appleton vigorously denied responsibility for that killing, and she believed him. The injection of a lethal euthanasia drug seemed too sophisticated, more like the work of a smooth operator like Kenneth Klein of March Investments. Mentally reviewing her stolen list of pool party attendees, Amanda was more confused than ever.

But did it really matter? They were going home, bowing out, and the more pressing problem was how to get two cars back to their condo. She feared Sara was too disabled to drive the Miata, and they had to take the Focus, with its smashed front grill because it was still loaded with Robby's inheritance.

Amanda was bone tired but too keyed up to sleep. She was hungry but too lazy to go down to breakfast when her cellphone rang. Caller ID said it was Linc Davis on the line.

"What's up, Linc?" She was surprised to hear from him.

"Mandy, Detective Winston just phoned with some good news. They recovered Vivian's diamond ring."

She sat up on the edge of the bed so fast her head spun. "How? When? Where?"

Linc laughed. "Would you believe some dumb

schmuck tried to pawn it in Charleston? Winston was thrilled that all those posters and bulletins he put out finally paid off."

"Where did the guy get the ring?" She couldn't make sense of it. Marty was dead, Appleton in jail.

Linc grunted in disgust. "That's the problem. It's been passing hand to hand for several weeks now. The jerk they arrested got it from a friend of a friend, with everyone promised a little piece of the pie once the ring got sold."

"So how will they trace it back to the thief?"

"Good question. All I can tell you is what Winston told me. They have a vague description of the original seller—all hearsay, of course."

Amanda was hyperventilating and accidentally elbowed Sara, waking her up. "Was the original seller a tall, blond, middle-aged man who looks a lot like me?"

Linc hesitated. "Not at all. Supposedly he was an older man, well-spoken, and well-to-do."

She was floored. If not Marty, then who? After a few more words with Linc, she quickly hung up.

"Now what?" Sara was sleepy and grumpy.

"I don't know, Sara. Can we go downstairs to breakfast and talk about it?"

## CHAPTER 53
*Talking hypotheticals...*

Clinging to the banister, Sara took the steps one at a time with Amanda ready to catch her should she fall. When they reached the base of the grand staircase, they passed through the lobby to an empty dining room, where Lois and Lou were quietly chatting together as they cleared the dishes and removed soiled tablecloths.

Amanda's stomach growled. "Oh, no. Are we too late to get served?"

Lois glanced up at them. "Not to worry, love. We still have some fresh coffee and leftover Danish in the kitchen, if you don't mind helping yourselves."

"Thanks, Lois," Sara said listlessly. She was more interested in rest and recuperation than food.

The kitchen seemed less like the Bates Motel by light of day. Amanda shamelessly filled a plate, while Sara settled for a tall glass of orange juice. Rather than returning to the dining room to eat, where they would be underfoot, they moved outside to the covered porch, where sun sparkled on the blossoming magnolia and purple phlox. The warm day coaxed a sweet, earthy smell up from the enchanted garden after yesterday's rain.

Amanda exhaled a sigh of contentment, until she noticed they were not alone. Max Eagle sat at one of the white wrought iron tables. As always, he was impeccably dressed as he sipped coffee and read *The*

*Wall Street Journal.*

"Join me, ladies?" He removed his wire-rimmed glasses and smiled affably.

"Love to." Amanda tried to hide her disappointment as she slid into a chair beside him. Telling Sara about the recovery of Grandma's ring would have to wait.

As Sara maneuvered into a chair, her sprained ankle gave way, and she spilled juice on Eagle's paper. "Oh, Lord, I am so sorry!"

"Not to worry, Dr. Orlando." Eagle calmly dabbed at the mess with a paper napkin.

Amanda and Sara helped.

When the job was done, Sara said, "How did you know my name? I don't believe we've ever been formally introduced."

He studied her through pale gray eyes. "Everyone in town knows about you two. I also happen to know what happened out at the quarry yesterday. You're lucky to have escaped relatively unscathed."

Sara said, "How would you know about yesterday? It hasn't been in the paper yet."

He shrugged. "I suppose the mayor told me or perhaps it was one of the commissioners."

The women glanced at each other, sharing one thought: Why was Max Eagle on the inside track? Sheriff Bill's investigation was ongoing and confidential. Who was blabbing to whom?

Eagle shook his bald head. "It's a shame about Marty Roach and Lonny Appleton. Talk about bumbling fools, those two were like a lame comedy act. It's too bad Apollo Partners got involved with Mayberry Acres in the first place. It would have gone much smoother without them. No one would have got hurt, and no one would be dead."

The man's unsolicited statement surprised Amanda. "What do you know about all that, Mr. Eagle?"

Before he could answer, Sara's cellphone rang, interrupting like a drunk at a church service. She apologized, turned her head away for a brief, private conversation. When she finished, she laid the phone on the seat of the fourth chair, where she could see it.

"Forgive me, please. That was one of my patients. I've put it on mute so we won't be disturbed again. Now what were you saying, Mr. Eagle?"

"I was remarking that Marty and Lonny were Dumb and Dumber. Kenny Klein at March Investments was foolish to bring them into it. He only invited them because of Marty's family ties to Judd Taylor."

Amanda found it beyond disturbing that Eagle was so in the loop. His odd gray eyes darkened like a storm cloud, and his fingers trembled on the handle of his coffee cup. "What's it to you, Mr. Eagle?" she asked quietly.

He licked his full lips. "I'm a major shareholder in March Investments. I own about thirty percent of their stock and sit on the board of directors. Naturally, the successful completion of Mayberry Acres is of special interest to me."

The mildly warm day did not explain the perspiration breaking out on Amanda's forehead. She noticed even Sara looked clammy and pale. "So I guess you were upset when you thought that Judd, my brother, and I did not intend to sell?"

His thin eyebrows shot up. "Actually, my sources understood that *you* were always willing, Miss Rittenhouse. Then your brother came around after the shooting incident, and now I hear Judd is ready to throw in the towel."

Amanda felt ill. Eagle's information was entirely too accurate. "You have excellent sources, sir," she began carefully. "I suppose we all understand how my family succumbed to coercion, but how did March Investments get three of the five commissioners onboard to approve your project?"

Eagle's laugh was oddly high-pitched. "Let's talk hypotheticals, dear. Commissioner Marty Roach was already in the bag. Theoretically, the others were open to bribery. Only Myron Landry remained hard-headed, but of course, that problem resolved itself."

"With a little help from a lethal injection," Sara muttered under her breath.

The words seemed to jolt Eagle. He pushed away his coffee cup as a tic started up in his left eye. In the meantime, Amanda was stunned by Sara sharing the information about the injection. It was a closely held fact, one Judd had shared in the strictest confidence.

Sara continued, "What I don't get is why so many people were willing to bribe, threaten, and even kill over Mayberry Farm. Sure, a couple of million bucks isn't chump change, but it's not all that much money."

Eagle took a deep breath and got his eye tic under control. "We were talking *hypotheticals*, remember? But you may as well know because the news is about to break that Mayberry Farm may be worth a great deal more than you suppose…"

## CHAPTER 54
*Going home...*

Eagle next described a secret bid from Simone Properties, a major developer of discount malls. They had been negotiating for months with March Investments to locate a complex in Mount Airy. The mega mall would include two hundred retail stores and fifteen anchor tenants. The building would be upward of 1.4 million square feet and attract more than seventeen million visitors each year.

Eagle explained that Concord Mills near Charlotte was the nearest competitor and that Mayberry Discount Mall would lure customers from Greensboro, High Point, Winston-Salem, Raleigh-Durham, and southern Virginia. It would require major new infrastructure, create hundreds of jobs, and breathe new life into Mount Airy.

"Andy Griffith wouldn't believe it." He guffawed. "But what's more American than cheap stuff for lots of people?"

"Is this really going to happen?" Amanda was dumbstruck. She visualized the traffic jams, the influx of the masses, and the Yount homestead bulldozed and buried under layers of concrete.

Eagle rubbed his pudgy hands together. "It's looking more likely each day." He explained about "ground leases" and "percentage rent," whereby March

Investments would lease out the land for ninety-nine years and demand a share of all tenant profits in addition to monthly rent. Simone Properties would pay the taxes, insurance, upkeep, and construction costs, while March Investments would sit back and collect the money for generations to come.

It didn't take a genius to know he was talking big bucks. "But what if it *doesn't* happen?"

"Life is a gamble, Miss Rittenhouse. If Simone doesn't come through, we execute the original plan for Mayberry Acres. That would be fine with me since I don't need the money, but I suspect you might be pleased with the discount mall scheme. It would make you a very rich young lady because if it works out, Kenny Klein would be forced to offer you a much better price."

While Amanda tried to suppress the string of dollar signs skittering through her mind, Sara sat very still, her green eyes laser focused on Eagle.

"So let me get this straight," Sara said. "In spite of all the violence aimed at securing this deal, it doesn't matter to you. Are you rich, Mr. Eagle?"

He stood, fastened the middle button on his expensive suit coat, and fiddled with his silk tie. "I am quite comfortable, yes. I'm a widower, and my wife, may she rest in peace, operated a very lucrative practice and left me well-off."

The picture of smugness, Eagle brushed a speck of lint from his sleeve and rotated his cold eyes toward Sara. "She was a doctor, like you, but she was a veterinarian."

For Amanda, the last missing piece of the jigsaw puzzle fell into place. Eagle had been at the pool party, where he had the motive and opportunity to murder

Myron Landry. "Did you ever assist your wife in her practice?"

"I did help, but only with the unpleasant duties she faced in her job."

The raw emotion in Sara's voice came out in a whisper. "Did you euthanize animals for her?"

He smiled and nonchalantly hitched one shoulder. "Yes, I did."

His answer was a blatant dare. He carefully folded his newspaper, picked up his coffee cup, and prepared to go. His calm demeanor scared Amanda to death, and she felt threatened. She wished grouchy old Lou would emerge from the kitchen with his baseball bat and protect them from this predator.

"So you killed Myron Landry?" Amanda's question landed more like a statement of fact.

"Prove it." He winked, then left.

The silence from the garden was profound. Sunshine glanced off the pink magnolias and purple phlox, but no bird sang.

"We can't prove it!" Amanda groaned.

Sara placed her phone on the table. "Maybe we can. I recorded the whole thing."

Amanda took both Sara's hands "My God, you are my hero! Let's take it over to Judd right now."

Sara slowly shook her head and touched Amanda's cheek. "No, babe. I'll email the recording to Judd and let him handle it. As for us? We're going home."

CHAPTER 55
*Returning to Mayberry...*

Monday, Memorial Day, exactly six weeks since Grandma's death, and they were returning to Mayberry. This time, they were caravanning—Sara and Amanda in the Miata convertible, with Mom, Ginny, and Lissa following in Mom's old Crown Victoria. Mom had returned from Vegas and was anxious to meet the family. Lissa, out of school for the holiday, was eager to meet Jana. Amanda's family had already met Lori, who had driven Sara home in the convertible a few weeks ago, thereby solving the problem of getting two cars back while Sara was too injured to drive.

Lori was a big hit. Sara had taken her into Charlotte to visit the police complex and introduced her to some top cops, which reinforced the girl's determination to go into law enforcement. Lori had hitched a ride home with some other Mount Airy residents, but her short visit had whet Amanda's family's appetite for meeting the rest of the Taylor clan.

Now they were driving to Judd and Ella's ranch house via a detour to Mount Pilot, where Judd had promised to deliver a "special announcement."

"I wonder what he'll say," Sara said as she drove.

"He probably wants to introduce us to his mother, Mavis, and his son, Micah."

The Taylors' son had been staying with Mavis since Marty's funeral. He was scheduled to fly back to

Florida after Memorial Day, so they had only a tiny window of opportunity to meet him.

According to the GPS, they were nearing Mount Pilot. Amanda checked the rearview mirror, still no sign of Mom following. They had parted company several miles back, but since tech-savvy Ginny had navigation on her phone, Amanda was confident they'd rendezvous eventually.

She then looked up toward the hills. "Oh, my God, what's that?" Looming in the near distance, atop a dark green mountain, sat an enormous, perfectly round knob of rock.

"It looks like a giant bundt cake with green icing!" Sara exclaimed. "Must be Mount Pilot." She Googled it. "Yep, it's a metamorphic quartzite monadnock, rising to a peak 2,421 feet above sea level."

Amanda didn't care. She was more interested in Mama Mavis's farm as they turned into her driveway. The long road was bordered with flat, fertile fields, terminating at a classic, upright, two-storied white farmhouse with a deep front porch. The wooden structure was likely built in the early 1900s but was freshly painted and well kept. A traditional red barn rose behind it, surrounded by pasture land, with the odd knob on the mountain overlooking it all.

"Nice place," Sara said. "Look, Judd's truck is here."

They parked beside the truck and several other vehicles they did not recognize. As they climbed out, Amanda saw two familiar figures tromping through a nearby pasture. She couldn't imagine what Michael and Miguel were doing there, but it was like déjà vu. The day she and Robby first encountered Judd, the M&M's had been working the fields at the rancher.

Before she could speculate further, Judd burst from the house, rushed down the steps, and gathered them into his arms. He was closely followed by a tall, handsome young man who stood shyly to one side, and a short, older woman who was as wide as she was tall. She wore a flamboyant tent dress, and her round, ebony face was dominated by a gleaming white smile.

After Judd finished hugging, Mama Mavis took over. When she pulled Amanda against her cushiony bosom, Amanda was enveloped by love and the smell of oatmeal cookies. In that amazing moment, she realized Mavis was her uncle Andrew's widow. Andrew, of course, had been Grandma Vivian's son. The whole concept was mind-blowing.

If anything, Micah was even more of a shock. His skin was café au lait, he was clearly African American, but he did not resemble his parents at all. Instead, he was the spitting image of Grandma Viv—same eyes, same facial structure, and same mischievous expression. It was like Grandma's genes had bypassed Andrew and his immediate progeny and landed in her great-grandson.

Sara saw the resemblance, too, and was uncharacteristically speechless as they sped through the introductions. When Mom, Ginny, and Lissa arrived moments later, it was clear that Mom also experienced the same incredulous reaction as she greeted Judd and the others.

They were rushed inside the house in a whirlwind of laughter and everyone talking at once. Amanda was only vaguely aware of the spotless, old-fashioned furnishings and tantalizing cooking smells coming from the kitchen. Somehow, she absorbed the information that Ella and the girls were back at the rancher, where they would all eat dinner, and that soon Mavis would be providing lunch.

Mavis suggested, "Micah, why don't you take Ginny and Lissa out to see the cows and chickens? They're city girls, so they might enjoy it."

"Yes, Grandma."

Once the three had departed for the barn, Mama Mavis served iced tea in the parlor. "Now, I'm fixin' to cook, so you go on and have your say, son."

With Mavis in the kitchen, Judd stood beside the fireplace, somewhat ill at ease with the formality but determined to make his announcement. Amanda noticed he had difficulty dragging his gaze from Mom. Undoubtedly, he was absorbing the fact that his white aunt was half-sister to his father, who had died in Vietnam before Judd was born. She also noted that as he shifted foot to foot, he had lost his limp and no longer wore the sling on his broken arm.

She had heard that time heals all wounds, but would time ever explain the improbable fact of this unexpected, wonderful new family?

## CHAPTER 56
*About the land...*

"It's all about the land—Mayberry Farm," Judd began. "I've decided to sell."

Sara drew a sharp intake of breath and touched Amanda's arm. Mom's eyes widened. It was not an unexpected decision, but still, after the rocky road they'd all traveled to get there, it was a landmark.

"That's why you see the M&M's out in the field. They're inspecting the soil and pacing off the acres, and they've agreed to come with me to start over here at Mama's place."

He explained that Mavis had come up with the idea at Marty's funeral. She didn't want Judd, her only son, to have to wait for her death to inherit the land but to use it "in the here and now," as she put it.

"Amen to that!" Mavis called from where she'd been eavesdropping at the stove.

Judd continued, "It's not as large as Mayberry, just shy of forty acres, but that's plenty big enough for our organic farming business. Ella and I plan to build a new house on this land, and we're still only fifteen minutes from Mount Airy, so Ella and the girls can keep their same schools, and I can keep my deputy job."

"You should quit that damned job!" Mavis hollered.

"I'm getting pretty old for heavy farming, Mama,"

Judd hollered back. "Maybe I should be a full-time law enforcement officer."

"Over my dead body!"

Amanda loved the banter between mother and son, while Mom laughed out loud.

"Who are you going to sell to, Judd?" Sara interrupted.

He sighed heavily. "Well, that's up to Mandy and Robby, as well, but right now, I'm thinking of selling to Kenny at March Investments. He's a cocky bastard, but it seems he had no part in the crimes committed by others. I reckon we have him over a barrel."

By "barrel," Judd meant that if the discount mall deal went through, they could ask for a much bigger barrel of money, and Kenneth Klein couldn't refuse them. They wouldn't know one way or the other until the following winter, which would allow Judd to harvest his current crops at the rancher.

"If the discount mall deal doesn't go through, that's okay, too," he added. "The original plan for Mayberry Acres would give us plenty of money to build, get the girls started at college, and move on with our lives."

Amanda butt in, "Whatever you decide is fine with Robby and me."

"Thank you, Mandy." With that, Judd gratefully sat and took his first sip of tea.

Throughout Judd's announcement, Amanda had been impressed by Mom's control. Her Realtor instincts must have been itching to grill Judd for details about the land sale, the site plan, contracts, and commissions. And yet she had held her tongue. Perhaps it was fear of losing control and succumbing to temptation that propelled Mom up and out of her chair: "If you will excuse me, I'm going to help Mavis in the kitchen."

At Mom's departure, Judd whispered, "Will you girls step outside with me? There's something I need to tell you…"

## CHAPTER 57
*A heavenly justification...*

Amanda braced herself. Judd's tone portended something ominous, and she'd had enough disruption for a lifetime.

Sara must have felt the same because the minute their sneakers hit the porch, she groaned. "What now, Judd?"

He looked out to where the M&M's were taking a break, sitting on the fence and passing something that looked suspiciously like a joint. Beyond them, Pilot Mountain was shrouded in a passing cloud. Next he pulled Sara into his arms for a crushing hug.

"Sara, how can I ever thank you for sending me that recording of Max Eagle? It set a fire under Sheriff Bill and got the investigation moving again."

"Glad to be of help," Sara responded coolly and moved out of his embrace. Of the two of them, Sara had always tried to distance them from trouble. Clearly, she was not eager to wade in again.

"So what happened?" Amanda had to know.

Judd studied his shoes and slowly shook his head. "I believe we could have nailed Max Eagle for Myron Landry's murder, but he got away."

"How is that possible?" Sara demanded.

"Max outsmarted us, and he has tons of money. I think he became wary the moment he left you at the Bee & Bee that morning and put his escape plan in order."

Judd told them that based on the innuendo in the recording, the sheriff had obtained a search warrant for Eagle's horse farm, which incidentally included his dead wife's veterinary offices.

"We found the lethal ingredients used in the euthanasia cocktail that killed Landry locked in a cabinet. Eagle hadn't even bothered to remove the key. His fingerprints were on the vials, but that didn't prove anything because Eagle admitted in your recording that he had regularly assisted in putting animals to sleep."

"He *got away*?" Amanda was incredulous.

"He sold his horse farm to Kenny Klein below market value and under the radar. The proceeds were electronically transferred to a bank in the Cayman Islands."

"So Eagle got away with murder." Sara was outraged.

Judd, equally frustrated, looked to the sky seeking a heavenly justification. "Like I said, Eagle was a rich guy. He caught an intercontinental flight to London and moved on from there. Between private pilots and God knows whatever other means of transportation, he's gone. Vanished into thin air."

The injustice was depressing all around, but Amanda said, "Too bad. Now Lois at the Bee & Bee has lost her best breakfast customer."

※※※※※

"But Max Eagle was kicked off the board of directors at March Investments. He'll never see one penny when we sell Mayberry Farm, and he's lost his life in the USA," Judd said.

Somehow, the conversation had reignited after they returned to the Taylor's ranch house and were awaiting dinner. The other adult women were helping Ella in the kitchen—laughing, getting to know one another, and having a high old time. Lissa was holed up with Jana in her bedroom playing video games, Lori was sitting out in the gazebo pouting over a breakup with Lily, Micah was strolling down the driveway chatting on his cellphone, and Sara and Amanda were once again alone with Judd on the back deck.

"I know you feel guilty, Judd, but don't beat yourself up over Eagle. He's not worth it," Sara urged.

"Yes, tell us something happy," Amanda said.

He brightened. "Okay, I have something special for you, Mandy." He went into the house and returned with a white plastic garbage bag,

She reached inside and lifted out Grandma's magic box. "Oh, wow! I'd almost forgotten about this!"

As she opened the little drawers in the oriental lacquered chest, pulling out costume jewelry mixed with safety pins and loose buttons, Judd said, "They finally released it from evidence, so I've been saving it for you."

Her ballerina pin had been in this box, the one that eventually went to Jana and incriminated Marty Roach. Amanda had gifted Jana with the pin and was thrilled to do so because Jana was Grandma Viv's great-granddaughter. The thought made her smile as she passed items back and forth to Sara and soon discovered a small key. At first she didn't understand the significance, then gradually, holding it in her palm, it came to her.

"My God, Sara, this is it—the second key needed to open Grandma's slant top desk! She left a note about this, remember?"

"Yes! The other key was in the sealed envelope Viv left for you in her self-storage unit."

Judd said, "I don't get it."

Amanda was beside herself. "Judd, you said you stored Grandma's old furniture in the barn. Is it too late to go see it?"

## CHAPTER 58
*Good and evil...*

Judd took them in his Ranger UTV. As opposed to the day they rescued Robby at the lake, he drove slow. The big tires still bumped over the rutted fields but did not jolt their bones. When they steered into the majestic forest, Amanda again recognized the spot where she and Sara had kissed and felt a sad nostalgia at the thought that one day in the not-too-distant future, all this would be gone.

She was sure Judd felt it, too. When he stopped at the old Yount homestead, she asked him, "Won't you miss all this?"

He sucked his lips into his mouth and grimaced. When he exhaled and squinted up at the cloudless, darkening blue sky, he said, "Damn right, I will. This farm's been my family's home for four generations, and you know how much Ella and I wanted to restore this old place..." He paused to help her and Sara from the UTV. "But after all that's happened, three deaths and the senseless greed tied to this land, it feels all wrong now, like it's poisoned."

Amanda was brokenhearted for Judd. As Sara took his arm and walked him to the wide front porch, Amanda hoped the decades of good memories would someday overshadow the recent horrors.

Sara said, "You know, this old house is a great design, but I've seen new, Craftsman-style homes that are reminiscent of the Yount homestead—only much better suited to modern living."

Judd nodded. "That's what Ella says. I caught her looking at floor plans online, and there's something to be said for fresh starts."

Amanda would never have uttered such a cliché but was glad that Judd was moving on. More pressingly, the sun was sliding downward in the western sky, dinner would soon be served back at the rancher, and she figured they had about one hour. "Judd, where is the barn?"

He held up one hand. "Wait, I have something else to tell you. It's about our grandmother's engagement ring."

She sat heavily on one of the steps. She wanted to go, but she needed to hear this. Sara sat, too.

"The guy who tried to pawn it in Charleston helped the sheriff determine the chain of possession. Marty stole it, but he didn't keep it long," Judd said, a pained expression on his face when he mentioned his deceased brother-in-law. "No, poor old Marty decided to bribe one of his fellow commissioners with the diamond. He was successful because the commissioner changed his vote to approve Mayberry Acres."

So Max Eagle had not been the culprit, Amanda's theory had been wrong. "Was this commissioner a chubby, well-to-do older guy?"

"Yes, a fat old guy who has been indicted and lost his job. Because the ring was recovered and he never got the cash, he likely won't serve time, but he's permanently disgraced."

"The big fish who *did not* get away," Sara said.

This was all fascinating to Amanda, and she had been thinking a lot about the ring lately because of something Linc had said, yet she really wanted to get inside that barn. "Please, Judd, can you just point us in the right direction?"

He chuckled and dug into his jeans pocket, producing a key. He explained how to jiggle the padlock on the barn door, how to access the lights, and then led them around to the back of the house. He pointed to an overgrown path bordered by blackberry bushes and sent them on their way.

The distance proved short. The moment she and Sara rounded the first bend, they saw it. The bank barn, built into a hillside, overlooked a steep valley. Looking at the decrepit structure, her first thought was that Judd was lucky to be getting the large, sturdy red barn at Mavis's place instead of this wreck. Her second thought: *Dear God, let me find Grandma's slant top desk.*

After a few tries, they eased the creaky oak door inward and were assailed by the smell of hay, old manure, and rotting wood. A large bird squawked and jetted past their heads to freedom, scaring them half to death. The lights proved to be an inadequate series of low wattage bulbs at the ends of cords also hung with strips of flypaper. A second-floor hay loft ran along the front wall, and luckily, several holes in the roof let in some sunlight.

The light streamed through dust motes to illuminate rusted farm equipment, milking buckets, and yes, toward the damp inner wall, a pile of antique furniture covered with a clear plastic tarp.

"Jackpot!" Sara headed for the furniture.

In seconds, they uncovered the pile and saw it.

"The desk!" They lifted away stacks of abandoned shutters covering the darkly varnished, delicate piece.

They carried it out of the shadows and placed it in the best available light.

Amanda already had the two keys in her hand. "The shutters protected it all these years." She inserted the first key at the crest of the slanted desktop and folded it down to expose the inner cupboards.

"Hurry, I can't wait!" Sara said.

The second key from the magic box unlocked the cupboard doors and exposed two long, narrow pigeonholes. Blindly reaching inside, Amanda removed a decorated tin box, a stack of letters bound with blue ribbon, and another stack bound with pink. Love letters, of course—one group from Thomas to Vivian, the other from Vivian to Thomas. The discovery brought a flood of tears to Amanda's eyes.

"Look at this, Sara." Her grandmother's handwriting at age sixteen was ornate with curlicues, the note paper still scented with floral perfume. The words included poetry along with confessions of undying love.

Sixteen-year-old Thomas's letters displayed a heavier, less practiced hand and included no poetry. He addressed Grandma as "My dear Miss Vivian," and his prose revealed not only passion, but also respect and disbelief at his "situation" which, of course, was the involvement of a young black man with the underage white mistress of the household.

It would take hours to read them all, but at a glance, it was apparent that young Vivian was the aggressor, while Thomas tried to hold back, giving her every opportunity to extricate herself.

"They were truly in love." Sara also had tears in her eyes.

"Romeo and Juliet."

"No, Mandy, their circumstance was much more dangerous."

The tin contained photographs of the young lovers together in the barnyard, on the porch, and picnicking at the lake. Each image reflected the sentiments from the letters.

"I wonder who took these," Sara said.

Amanda was certain. "It must have been Thomas's mother, Mayberry, the one this farm was named for. Remember, Judd told us: *the old woman whose full lips were like the blackberries in May?*"

"I don't think I heard that."

It didn't matter. In Amanda's mind, Mayberry was the photographer. She recalled her grandmother Viv's instructions: *What you find in Aunt Alice's desk is yours to share with the others in our family but only when they are ready. Until then, keep this letter and its contents to yourself. I trust you on this. Love, Grandma.*

Well, her family was now ready to share this discovery. Not only had everyone come to love the Taylors, but they cherished the connection. This treasure trove not only explained the ancient love affair, but would also make everyone proud of Grandma's courage and conviction at such a young age.

Grandma would be proud, too, of the amazing people her union with Thomas had produced. The great tragedy was that Grandma had never learned to know them. But she had provided for them during her life and after death—a death in essence caused by the residual prejudice and greed also passed unresolved through the generations.

These unresolved intersections of good and evil, however, were not uppermost in Amanda's mind. Instead, she thought about what Linc had recently told her about Grandma's engagement ring: *Vivian wanted the ring to go to either you or Robby. Whoever gets married first shall have the option of giving it to his or her spouse.*

At the time, Amanda had thought little of the bequest. It was simply Grandma laying down a challenge from the grave. She looked over at Sara, who had a bemused smile on her full lips as she studied a photo of young Vivian with Thomas. Sunlight played on the glossy black wing of Sara's hair and caressed the porcelain curve of her cheekbones.

Maybe someday soon Amanda would find Grandma's courage to pop the question and grab the brass ring which, as a metaphor for Sara, was far more precious than brass, gold, or diamonds. It was priceless.

## About the Author

Kate Merrill is a longtime art gallery owner who lives with her wife, two cats, and a dog on a lake in North Carolina. When she's not writing, she enjoys swimming, kayaking, and allowing her strong-willed golden retriever to take her for a walk.

## *IF YOU LIKED THIS BOOK...*

Share a review with your friends or post a review on your favorite site like Amazon, Goodreads, Barnes and Noble, or anywhere you purchased the book. Or perhaps share a posting on your social media sites and help spread the word.

Join the Sapphire Newsletter and keep up with all your favorite authors.

Did we mention you get a free book for joining our team?

sign-up at - www.sapphirebooks.com

# Other Books by Kate Merrill

**Romance**
*Northern Lights* (as Christie Cole)
*Flames of Summer*
*Beloved Enemy* (as Elizabeth Whitaker)
*Framed*

**Diana Rittenhouse Mystery Series**
*A Lethal Listing*
*Blood Brothers*
*Crimes of Commission*
*Dooley Is Dead*
*Buyer Beware*

**Amanda Rittenhouse Mystery Series**
*Murder at Metrolina*
*Homicide in Hatteras*
*Assault in Asheville*
*Murder at Midterm*
*The Mayberry Murders*

**Miss Addie's Gift: Portrait of an American Folk Artist**

**Too Many Damn Yankees in Queen Charlotte's Court**
**A collection of Short Stories**

Kate, a longtime art gallery owner and passionate writer, lives with her family on a lake in North Carolina. When she is not writing or creating driftwood sculpture, she enjoys swimming, boating, and playing with her cats.